THE SCARS
THAT DEFINE US

THE DEVILS DUST
book Two

M.N. FORGY

THE SCARS THAT DEFINE US
Copyright © 2014 M. N. Forgy

Edited by Hot Tree Editing
Cover design by Arijana Karčić, Cover It! Designs
Formatted by Max Effect

I dedicate this book to those who were dragged through life's unforgiving hurdles, and came out on top.

Wear your scars with pride.

Live with no regrets.

1

Dani

THUNDER ERUPTS FROM ABOVE AS THE DARK, OMINOUS, SKY OPENS up, allowing sprinkles to cascade down. I blink, the rain clinging to my eyelashes as I stare at the club from afar. The smell of wet pavement is heavy in the air as the rain pounds against the asphalt. I've been considering my options, my fate. I've been standing here for an hour, knowing that walking into the clubhouse could seal my future with a bullet to the head, possibly by the one I love most, Shadow, but going back to the life I had before would grant me a destiny of only surviving; I wouldn't be living.

I was just as shocked as the club was when my mother and her boyfriend Stevin showed up at the bike show with a team of Federal Agents. Not only did I feel betrayed, I felt hurt. How did I not know my mother was a part of the FBI? That bitch kept me for two and a half days trying to pry information from me as a witness. After they got nowhere, they tried to keep me as a possible suspect. Stevin and my mother were the laughing stock of their work force.

"Look, we have wasted a lot of our resources on this club. When the informant was shot, we had to go in, breaking our six-month cover in the El Locos. Only one of the Devil's members had a gun, and he tested negative for gunshot residue. We don't have any evidence, and we won't get any; they cover their asses too well to get caught. I'm calling it quits." The conversation carried from behind the door, which led to my interrogation room. The detective speaking sounded agitated, like the one who had been questioning me all day.

"I know I can get her to talk. Just give me some more time," my mother pleaded. Her consistency at making me her rat angered me. It also showed me just how much my mother hated me; she only kept me around in her life for this exact purpose; bringing down my father and his club and making his daughter, me, the one to do it. It's not going to happen, though; I'll die in the hands of my father's motorcycle club being honest rather than live and being a rat.

"She is your daughter, Sadie," the agent said in distaste.

"Blood doesn't make her my daughter," my mother spoke harshly. That should hurt but it didn't.

"No judge is going to sign off on detaining her any longer," the FBI agent replied sternly.

"It's over, Sadie; it's time to let go. We gave it our all. I gave it my all, for you," Stevin said softly.

Three hours later, here I am.

The rain starts pounding on my shoulders as the wind picks up, its velocity so hostile, I have to firmly plant my feet to the ground to keep from blowing away. That wouldn't be a bad thing right now. Away sounds better than here, but I have nowhere else to go.

"You!"

I look up and see my father Bull, Locks, and Bobby all standing outside the clubhouse. Shit, how long have they been standing there? Bull stands in front of the others with his hands on his hips, the rain slamming down on his leather cut; his cut claiming him as a Devil's Dust member. My father is the president of the club. I should be fine, but with the look he has on his face; I'm not so sure my safety is on the top of his priorities. I take a deep breath, possibly my last, and move forward hesitantly.

"That's far enough," Bull says, his voice cold and threatening.

I stop a few feet in front of them, my body trembling with fear. I straighten my back to appear unaffected, but it's no use. I'm scared to death.

"What the fuck are you doing here? You got a death wish?" Locks barks, his hand planted firmly inside his cut, no doubt on a gun. Locks, being the Vice President, could shoot me right here in the courtyard and get away with it.

"I -" I choke, "I'm not one of them," I say timidly. The wind's so loud it's hard to speak above it.

I look in Bobby's direction, curious as to where Shadow is. He should be here protecting me. I want to believe Shadow will keep me safe, that he will shield me from the throes of violence from the club. However, if I close my eyes, I can still see his face when the look of distrust slithered across it.

Bull looks me in the eye from a distance, his eyes darting up and down trying to read my body language. We stand silently. The wind howls and thunder claps from above. My eyes plead for him to believe me, believe that I had nothing to do with my mother and her plans to take down the club. My worst fear of all surfaces he won't kill me; instead, he will send me away and I'll have to go back to my mother or live on the streets.

"I have nowhere else to go," I cry above the thunder.

"Bobby, check her."

"Check me?"

Without warning, Bobby stomps forward, grabs the hem of my shirt, and lifts it up, exposing my bra. The cold rain blasts against my flesh like razor blades as he pats my back, legs, head, and every other inch of my body.

"Clean, no wire," Bobby informs.

Wire?

"I'm not one of them!" I yell in frustration.

The wind gusts, and lightning cracks loudly from above as my heart bleeds for them to believe me.

"Let's take this inside." Bull nods toward the club.

Bobby pushes me in the small of my back toward the clubhouse, making me stumble. Everyone treating me like a rat has me second-guessing going inside, but with the grip Bobby has on my arm, I don't think I have much of a choice anymore.

◆ ◆ ◆

I'm sitting in the spot at the wooden table where I always sit. It seems I'm always in trouble when I'm sitting at this table.

"What did you fucking tell them?" my dad questions. "And, Dani," he pauses, "I want everything." His voice is demanding, and his menacing eyes penetrate my soul. Gone with the loving, caring father he was before, before my mother tried to bring the club down. I can't believe she had the nerve to make it look like I was part of it.

His voice is cold and laced with warning, making me think hard before answering.

"They asked if I knew Ricky, the boyfriend of Shadow's mother, Cassie. I said no. The agent showed a picture of Shadow carrying me out of Ricky and Cassie's house, when you guys rescued me from being kidnapped, making me out to be a liar. So I said I woke up to Shadow carrying me and I don't know or remember anything else." I stop to look around the table at Locks and Bobby, their faces not giving any indication they believe me or not. "I didn't tell them anything. I swear."

"She's a liar, Prez," Locks says as if I'm not even in the room. My hands begin to tremble with fear; if my dad listens to him, I won't be alive much longer.

"She's my blood." My father speaks with emotion. It takes me back. Maybe I have hope on my side after all.

"I think she's telling the truth," Bobby says, looking right at me, his words making me smile slightly.

"What the fuck would you know?" Locks snaps.

"I got to know Firefly a little bit, and I think I would have seen something along that time to indicate she had something to do with it, and I didn't," Bobby insists. The name Firefly catches me off-guard. I remember when he gave it to me how ridiculous it sounded. Yet, I fell in love with it after Shadow said it was perfect for me; that I was his light in his cruel, dark world. *Shadow. Where is he?*

"Vote," Locks demands.

Vote? What the hell does that mean?

Bobby and my dad both look in his direction, Bobby's face unreadable and my dad's angry.

"Fine, but until then take her to your room, Bobby. Get all the guys rounded up. I want this shit aired out now." Bull moves his hand toward the door, indicating Bobby to take me away.

I stand up, the chair scraping the hardwood floor with a screech. I make my way out of the doors, not looking back at the table, which will hold my fate.

"I don't need to stay in your room, Bobby. I can stay with Shadow in my old room," I declare, shaking his grip off my shoulder as we head toward the hall.

"No, you need to stay with me, Firefly. It's for the best," Bobby whispers softly as he tries to grab hold of my arm again.

"You can shove that thought up your ass, Bobby. I'm not staying with you. Shadow wouldn't allow it." I look at him over my shoulder with raised eyebrows. He looks shocked at my crude tone, but if I've learned anything by all this, it's that you can't be soft. Soft means you're weak, and weak can break you.

I open the bedroom door to mine and Shadow's room and see Shadow lying on the bed naked, a sheet wadded around his crotch.

There are empty beer bottles on the floor, and the nightstand has drugs laid out across it.

"Shad-"

"Who the fuck are you?" a female voice interrupts from the en-suite bathroom the bedroom holds. Snapping my gaze from Shadow to her, I notice a tall, skinny woman. She has dark-brown hair which is long and tangled; overall, it's just disgusting. She is tying up her slutty dress around her neck like she had been naked just moments before. My gaze slides back to Shadow, who looks like he's seen a ghost. I suddenly feel sick to my stomach, and I want to claw my heart from my chest from the unbearable ache spreading from it.

"What the fuck is she doin' here?" Shadow asks Bobby as if I'm the stray dog who came in from the rain.

That is the first thing that comes out of his mouth? No "I'm sorry, baby; it's not what it looks like"? No, he doesn't even try to hide that he just messed around on me.

"Meeting now," Bobby says, pulling me from the doorway. "Come on, Firefly." I pull my arm from him and stare at Shadow, my eyes beginning to glaze over with tears. How could he? I want to jump on the bed and beat him in the head with the alarm clock sitting on the nightstand, but I can't even move from the hurt radiating through my veins.

"It's all right, Firefly. I got you. Come on." Bobby pulls me with a little more force to get my feet moving before he closes the door and opens the one directly across the hall.

◆ ◆ ◆

"You were gone for a few days. Everybody thought you were in on it, including Shadow," Bobby explains, as I sit on the bed dumbfounded. His blue jeans hang low on his hips, and his white shirt is bunched upward on his hard stomach. I avert my eyes to the trashy floor.

"My mother kept me, trying to use me as a witness," I say flatly. Suddenly cold, I pull my leather jacket tightly around my body. Bobby nods in understanding as he hooks his fingers into his belt loops.

"Hell, they let the brothers go pretty quickly when they couldn't prove they had anything to do with Cassie's death. They didn't have shit on 'em," Bobby says, crossing his arms and widening his stance. I forgot I saw him running with a gun after Shadow's mom, Cassie, had been shot. I guess he got away. I am still in shock my mother used Cassie as a criminal informant. My mother is like a venomous snake, slithering her way in any way she sees fit. Cassie almost killed me, pissed that Shadow had killed her boyfriend Ricky. She wanted to take Shadow's only love, me. She got her wish, only it was my own flesh and blood who did the taking.

"You killed Cassie," I state. Bobby shrugs and looks the other direction. "You saved my life, thank you," I add quietly.

"I did what had to be done." He looks right at me, his stare letting me know it was for the club, not me. We sit here silently, the air filled with so many questions but silence filling the unknown instead.

"I just need to tell Shadow I didn't have anything to do with my mom's cancerous plans. Everything will go right back the way it was," I say to myself more than to him. I'm delirious with hope, not seeing the betrayal of Shadows actions clearly.

"You don't actually believe that, do you?" Bobby looks at me like I'm an idiot. I shrug, knowing this is not going to be a simple process of forgive and forget with Shadow. His mom ruined him of trusting and loving easily, neglecting him and making him fend for himself at such a young age; makes him question who he can trust in this world if he can't even depend on his own mother.

"No," I respond, throwing my head in my hands.

"Look, stay in here, get a shower and I'll come back and fill you in later," Bobby explains, grabbing the door handle to the old, wooden door.

I look around the room. It's a mess. I'm sure the bathroom isn't any better.

Before I say another word, Bobby leaves and shuts the door behind him.

Looking at the dirty room around me, my heart suddenly ceases beating. A sob escapes my mouth as I realize the extent of the hell my mother has left for me to endure. If I ever see her again, I might kill her, make her bleed as my heart is bleeding right now and Shadow, he just messed around on me without a hint of shame. I look down at my arms and see the leather jacket claiming them, my jacket claiming me as Shadow's property, telling the world I'm his ol' lady. My chest feels heavy and begins to sweat. I'm suffocating. I pull on the leather jacket, scratching and screaming to get the damn thing off. I'm not anything of Shadow's anymore. I get it off and throw it across the room as if it's a plague. A violent scream erupts from my throat in despair.

Fuck Shadow!

My lungs take a second to regain airflow as Bobby slams the door shut. The last fucking person I thought I would ever see just walked into my room, Dani.

I think she was in on the bust with her mom, using me to get information on the club and using me to get back at her mother in the process. Even with all that, I can't get her out of my head. I still love the woman who used me and betrayed my club. How am I supposed to deal with that feeling of treachery? The only way I know how is drugs and women. It's not working, though. It used to work before I knew Dani, before she became my Firefly, lighting up the dark torment, which was guiding my self-loathing. She was my drug rather than the drug of killing. Killing gave me control, made me feel like I had a handle of myself, of my life. Now nothing helps, no matter how many drugs I take or the amount. I snorted so much cocaine yesterday my nose bled, and the sight of women just makes me angry. Nothing can make me feel like Dani did, and nothing can numb the pain she caused.

"That your girl?" Mandy, or was it Sandy, asks me.

"Get your shit and get out," I say, sitting up on the bed. Just seeing her makes my jaw clench.

"She the reason you can't get it up?" she asks, her hands on her hips.

Like I said, even the sight of other women angers me. I still try to entertain the idea I want pussy but once I get them naked, I can't stand to look at them. Knowing it's not Dani and the fact that the only woman I want is a fucking traitor makes my stomach turn. Once I got this slut in here, I couldn't even touch her, making me angry at myself. Dani did this to me. She broke me beyond repair. My fucking Firefly threw me into a darkness I can't escape.

"Bitch, if you know what's good for you, you'll get the hell out, now." I point at the door. "Just your presence makes me want to kill you, let alone the idea of fucking you," I say coldly. Her mouth forms a gaping 'O' perfectly; I'm sure she would give amazing head. I watch her turn in anger as she slams the door behind her.

I get up, get dressed, put on yesterday's clothes and throw on my cut. Running my hands through my hair, which is in desperate need of a trim and wash, I walk out the bedroom door. I stop and stare at the door across from me, knowing it holds Dani the remedy to my pain, but a toxin to my mind. How could she play me so well? I'll never forget the feeling I got when her mother picked her up off the ground yelling about how she was a witness. I was told Dani was telling them everything, but I hoped it was a lie and they were just trying to get me to rat myself out. There are no words to describe it, but what boggles my mind more than anything is why did Dani come back?

◆ ◆ ◆

I sit in my spot at the table and instantly smell Dani's perfume. Her smell of peaches fills the air, making the hair on my neck stand on end. I look across the table and see Bobby staring back at me, his face in a scowl. I'm sure he's not happy that he and Dani just walked in on what looked like me fucking around. Fuck him.

"Dani's here," Bull says, cutting to the chase as he lights a cigarette.

"What?" Hawk's scratchy voice asks, along with everyone else who is just as surprised.

"Yeah, apparently she was just as startled about the whole shenanigans her mother had up her sleeve as we were," Bull informs us as he takes a drag from his cigarette.

"I think she's a threat to the club. She needs to be taken care of," Locks says, loathing high in his voice. Instantly, I'm reminded that Dani knows the darkness, which tempts me. If she said anything to the Feds, I will be on death row for sure.

"You know what we do with threats." Old Guy nods in my direction, indicating they send me after threats to ensure they never have the chance to talk. I kill them and, as sadistic as it sounds, I usually enjoy it.

"Firefly is not a threat," Bobby clips, eyeing Old Guy. What was Dani thinking coming back here? I kill threats. If this goes south, Bull could order me to kill Dani. Can I kill her?

"Regardless of her mother, Dani is not like her. She has Devil's Dust in her. We've all seen it come out while she's been here," Bull says, catching everyone's attention. "That fight between her mother and her that day was intense. Dani's my blood, and she has nowhere else to go."

I smirk at the memory. Dani just about killed her mother that day. It was great watching her come into her own; who knew a beauty such as herself could be so brutal.

Everyone goes silent as Bull looks at me. He knows the shit I have been dipping in the last couple of days. Seeing how he thinks Dani is innocent, I am no doubt on his shit list.

"Dani is not like her mother. I can tell you that," Bobby says smiling. What does he know? Why in the hell is he protecting her so much?

"So, what do you want from us?" Hawk asks.

Bull sits, rubbing his scruffy jaw as he thinks.

"After the storm she goes," Bull pauses and looks at me. "She can stay with Bobby for now, get her on her feet. I'll keep her away from the club until everyone feels comfortable around her," Bull says to Bobby, who nods in agreement. "I'll have Tom Cat transport her wherever she needs to go." Bull looks at me, his eyes angry and waiting for me to object. I look away and stare at the wall, not sure what I'm feeling entirely. "Things will surface whether she was involved or not. If she was," Bull looks at me with sorrow, "then we'll handle it. Everyone in favor?" he asks. Everyone says aye but Locks and me. I sigh loudly; this entire situation is a clusterfuck. *What if I'm sent to ensure her silence?* The thought angers and frightens me all at the same time. I don't know if I can trust Dani, what if she is responsible for trying to take down the club? I don't know if I can allow someone to harm Dani if that is the order to the situation, making me go against my brotherhood to save Dani. Bull slams the gavel down, declaring the vote over.

"This is Bullshit," Locks bellows, his face wrinkling with anger as he scrunches it at Bull with disbelief. Locks face is blistering-red, making his long, blond hair and mustache appear lighter against his skin.

I'm not sure why I didn't agree entirely. Maybe because my head is telling me I need to wash my hands of Dani for being a threat, but my soul still reels for her. Until I know the truth of her involvement with her mother, I need to keep her backstabbing ass away from me. Keep it in my head that she's a threat and nothing more.

Dani

Inside Bobby's greasy bathroom, which is anything but sanitary, I grab a shampoo bottle to wash my hair. The smell releases tones of vanilla and coconuts; it smells like Bobby. I wash my hair and body, wondering how I allowed myself to get in this mess. What if the voting goes against me? Will someone drag me out of the shower by my wet hair and shoot me in the courtyard? I groan at the thought and turn the water off. I push the shower door open and take the red towel hanging from the towel rack. Wrapping it around myself, I notice the ends are tattered and its small size. I wonder if Bobby has any clean shirts I can borrow until I get my things. I walk out of the bathroom and notice Bobby walking through the bedroom door with a suitcase in hand.

"Shit. Sorry, Firefly," Bobby says, noticing I'm indecent. His tone is apologetic, but his eyes never leave my half-naked body. Blushing, I try to pull the small towel tighter.

"Here are some things I grabbed from the apartment. I'll give you a minute to get dressed, then we'll talk." He gives me one last glance, his eyes squinting with desire. My mouth parts with surprise. "Bobby!"

He smirks and shuts the door.

Opening the suitcase, I find my things shoved in there, no doubt from Bobby. I notice an unfamiliar white paper bag and grab it. I empty its contents on the floor and find a pack of birth control. The little pink case reminds me that Shadow was going to ask Bobby to have Doc write me a prescription for it a few weeks back. Poor Doc,

I bet she gets tired of working as a doctor for the club. I wonder how many girls she puts on birth control who crawl through here. I throw the pack back in the bag. I started my period a few days ago, and with recent events, I'm not going to be having sex anytime soon, so what's the point in taking them? I find a black bra with matching panties, and a grey tank with ripped shorts and quickly put them on, unsure when Bobby will bust through the door again.

"Hey," Bobby says, entering the room as soon as I put on my last piece of clothing.

"Hey," I respond, throwing my hair in a messy ponytail.

"So, it looks like you will be staying here until the storm passes," Bobby states, crossing his arms, his bare arms rippled with tattooed muscle.

"Okay," I say, my tone encouraging him to continue.

"After that, you are going to stay with me back at the apartment until everything is figured out."

He means until the club is convinced about whether I had anything to do with the FBI or not.

"What about Shadow?" I ask, curious what he thinks of all this.

Bobby turns his head to look at the wall.

"What?" I question, sensing something is off. "How did the vote go?"

"You're here, aren't you?" he asks, picking some trash from the floor.

"Yeah, but did Shadow vote in my favor, or whatever it was you guys were voting for?" I ask, curious.

Bobby stops and looks at me, his blue eyes hiding the truth he doesn't want to tell me.

"I can't talk to you about club business, Firefly," he says, turning his head quickly. His avoidance tells me what I already know; Shadow voted against me, but what was the vote? Did he vote to kill me? Did he want me out of here?

I turn my gaze toward the floor and close my eyes with hurt. This ache in my chest is really starting to become unbearable.

Every time Shadow takes a blow at me, my heart shatters that much more.

"Did you vote against me?" I inquire, looking at Bobby, wondering if I had a friend in this Hell.

Bobby looks back at me and smirks, my persistence making him shake his head, but his smile letting me know he has my back.

◆ ◆ ◆

For the rest of the day, Bobby insists I stay in his room. Knowing there's a possibility Shadow voted against me, that he may be tasked to kill, or even want me to leave the club, eats away at me. Despite keeping as busy as I possibly can in Bobby's room, my thoughts constantly switch to him, but I still want to punch him in the head for being a prick. The lights flicker, pulling me from my thoughts, with night upon us the bedroom darkens for seconds at a time with the harsh storm surrounding the state.

The door creaks open, the thing barely hanging onto its hinges.

"Hey, you all right?" Bobby questions, coming into the room.

"The storm seems pretty bad," I say, pointing at the light flickering from above us.

"Yeah, it's pretty nasty," he responds, throwing some black sheets on the bed. "Here are some clean sheets."

"Thanks," I say, touching the dark, jersey-knit fabric. "Where's Shadow?" I word-vomit.

Bobby stops in his tracks. "He's across the hall in his room." His voice is hesitant. I can tell he wants me to keep my distance.

"Oh," is all I muster. I know I should stay away from Shadow, but I can't help but want to run in his room and be with him. My head and heart are so conflicted.

"All right, well... night, Firefly," he says, stepping out of the room.

"Wait. Where are you going?" I ask. I hate being trapped in this room by myself.

"Gonna sleep on the couch. Let you have the bed to yourself."

"Oh, thanks." I smile in appreciation.

"Night, Firefly."

"Goodnight, Bobby."

◆ ◆ ◆

I wake in a hot sweat, the wind whistling against the building and the thunder clapping. Dreams of the kidnapping still haunt me when I sleep. I wonder when I'll be able to finally sleep through the night without a reminder of Ricky's voice. I slip off the bed, out of breath and flip the switch to the lights but they just flicker on and off. The electricity is unstable from the violent storm. It explains why it's so muggy in here. I open the door and peek into nothing but still blackness. "Bobby!" I whisper loudly, but there's no response. I could run, just grab my shoes and high tail it out of here. I look across the hall at Shadow's door and know I can't leave. If I run, I will look guilty, and they will find me. I tiptoe into the blackness, my hand trailing against the gritty wall to help lead the way. The lights flash on and off, giving me a chance to navigate down the hall and into the kitchen. I find the sink by chance and trail my hands along the counter to the rack with clean dishes. I stumble upon a glass sitting on the draining board, I fill it with water then lean against the sink and enjoy the cool liquid splashing down my throat. My body is beading with sweat. *How can anybody sleep? It's so hot.*

"Fucking lights!" I hear as Shadow flings open the kitchen door. We both stop and stare at each other as the lights flicker on and off. My body goes stiff, and my heart races as Shadow stares back at me, his eyes sinister and dark, piercing me. Thunder booms and the lights go off. Frightened, I toss my cup in the sink, the glass shattering as it hits the stainless steel. I make my way quickly in the darkness toward the kitchen doors to get away. The last place I want to be is in a dark room with Shadow.

I trip over a stool as the lights flicker on briefly, my hands falling against the dusty floor with force, making my palms burn from impact. I look up and notice Shadow near the sink where I was before, the lights giving away my location. His eyes catch mine before the room goes black again, and I crawl toward the door in the pure blackness. When my hand touches it, the lights flicker on and Shadow is standing where my hand is touching instead of the door. I open my mouth to scream, and he smacks his hand against my mouth to quiet me as he pulls me up violently and jerks me against his chest.

2

Dani

"**D**ON'T SCREAM," SHADOW WHISPERS INTO MY EAR, HIS TONE alarming and menacing. "Do you understand what I just said to you? If I let go and you scream, you're not going to like what I do next."

I nod in understanding as my heart rams against my chest in fear. He slowly releases his hand from my mouth. I throw his arm holding me against him off me, while I push away from him. He's wearing black jersey shorts with no shirt, his dark hair sticking to his forehead from the heat. Even when I'm not one hundred percent sure he's not going to kill me, I find him lick-worthy. His chest glistening from little droplets of sweat forming from the heat.

"Why did you come back here, Dani?" he asks, his tone harsh. The lights flicker, giving him an eerie glow. One side of his face is shaded with the dark while the other is flashed with the small gleam of lights, which turn on and off briefly. His face is drawn down, his eyes hooded with an impending death glare. His lips smirk to the side as he reads my frightened body language.

I straighten my back and try to act unaffected. "What was I supposed to do? Go back to New York with my mother?" I don't try and hide the bitterness in my tone.

"Coming back here was stupid. Only reason you're still here is because your father is the president. Otherwise, your ratting ass would be six-feet-under." Shadow's words hit what's left of my heart. I can literally feel my shattered heart lifting walls of defense and scarring those made from love.

"Fuck you, Shadow. I'm not a rat," I spit.

"Right," Shadow says sarcastically. "So, I'm supposed to believe you didn't tell your mother anything?" He puffs his sweaty chest out and hooks his thumbs in the elastic of his shorts.

"You mean how you are a hit man?" I ask scowling. "If I had, would you still be standing here?"

Shadow huffs at my statement; he clearly doesn't believe me.

"So, I should just trust you?" Shadow scoffs. "Trust the girl who was whisked away by the FBI, who claimed she was a witness. Trust the girl who took my soul and smothered it with her lies?" He cocks his head to the side and smirks. "I don't think so, babe."

I flinch at his cruel words, feeling the snap of my last string of caring. I smile, disgusted by his hurtful words. "Shadow, I never had your trust to begin with, so believe whatever the hell you want."

Shadow's face falls from amusement to an expression of anger. His jaw hardens, and his eyebrows cave inward. I shiver, regretting my sudden sprout of bravery.

"Dani, I can tell you this. You don't want to piss me off," he says with hooded eyes.

"Pretty sure I already have." I scowl at him, telling him what we both already know. I am the enemy, not only to him, but also to everyone in this club.

He stares at me, the power in his eyes ominous. I wonder how I got myself into this situation. How did I believe Shadow and I would ever be anything more than a train wreck?

"You promised me we wouldn't be that couple," I say, trying to hide the hurt that he slept around on me, but I'm not strong enough. I shift on my feet and slant my head to the side, looking at the gritty floor, which lights up and goes dark for seconds at a time. "You said you weren't that guy," I continue.

I look at him, waiting for what he has to say to his broken promise. His eyes change to those of regret, before hardening so quickly, I question if it even happened or if I just imagined it.

Shadow chuckles, widening his stance and folding his arms across his sweaty chest. "You mean an outlaw from a motorcycle club broke a promise? Lied to you?" He laughs. "That's a shocker."

My body is hit with a surge of adrenaline straight to the heart. I thought Shadow was different, that he was the one, but I was clearly wrong. He is the opposite. He was just the one who broke my heart.

"Firefly, are you in here?" Bobby asks, pushing through the doors to the kitchen.

Bobby looks between Shadow and me. "You all right, Firefly?" Bobby asks with concern, his lips pinched and eyes lifted with worry.

Shadow glares at Bobby as he enters the kitchen.

"Yeah, I'm fine." I make my way to the doors but stop short, right in front of Shadow.

"Fuck. You," I whisper.

Shadow bites his bottom lip as his eyebrows furrow, giving a light wrinkle between them. Bobby pushes on my back and directs me back to my cell.

◆ ◆ ◆

The next day, the storm is over for the most part. Some rumbles of thunder linger, but we have full-functioning electricity and the air conditioner is back on. Bobby brought me breakfast and lunch along with a clean towel for showering. I'm hoping tomorrow we can head to the apartment; I don't want to be around Shadow or this club any longer. After looking at my sixth motorcycle magazine, I have had enough of being held captive in this room. Maybe Bobby can whip me up one of his whiskey drinks or something. Spending the day numb and drunk doesn't sound bad. I look in Bobby's dresser for some kind of weapon in case I run into Shadow again. I don't know if I can bring myself to hurt him, but I'd like to think I would if I needed too. *Crap.* There is nothing but spare bullets in his drawers. After coming up empty-handed with nothing to use as a weapon, I open the door slowly and poke my head out, looking for any sign of Shadow. I don't hear anything. It's completely silent, which is odd; there are usually guys hollering and girls giggling.

I enter the bar area and Babs is standing behind the bar looking at a magazine. Her red hair is pinned up with curls flopping down everywhere. She's wearing a long, black sleeved shirt with black pants. Not something I peg her for wearing—weird.

"Hey, there, how ya doing?" she asks, slapping the magazine closed. Her eyes and tone seem surprised to see me.

"I could be better," I say, sitting down, not sure if I can trust her. She seems to play the motherly role of the club and is feisty with her forward attitude. I wouldn't doubt her for a second to try and eliminate me for being a possible threat to the club.

"Where are the boys?" I ask, looking around the empty space.

"On a run," she says flatly.

"A run? It's still storming," I say, pointing toward the glass doors.

"That won't stop them dumbasses," she says with a smirk.

The doors to the kitchen suddenly slam open.

"All right, we're set. You ready?" Vera says, walking up beside Babs with a set of keys in her hand. Vera's reddish-brown hair is pulled up in a high ponytail. Her tight, black shirt is tucked into short, ripped jean shorts, which are topped with her property patch deemed by Old Guy. I've only met Vera once, right before the bike rally where everything went to shit. She wasn't too friendly if I remember right. Old Guy, her significant other, I met before as well. He didn't try and hide his attraction toward me when we first met, he was very forward in his advances. Vera's eyes lazily find me sitting at the bar before scowling.

"Great, what are we going to do about her?" she asks, her eyes never leaving mine.

"What?" I ask, sounding a little nervous.

Babs smiles wolfishly. "Bring 'er along."

"What?' Vera asks, confused.

"She says she's innocent, that she's one of us. Make her prove her loyalty," Babs says, looking at Vera.

Vera smiles. "To us anyway. The boys will have to decide if she's loyal on their own."

"You want to clue me in on what you guys are talking about?" I ask, getting a little peeved they are talking as if I'm not even in the room.

"I have a niece who's almost eighteen. Her name is Silvia. She just got released from the hospital last night because her boyfriend decided to use her as a punching bag," Babs says, shaking her head in dismay and slowly sliding her tongue over her upper red lip.

"Dislocated her jaw," Vera says, stepping around the bar. "Babs brought it to Locks' attention, so he could bring it to the table, but he told her no." Vera's tone is angry and hostile at Locks' decision. Seems Vera has Babs' back and is upset Locks didn't stand behind his wife's request to involve the club.

"So, what does that have to do with me?" I ask, shrugging.

"We, and now you, are going to go scoop up this douche and teach him what happens when you fuck with one of our own," Babs says, putting her hands on her hips, her tone proud.

"And Daddy and Lover Boy cannot find out about it," Vera patronizes.

I look at both of them, considering my options. I could use the brownie points with the ladies at this point. It's not convincing Shadow of anything, but at least I'll have my foot in the door. Showing the ol' ladies I can keep a secret would do just that, and if there is anything illegal about to happen, it will prove I am not with my mother and her clan of agents.

"I'm in," I say, standing.

"Like you had a choice," Babs laughs.

"If you said otherwise, I would have had to beat the shit out of you and throw you in the closet till we got back," Vera says, her tone serious.

"Vera!" Babs snaps.

◆ ◆ ◆

I'm sitting on a bench in the back of one of the club's black vans, with a couple of other ol' ladies wearing cuts. Babs is driving and Vera has the passenger side. I'm sitting next to Cherry, and Molly and Pepper are sitting across from us. I remember seeing them briefly right before the bike rally, when the raid happened, but I don't know much about them.

"You cool?" Molly asks, throwing her brown hair into a tight bun.

I nod, not sure what to say or expect.

"She's fine," Cherry says, nudging me in my shoulder. "She's got it in her blood."

"I'm Phillip's ol' lady, by the way," Cherry says, putting her hand out to shake.

I shake it. "Don't think I've met him," I respond, trying to put a face with the name.

"Yeah, he's doing time right now," she says, looking down. Her strawberry hair skirts across her face, hiding her kind eyes.

"Oh, I'm sorry," I reply, trying to sound as sympathetic as possible. I wonder what he did, but I don't ask.

"No worries, he should be out in a few months."

"That shit you were in," Pepper adds, pointing at me. "They say you didn't have anything to do with it. Did you?" she asks flatly.

I shake my head. "No, that was all the work of my bitch of a mother." I roll my eyes.

All the girls start laughing, catching me off-guard.

"What?" I ask, confused.

"You sound just like him," Cherry says, smiling big.

"Like who?" I ask, looking around at the other girls.

"Like Shadow," Molly says, laughing.

I look down at my hands. Shadow. Just his name is like a punch to the gut, and it hurts.

"We're here, ladies!" Babs yells over her shoulder.

"Where?" I ask.

"Silvia said this is where the fucker deals," Bab's explains, the word *deals* catching my attention. *Like, drug dealer?* My eyes widen with fear, wondering what we will face when we get out of the van.

We sit in silence for a few moments as Babs and Vera scout the place. The van doesn't have any back windows so I can't see a thing.

"Why'd he hit her?" I ask to no one in particular.

"He needed a reason?" Pepper smarts.

"No, I just mean-"

"He accused her of getting into his drugs, demanded she pay for what she took. She swore she didn't take anything, and he snapped," Babs informs.

"There he is." Vera points out the front windshield.

Molly pulls the back van door open and hops out. My heart is pounding so hard I can hear the rush of blood pooling in my ears as I follow. The adrenaline races through me like a virus, consuming my righteous upbringing, enforced from my mother. I smile at the intrusion of corruption, welcoming the feeling of being malicious. I look around and notice we are behind a big building. Thumping music plays from the inside, it's some kind of club with green lights skirting the rooftop. The sky illuminates with leftover lightening and low rumbles of thunder, the storm reminding us of its presence. I follow the girls who are approaching a younger guy. He has on a green bandana pulled backwards with a dirty, white t-shirt and baggy jeans.

"You Darin?" Babs ask, pointing a bat at him.

"What the fuck is it to you?" he mouths, tilting his chin up, his hand in the waist of his jeans

"This is for Silvia!" Babs yells as she swings the bat so fiercely locks of her hair fall loose. He falls to the ground, passing out.

"Dani, grab his gun," Babs orders, pointing to the guy's crotch with the bat. I hesitate as I stare at blood dripping from Darin's head and down his face.

"Do it!" Vera yells, snapping me from the blood. I jump forward, reach into his jeans and fish out a polished gun. It's heavy, and it feels powerful just sitting in my idle hands.

"Girls, grab his feet. Vera and I will get his arms. Dani, get the door to the van," Babs commands, handing me the bat. I carry the bat and the gun; the rush of danger flowing through each of my hands makes my palms twitch.

Once we got the unconscious Darin in the back of the van, we drive off like a bat out of Hell. Babs is driving so fast I nearly fly across the back of the van on a turn. We drive for about twenty minutes before Babs pulls over and hops out.

I climb from the van, hear waves crashing, and smell salt. I look around and notice a rundown building but not much else. Babs snaps her fingers at me, so I hand her the bat as I palm the gun.

Babs grabs the still-unconscious Darin and drags him by his feet, his head hitting the ground with a loud thud. A low moan escapes his lips as he wakes.

"What the hell?" Darin moans, reaching into his pants. A sudden feeling of courage striking, I give his foot a firm kick.

"Looking for this?" I ask. The thought that a guy could lay such harm to a girl has me feeling animosity.

"You are dead bitch," he says, looking at me with a promising grin. His smile is big, showing off bloody teeth where the blood from his head wound has dripped down, but his eyes are narrowed in warning. His threat has me pulsing with rage; I'm tired of threats.

"So, you like to beat girls?" Vera asks.

Darin laughs maliciously. "That bitch had it coming. She knew better than to get in my stash," he says matter-of-factly.

"Dani, shut him up," Babs says. I look at her, shocked. *Does she want me to shoot him?* Thinking on my toes, I grip the gun and hit him in the mouth hard. The sound of metal slamming into his jaw makes the hair on my neck raise. He yells in pain, grabbing his split lip the impact caused.

"What's wrong? I thought you liked to fight?" I ask, a surge of bravery rising, making my hands tremble with nervous excitement.

He looks up at me from the ground. His shameless eyes hold me in place as he wipes the blood from his mouth with the back of his hand and starts to chuckle. It pisses me off. Violence creeps its way into my system, eager for me to show my true colors, not only to the girls, but to myself.

"Damn girl," Cherry laughs. "I can see why they call you Firefly," she says, looking at me with a smirk.

"Silvia knows if she wants drugs to come to me. Either way, you don't hit girls. Especially ones associated with The Devil's Dust," Babs says, kicking him in the ribs hard.

"Dani, you want to prove yourself? Show him what happens when you mess with The Devil's Dust," Babs says, handing me the bat. I hand her the gun and grip the bat tightly, my fingers slipping from the sweat gathering in my palms. I look at the guy who is bleeding; his eyes dull from severe drug use. He reminds me of Ricky and Cassie who kidnapped me. Kidnapped me because of my mother who made Shadow's mom a criminal informant. My blood boils at the connection; maybe I need therapy from the traumatic experience they put me through. I swing the bat with an emotional yell as a loud crack follows, splitting his kneecap. Darin rears up and grabs his knee, screaming in pain. I smile, feeling relief, screw therapy, this will do.

"That 'a girl!" Molly laughs, kicking the guy in the gut.

I grip the bat harder and slam it down across his arm, the adrenaline feeling like a drug.

After a beat-down that guy will never forget, we all jump back in the van and head back to the club, leaving a bloody, unconscious thug in an empty parking lot, not knowing if he is dead or alive. On the drive back, the girls all start replaying everything that happened, but all I can feel is shame. Coming off the high of rage, I feel the leftover guilt eating at my conscious. *What the hell did I just do?*

Babs parks the van next to the garage and we all hop out.

"You did great kid," Vera says, patting me on the back.

"Yeah, this shit with your mom will fly over soon," Cherry remarks sweetly.

"Welcome to the pack," Pepper says, smacking my ass.

I smile lightly as they all head into the club, acting as if nothing savage just happened. It's crazy when you think about it. The hurdle of life's abandonment scarring us, we wake up every day in the hope of redemption, that today will be better, but it's a lie. In reality, you have to swim to survive, even if it means drowning the innocent to get to the shore of hope.

I head to Bobby's room and notice blood on my hands, so I walk into the bathroom and turn the shower on hot. The room fills with steam as I look into the mirror and notice blood spatter all over my face and clothes. I undress quickly and jump in the shower to rinse off. The warm water rushes down my body, rinsing the traces of blood away as if it hadn't happened. Looking at the water of blood and sins washing down the drain, I think about my mother, how distraught she would be if she found out I was a part of kidnapping, battery and assault, possibly murder. Breaking her upbringing of an untainted daughter. A laugh escapes my mouth, a vicious laugh

THE SCARS THAT DEFINE US

so hard my belly cramps. My laughter begins to falter as I realize proving myself to the girls tonight unleashed something far darker than I could've ever imagined. It is dangerous, manic, and it craves the throes of violence. It's exactly what my mother tried to keep me from discovering my whole life.

◆ ◆ ◆

Waking up this morning, I feel different. I feel the innocent, fragile mind that was my norm vanish into the wind, like pieces of a dandelion blowing into the darkness and fluttering down into a world of angst and bravery. White wings which were once my sign of innocence have molted into dark, ominous feathers, piecing off one by one.

I have Bobby take me to the apartment first thing; luckily, I don't run into Shadow. When I walk into the apartment, it is much cleaner than the last time I was here. I remember coming here after Shadow and I had our getaway; the place was trashed by Bobby. I close my eyes tightly trying to push out the images of Shadow and me at the beach house. Will the pain of his betrayal ever wear off?

"So, I'll put your things in my room just in case Shadow decides to show up," Bobby says, packing my crap into his room. I follow him and notice his room has a similar layout to Shadow's, only different colors. Bobby's bed is unmade and has a red comforter with white sheets, and its size is just as big as Shadow's. Bobby's dresser is white with a huge back mirror and his room has clothes thrown from one end to the other. I can't even tell you the color of carpet he has, or if he even has carpet. It's just a sea of dirty clothes.

"Needs cleaning, but its home," he says, smiling.

"Thanks, Bobby. You have been a life saver in all of this," I say, my tone appreciative.

Bobby shakes his head. "Just doing what was ordered." He glances at me with an unreadable look.

"So, first step is getting you a job," Bobby says, rubbing his hands together.

"Oh, goody," I say dramatically.

"I'll pick up some newspapers in town, see if anything sparks your interest," he says, smirking.

"That would be great, thanks." I tilt my head to the side with a smile of appreciation.

"Yeah, no problem," Bobby says, grinning a panty-dropping smile. He scratches his chest, the act bringing his shirt up and showing his rock-hard abs. I suck in a tight breath and look at the dirty clothes around my feet; anything to keep my mind off how horny I am and how Shadow is not here to relieve it. My blushing cheeks giving away I find Bobby attractive, he chuckles and walks into the living room. I take a steady breath and follow.

"There should be food and shit in the fridge if you get hungry. I'll be back later," he says, heading toward the door.

"Oh, and Firefly," he hesitates, pausing at the door.

"Ya?" I dart my gaze from the fridge to the door where he's standing.

"Keep your ass in this apartment," Bobby demands, his hand pointing to the floor, his harsh tone making me jump. Before I can ask why, he slams the door shut.

3

Shadow

I PULL MY .45 UP AND AIM AT THE TARGET ACROSS THE GRASSY FIELD, take a deep breath and apply pressure to the trigger. Instantly, the gun fires and recoils, giving me a brief second of relief, but not enough to curve my dark craving: killing.

"Hey, fucker."

I look over my shoulder and see Bobby walking up behind me. I nod at him and aim my gun back at the target.

"You going to ignore me forever?" he asks.

Annoyed, I lower my gun and scowl at him.

"I'm not ignoring you, just been busy," I reply, but it's a lie. Ever since he has taken Dani under his wing, I have avoided him any chance I could.

"Yeah, whatever," he says, lying his gun out to load. "What's the deal with you and Firefly?" he asks. I look at him in disbelief. *How the hell is he going to ask me that? Especially while I have a loaded gun in my hand.*

"Not much to tell; she's a fucking rat," I declare, firing my gun at the target. Just saying those words makes my stomach knot. I'm not sure if it's because I feel it's far from the truth or because I feel she may very well be a threat. Either way, I have to try to keep my head focused; she's not to be trusted.

"You still think she's not telling the truth?" Bobby asks, aiming at the target and firing. Looking at Bobby, I can't help but notice his aim is a little off.

"Raise your gun up an inch," I tell him.

"I have seen how bitches manipulate and deceive to get what they want. Fool me once." I aim my gun at the target. "That's all you get," I whisper. I fire the rest of my rounds in a rage, hitting the target every time. It's the truth; women will do anything, use any weapon they see fit to get what they want. Not me. I won't be one of those guys left in the storm of a deceiving female.

Bobby shakes his head." I think you're wrong, brother."

"Don't much care what you fucking think, Bobby," I spit, his attitude sparking flames of uncontrollable anger.

"Right so that little altercation between you and Tom Cat was nothing?" Bobby smarts. I turn and glare at him, of course he would have seen that.

After Bull appointed Tom Cat to transport Dani, I saw Tom head towards Dani's room later that evening. I couldn't help but stand by her door and see what the fuck he was doing in her room. Dani was sitting on the bed, her body slumped over. She looked extremely sad, and it killed me. I know I caused that sadness, a part of me wanted to comfort her. But I couldn't get passed that she might be a threat. Tom Cat rested his hand on Dani's shoulder gaining her attention. The innocent touch sparking a jealous rage within me. He introduced himself, his tone cheery, and friendly. It pissed me off. After he left her room I followed him to the court yard.

"Tom Cat, can I get a word?" I ask.

"Hey brother, what's up?" he questions, placing his hands on his hips.

"You driving Dani around, huh?"

"Yeah, apparently," Tom Cat says, grinning from ear to ear. He lifts his eyebrows in a gesture that has me furious. I feel jealous and angry, and I fucking hate it. I slap my hand over his shoulder, and dig my fingers deep into his flesh.

"Don't think about trying anything," I seethe. "You are to drive Dani where she needs to go, and keep your fucking mouth shut," I whisper, my tone harsh and threatening. I tighten my hold on his shoulder, making my knuckles turn white from the pressure. "Do you understand?" I ask.

Tom Cat winces from my hold. "Yeah, man!" He bellows with pain.

"And if you see anything tying her to her mother, you come to me first," I demand. Tom looks at me like I'm insane, his eyes wide with uncertainty. I glare, and tighten my hold. Tom's knees buckle from the force, making him finally nod in agreement. I release my hold on him, and walk away. I still care for Dani, and it fucking hurts.

"What the fuck-ever, man," Bobby says, breaking me from my thought. He throws his hands at me and walks away.

Fucking Dani. If it wasn't already bad enough, now she's turning my fucking brother against me. Never should have got involved with her ass.

A week has gone by, and I have been locked away in this damn apartment like a prisoner. Bobby has brought me all kinds of newspapers and I have even looked on the internet for a job, but unless I want to be a dog walker or receptionist at a tanning salon, I can't find anything, which sparks my interest. Not for a career, anyway.

I have cleaned the apartment from one end to the other, all except Shadow's room; I can't bear to walk in there. Just looking at the door alone sparks images of Shadow and me in a lover's ecstasy.

I push through the double doors, which lead to the balcony of the apartment and lay in the sun lounger. The one advantage of being here is getting to sunbathe on the balcony.

I position my black bikini top and notice I have tan lines. I lay on my stomach and untie the back of my top in attempt to get my tan even. I really wish I could find my iPod. My emotions are running so hot and cold right now I can't make out how I feel about anything in my life. Music would help settle my racing thoughts.

◆ ◆ ◆

"Hey, I brought Chinese food." I spring up to the sound of a voice and see the sun is setting and Bobby holding a brown paper bag.

"Fuck me," he mutters, looking at me with heavy eyes. I look down at what he is staring at and notice I am topless.

"Shit!" I yell, grabbing my top. I press it to my chest and run toward the bedroom.

"Shit. Shit, Shit," I chastise myself, running into the room and slamming the door. I grab a red shirt from the closet and slip it on. It hangs off my shoulder and goes to my hips.

"Ouch!" I scream at the piercing burn coming from the fabric scratching at my skin. I go to the bathroom and look into the mirror. Noticing my face is a little red, I turn and pull the shirt up and see my back is really red. I can't believe I fell asleep out there; now I'm burnt to a crisp.

"Everything okay, Firefly?" Bobby's tone is concerned as he

comes into the room.

"Yeah, I'm just sunburnt," I say, lowering my shirt. Bobby walks into the bathroom, his large body taking charge of the room. He leans down, opens the bottom cabinet to the sink and pulls out a bottle of green aloe.

"Turn," Bobby demands, twirling his finger for me to turn my back toward him. I turn slowly, still a little embarrassed he just saw my naked breasts. Bobby pulls the back of my shirt up and plasters his large hands on my back. The green jelly feels like ice, making my body wince from his touch.

"Sorry," he says, rubbing the aloe in. "Falling asleep on the deck is easy to do. I've done it a time or two," he says, rubbing the jelly upward. My eyes catch his in the mirror; his blue eyes are staring back at me. My breath catches when his fingers graze the soft tissue of the side of my breast. I look over my shoulder, gaze at Bobby, his eyes daring, and hooded. My stomach flips at the thought that Bobby might find me attractive, that he may want me, but with the mess I'm in, I can't pull him down with me, and as messed-up as it seems, I still love Shadow. As if Bobby could read my thoughts, he pulls away the same time I do.

Bobby clears his throat as he wipes his hands on his jeans. "I got us some grub, you hungry?"

"Yeah, starving, actually," I respond. The situation feeling awkward, I make my way out of the bathroom.

I walk into the living room and sit on the floor as Bobby hands me a container of Chinese food. He sits next to me on the floor, crossing his long legs at the ankles while he plunges his fork into his own container.

"I grabbed us a few movies. This one is supposed to be funny," he says, grabbing the remote off the couch.

"I could go for a laugh," I say, looking into my plastic container and finding Lo Mein noodles, my favorite.

We sit in silence, watching TV and eating dinner. Every now and then, one of us will laugh when something silly happens in the movie.

"Need a drink or anything, Firefly?" Bobby asks, standing up and heading toward the kitchen.

"Yeah, sure," I say, slurping a noodle in my mouth.

Bobby hands me a beer and sits on the floor. "Thanks, Bobby," I say. "Bobby, is that your real name?" I inquire, taking another bite.

"No," he replies smiling. "Not a fan of my first name. That's the reason why everyone calls me Bobby," he explains while taking a huge swig from his beer.

"Ah, come on, tell me." I nudge his shoulder, trying to urge him to open up.

Bobby chuckles. "Robert," he says, taking a mouth full of noodles.

"Robert?" I question with a raised brow.

Bobby nods with pursed lips. I observe his features, his blond, wavy, surfer-like hair and blue eyes; his big, beefy arms with tattoos; I even notice his big, plush lips.

"Yeah, you don't look like a Robert," I laugh with a scrunched face.

"Yeah, my whole name is Robert Zane Whitfield," he says with distaste.

"I like the Zane, but not a fan of the Robert," I say smiling.

"I've been called worse things," he jokes.

Sitting quietly, I notice I haven't seen Doc around, or heard much about her from Bobby, either.

"Where's Doc?

Bobby shakes his head. "She's complicated."

"More complicated than Shadow and me?" I ask with a grin.

Bobby laughs. "Possibly."

He sets his empty container next to the couch behind him as he wipes his mouth with his hand, the sound of the scruff rubbing against his palm.

"We start getting along great, but she always pulls back."

Bobby's tone sounds defeated, like he can't figure it out.

"What happened?" I ask, setting my empty container down.

"I told her I wanted to meet her daughter one day." He looks up at me with a whimsical look. "She froze, told me it wasn't in her best interest to allow me to get involved with her daughter or for us to go that far in whatever we have." He cracks his knuckles, the sound of it making my body shiver.

"That sucks." I try to offer something more empathetic, but really I can understand her decision. Bobby is involved in a club, which is criminal and makes enemies left and right.

"Think I'm just a fuck buddy to her," he says, running his hands through his golden hair. "Fine with me, though," Bobby laughs, gaining an eye roll from me. Sneaking a look at him, I notice his eyes squint at the corner with concern. I wonder what their story is.

We finish our beers while continuing small chitchat. I learned Bobby hates surfing, loves football, but hates baseball. He loves animals and will eat just about anything. His whole attitude is different from Shadow; Bobby is carefree and light, where Shadow is dark and complicated.

After the third movie, I can barely keep my eyes open and start to nod off.

I wake up to large arms under my legs and neck, lifting me from the floor.

"Where are you taking me?" I ask half-asleep.

"Taking you to bed, Firefly," Bobby says, his voice awake and alert. I feel my body shift with every step. His body is hard and lean against mine, making me feel small. I can't help but notice the smell of exhaust and coconuts in the crook of his neck.

I feel my body placed on the bed and the blanket pulled over me.

"I enjoyed tonight, Bobby. Thanks," I mumble. It was nice having some kind of human interaction. As much as I wish it was Shadow, I think it's time to realize that Shadow and I wouldn't be anything less than carnage.

"Yeah, we should do it again," Bobby says, his tone sincere. He heads toward the door and begins to close it.

"Night, Firefly."

Shadow

I sit in my usual seat in the back, away from other customers and the action. The leather is cracked in my chair and it smells like cheap perfume, but it's not as loud back here. It doesn't really matter where I sit, though; the girls always seem to flock toward me. The lighting is dimmed to a seductive glow, the air filled with fog and the room littered with half-naked girls, horny men, and loud music.

"Hey, Shadow," one of the strippers says, walking my way.

"Hey, Jasmine," I say casually. Jasmine has dark hair, green eyes and is wearing a black, sheer robe over her naked body. It doesn't leave much to the imagination, as I can see everything. I notice Bobby sit in the chair next to me. I look over and give him a nod as he stares Jasmine down.

"Haven't seen you here for a while," Jasmine says, sitting on my lap uninvited. I look at her face as she turns and smiles at me, her green eyes catching me by the balls. I came here hoping to escape Dani, and I still manage to fall face-first into her.

"Hey, babe, why don't you get us our usual," Bobby suggests to Jasmine.

Jasmine gets up from my lap instantly. "You got it, babe," she throws over her shoulder as her eyes flirt with Bobby. Her green eyes make me see Dani rather than this slutty stripper. I squeeze my eyes shut and try to shake away anything Dani out of my head.

"You asked me to come here, Bobby, so what's up?" I ask, eyeing the girls on stage dancing for a quick buck. A blonde, busty girl winks at me as she grips the chrome pole and swings her legs around it, making her whole body circle it.

"Just worried about you, man; thought you could use getting out," he says with sincerity. I don't need his empathy.

"Worry about your own shit, I'm fine," I say, my tone cold and angry.

"Whatever you say, brother," Bobby chuckles. He knows I'm anything but fine; sometimes I hate how well we know each other.

"How is Dani doing?" I ask.

"She's all right. She's trying to get a job right now," Bobby says, adjusting his pants as the blonde grinds the pole center stage.

"Can't find one?" I ask, looking in his direction. I find it hard to believe we can't get her a job. We have connections everywhere.

"Nah, not any she wants," Bobby answers. "I think she's looking for a job she can settle down and make a career with, I'm not -"

"She wants to dance," I say, interrupting Bobby. He eyes me awkwardly. "Like ballet. She told me she loves to dance ballet. She was going to help teach little kids or some shit in New York before her mother stepped in." I look over and see Jasmine hand Bobby his drink before handing me mine.

"So, Shadow, you going to take me in the back and show me a good time?" Jasmine asks, eyeing me with those green eyes. Looking into those pools of green, all I can think of, all I can see, is Dani. How much I miss her. How I want to smell her scent of peaches and feel her wrapped around my cock.

"Yeah. Let's go," I say, standing up. She links her skinny little fingers through mine and pulls me toward the back into a private room.

The sun is out and burning bright as we ride into town. Bobby woke me up after sleeping until noon, telling me he had a job lined up for me somewhere. I'm nervous; who knows what kind of job Bobby found. I can't help but notice the unease I feel riding on the back of his bike. I hate feeling like I'm breaking a club law when I don't even belong to Shadow anymore. The motorcycle roars forward, snapping me from my thoughts as we turn into a parking lot full of businesses. I climb off the bike and hand Bobby my helmet.

"There it is," Bobby says, pointing through the lot. I look in that direction and notice a two-story building. It has a large, glass front and the foundation is made of clay-colored bricks. I look at the sign and almost lose my lunch.

'Of The Ballet'

It's a ballet studio.

"Shadow mentioned something about you liking ballet, so some strings were pulled to get you the job," he says, putting his helmet on the bike.

"Who pulled some strings?" I ask as I stare at the building in awe.

"Come on, you're going to be late," he states, tugging on my arm and ignoring my question.

I walk in the door and a bunch of little girls in leotards, smiling and giggling, run out with their parents. I notice mirrors plastering the walls, with ballet barres along them. The ceiling is high with windows along the top, filtering in a generous amount of sunlight. On the right of us sits a curved desk with a pair of ballet slippers hanging in a display case on the wall amongst medals and awards.

"Ah, you must be Dani?" a voice from behind a desk asks.

"Yes," I say, smiling, standing on my tiptoes to see over the desk.

A woman stands from behind the desk and walks toward me. She is tall and thin with a pale complexion. Her blonde hair is pulled into a tight bun, and she has honey-colored eyes.

"Nice to meet you. I'm Mila." She darts her thin hand out to shake.

"Hi," I say, shaking her hand back.

"You're here about a job, right?" she asks.

"Yes," I respond with a kind smile. She leans to the side and eyes Bobby standing behind me before looking back at me.

"Do you have any experience?" she asks.

"I have practiced ballet since I was a little girl," I inform.

"Right. Show me," she says, crossing her arms, no humor to be found in her tone.

I look over my shoulder and see Bobby standing there watching me, so I look back at Mila and take a deep breath.

I stand in the fifth position, the sides of my feet touching, and my toes pointing to the opposite foot's heel. Balancing on my left leg, I slowly lift my right foot off the floor at a forty-degree angle. I turn out my right hip and straighten my right kneecap. Then, I lift myself to stand on my toes, my left foot into an en pointe—as much as I can without the proper shoes—while I point my toes on my right foot. I lift one arm up while bowing the other out from my body. I smile because even after not practicing for as long as I have, my body immediately remembers. I let my frame ease as my foot screams from my en pointe, and my calves burn from not being used in a while.

"Arabesque, very nice," she says smiling. "We have different ballet slippers in the back you can use, along with a leotard until you can buy your own," she says, pointing toward a door to the side of us. "I'm going to start you off with the younger girls, three times a week. When we need filling in, you work with the older girls. You start tomorrow," she explains, handing me papers to fill out.

"Thank you so much!" I enthuse, shaking her hand just a little too eagerly. I cannot believe I just landed my dream job, finally getting to do what I love. I never thought I would wear another pair of ballet slippers again.

"You're welcome. Get those papers filled out before you return, Dani." She turns and walks back behind her desk just as the phone starts to ring.

"Yes!" I yell out and slap Bobby's arm. "I got the job. I cannot believe it." I say, letting out a breath as we leave the studio.

"Sounds like we need to celebrate, Firefly," Bobby says, smiling wolfishly.

"Hell yes!" I say, laughing.

Looking at the reflection in the mirror, all I see is a monster staring at me, an ugly regret looking back. When Jasmine took me in the back room at the strip club last night, all I could see was Dani's green eyes looking over the shoulder of a complexion that reminded me of my Firefly. I closed my eyes and imagined her laugh, her smile and smart mouth. Then the bitch spoke, and I opened my eyes and saw anything but Dani; I saw a mistake smiling back at me. I pulled my pants up and got the fuck out of there, leaving Bobby behind. I came straight back to the club where I drowned myself in whiskey and cocaine.

Without Dani, my days seem cold and long, waking up to a constant emptiness surrounding my soul. I know I still love Dani, but my head can't get around if I can trust her or not. I try to numb myself from the truth, but I can't seem to get over this hurdle of betrayal lingering deep within my fucked-up soul. I look from the sink and see my blue eyes in the mirror. Looking into them, I imagine Dani's fierce, green ones.

I roar with anger and slam my fist into the mirror. My image of obsession shatters into pieces, falling into the sink. Bursts of stinging and burning fill my hand instantly; I look down and see trails of blood dripping from my hand. I relish the feeling of pain somewhere besides my fucking chest, as the blood reminds me I'm still alive even though I feel like a walking corpse. I want Dani, but I have to know she's not a threat. Not a sealed fate to prison or death row because once I have her again, there's no way I can hold back.

I walk into the hall in search of a towel to wrap around my bleeding hand when Bull's voice stops me.

"So, she got a job, huh?" He pauses; he must be talking about Dani. "That's great news. You coming back here later? Think we are going to let loose; the brothers could use it after everything that's been going on." He pauses again. "How are you guys going to celebrate?"

I'm guessing Bobby's taking Dani out to congratulate her on getting the job, and the thought pisses me off.

"Well, sounds like fun. Let me talk to her." He pauses. "Hey, Doll, I heard you got a job. I couldn't be happier for you. I'll try and stop by sometime and see you," he says softly before hanging up.

I round the corner, hoping the act of my eavesdropping isn't apparent.

"What the fuck happened to your hand?" Bull asks, pointing to my bloodstained hand.

"Nothing," I respond coldly.

As soon as we left Of The Ballet, Bobby drove us to get liquor, where I was told I wasn't allowed to pick because I apparently have shitty taste in alcohol and pick chick drinks. He grabbed two bottles, one amber-colored and another some kind of tequila. We stopped and picked up some take-out before heading back to the apartment. I'm glad fate has decided to finally hand me a stack of cards in my favor. Landing this job may allow me to finally get my life on track and move forward. My chest tightens; the thought of having to move forward without Shadow in the play hurts. I don't understand how he can just wash his hands of me so easily; did he feel nothing for me? We did fall for each other very quickly. How well can you know someone in that short amount of time?

"Here, take this shot, Firefly." Bobby hands me a glass of tequila in between scarfing down noodles from my take-out box. We've been back at the apartment for about an hour now, and we haven't stopped drinking since we walked in.

"This is my third one. You remember what happened last time you handed me shot after shot?" I remind him as I throw the fire down my throat. I got so drunk last time, but it was an experience I'll never forget.

"Yeah, that was some funny shit," he says, chuckling to himself. "Oh, I got something for you," Bobby says, moving to his cut slung on the back of the couch.

"Oh, yeah?" I ask excitedly. I follow him toward the couch with a shot in hand.

"To keep you safe," he says, handing me a sleek, black gun. I set the shot glass on the coffee table and palm the gun, my hand instantly sweating.

"It's an untraceable pistol, so don't get caught with it," he says, smiling. "Here is how you turn the safety off." He clicks a button on the side and looks at me to see if I understood what he just did. He then pulls the top of it back, making a loud clicking noise. "And this is how you load it," he instructs, handing it back to me.

"Never aim at someone unless you have every intent of killing them," he says seriously. "I'll try and get you to the shooting range to shoot sometime." He sits back down on the floor where I was sitting moments before.

I eye the gun placed in my hand. It makes me nervous holding it, but I feel powerful with it. I hold another's fate in my hands with this gun.

I put the safety back on and place the pistol on the counter for now.

"I can't believe you skipped the party to stay and mingle with my lame ass," I tell him, downing another shot. I wince from its brutal assault in my throat, gaining a laugh from Bobby.

"Gah, I'm going to regret this in the morning," I say, smacking my lips. I can feel the numbness creeping up the sides of my mouth from the alcohol, letting me know it is taking effect.

"My mom always had a saying: No regret in life, no fear in love." His face lights up as he speaks. He holds a shot glass in a toast before tossing the amber liquid back.

"Your mom?" I ask.

"Yeah, she and my pops passed away in a car crash a while back," he says sadly.

"I'm sorry to hear that, Bobby. Were you guys close?"

Bobby nods. "Very. My pops would say, 'live life to the fullest and never see anything as a regret, but as a lesson. That when you love, love shamelessly and not with fear.' So eventually, my pops would say, 'no regret in life,' and my mom would chime in, 'no fear in love'," Bobby says, his lips curved in a smile.

"But we are here to celebrate, Firefly. Now, drink up," he orders, handing me another shot.

I hold it up. "No regret in life. No fear in love," I chant as I swish it back and yelp at the burn gliding down my throat. My body is starting to hum, and I feel my body temperature rise. I watch Bobby pull his shirt off as he is starting to feel the alcohol take effect and make him warm, as well. He struts over to the stereo and turns on some music. Justin Timberlake swoons through the speakers as Bobby slides to the left, his hand cupping his jean-clad crotch as he sings with the music. I can't help but laugh at him. Seeing a man as muscled as Bobby, covered in tattoos, dancing to Justin Timberlake is a sight to be seen, but damn if Bobby doesn't pull it off, he looks very alluring in my buzzed state of mind.

"Come on, Firefly. Get up and dance with me," he beckons, holding his hand out. I jump up in my giddiness and start singing with him, but my words are slurred and my feet stumble. His hands claim my hips as we dance to the music.

Four shots and three beers later, I'm smashed. Bobby, who has had way more than me, is even more wasted. He turns and pulls a brown wooden box from under the couch after tossing an empty beer bottle randomly across the floor.

"What's that?" I slur, my vision starting to blur. Actually, it's been a little fuzzy for a while, now that I think about it.

"This?" he slurs back.

I nod heavily.

He opens the lid, and I have to stare closely because of my blurry vision. I see a blue and white swirled glass pipe and a baggy containing what I think is weed.

"Ever tried it, Firefly?" he asks, packing the glass with the green stuff from the baggy.

"No." I shake my head, making the room spin. I close my eyes hoping when I open them, everything is still.

He lights the little glass and sucks in the smoke from the other end. "Here," he says, his voice high-pitched from holding the smoke.

"Uh, I've never done drugs before. I don't know," I hesitate, nibbling on my bottom lip.

"If you don't want to, I won't force you," he says calmly, letting out a puff of smoke.

"What if my job has drug testing?" I slur.

Bobby almost chokes on the smoke he's holding. "Nah, I doubt it," he laughs. "Mila dips her fingers in a lot worse than pot."

I have never tried weed, but I always wanted to. *What do I have to lose?* I grab the glass pipe and inhale deeply.

"There you go, Firefly. Let your freak flag fly," he chuckles.

I hold the smoke in my lungs, feeling the burn rise slowly. It's harsh on my lungs and feels like fire in my throat, making me exhale its earthy smoke. I start choking, the burn in my throat not letting up.

"That was a pretty big hit," he says, putting the things back in the box.

"Is that bad?" I ask, still coughing.

"Nah, but you're probably going to be high as a kite," he slurs.

I sit back, my body feeling light and dizzy. I feel my drunken state rise from the effects of the weed, making it hard not to throw up or pass out. I close my eyes and try to focus on where I'm sitting, mentally telling myself the room isn't spinning. I drown in the effects of feeling like I'm floating on a pool of clouds and dive into blackness. My numb body falls forward with a hard hit, but I don't have it in me to give a damn.

4

Dani

I WAKE UP TO THE SUNLIGHT BLARING INTO THE LIVING ROOM. I'M lying on the couch with a blanket thrown over me. I pull myself into a sitting position and moan from the pain riddling through my shoulder. When I look over, I notice a good-sized bruise.

"You did that when you passed out last night," Bobby says. I peer up and see him leaning against the doorframe. His blond hair is wet and his chest is bare; the only thing he's wearing is a white towel wrapped around his waist.

"My head hurts just as bad," I croak. I smack my lips together and swallow; my mouth feels dry and sticky.

"Here, drink this," Bobby orders, sitting a glass full of red liquid on the coffee table.

"What the hell is that?" I ask, pointing to the glass.

"Your hangover remedy. Drink it, shower, and you'll feel better," he states, laughing.

I reach over and grab the cold glass. I sniff it and smell tomato and lemon. I gag instantly.

Bobby chuckles and walks down the hall.

I take a deep breath and try to take a sip. As soon as the cool liquid hits my mouth, I feel vomit rise in my throat. I get up and take off toward the bathroom, running past Bobby to get to it.

◆ ◆ ◆

It's my first day at my new job and I love it. The little girls are so cute. I tell them to do a position and they just twirl and ask if they look like a princess. I can't help but laugh and twirl with them. Thankfully, I don't have a hangover and feel okay to spin. Bobby had to feed the red remedy juice to me sip by sip this morning, but he got it down me and I started feeling better.

"Aren't you a little too old to be a sugar plum fairy?"

I turn from the little dancing girls and see a gentleman dressed in a very expensive-looking suit. He has short, light-brown hair and vibrant, brown eyes, a chiseled jaw and thick lips. His arms are lean, and his frame looks a little muscled but not by much.

"Excuse me?" I ask, my head tilted.

"I'm Kelsey's father, Parker," he says, running his hands through his hair with a grin. His tone is smooth and accented.

"I'm Dani," I smile.

"Is that short for Danielle?" he asks with a handsome grin.

"Yes, it is."

Parker eyes me from head to toe in my leotard; his chocolate eyes taking in everything, making me bite my bottom lip uncomfortably.

"Well, Danielle, I'd love to have dinner with you sometime," Parker says, his tone flirty and his dark eyes intimidating. He walks to his daughter Kelsey and grabs her hand.

"I don't know—"

"Don't think of it as a date. Just a night to enjoy yourself," Parker interrupts, walking up to me. His stride is precise and calculated his tone deep and reassuring. It would be nice to go out and get Shadow off my mind, along with the club. Looking at the way things are going with the club and the fact that there is no sign of me gaining their trust, I should think about moving on. I look down at Kelsey who is spinning back and forth, as her dad holds her hand firmly.

"That sounds great," I say with a hard swallow.

"Perfect," he exclaims, his mouth turning upward into a gorgeous smile. He slides his hand along the side of his head, smoothing down his hair trying to curl just above his ear.

"Where should I pick you up?"

I walk over to the desk, write down the address of the apartment, and hand it to him.

"I'll see you tomorrow at eight, Danielle." He leans in and pecks my cheek lightly. I can't help but smell his scent of mint and aftershave as he leans back.

He winks at me and leaves as Bobby is walking in.

"Who is that douchebag?" Bobby inquires loudly, not caring if Parker or the little girls hear him.

"A night out," I say, raising my eyebrow.

"No shit?" Bobby asks, stepping back toward the door to get another look at Parker. "The fucker has money."

I step over to the door and look out. Parker and his daughter are climbing into a nice black, sleek-looking car.

"His name is Parker, and it's just a night out," I say, reassuring myself that it's nothing more.

"That is an Aston Martin, very expensive," Bobby states, tapping his knuckles on the glass. "What do you see in that prick?" he asks, his tone laced with revulsion.

Looking at Parker, he would be any girl's fantasy. He's handsome, appears to be a gentleman, and seems intelligent. Why I am not sold on the idea has me puzzled.

"I don't know," I whisper against the window, my breath fogging the glass as I breathe against it.

I feel Bobby staring at me, but I don't look. I just watch Parker leave the parking lot, wondering what the hell I'm thinking.

"It's good for you to get out. I'm sure you'll have fun," Bobby remarks, his hand patting my back. His encouragement to get back out there has me pulling from the glass and looking at him a little shocked.

♦♦♦

I settle for a red dress with a high neckline, the hem stopping just above my knee. Shadow bought it for me on our trip; he said I would look sexy as hell in red. I sigh. Tonight is to forget about Shadow, to just forget about the pain. I hear knocking come from the door, so I grab my silver heels and slip them on as I make way to answer it.

"She's not ready," I hear Bobby say in the living room, his voice cold and dripping with hatred.

"All right," Parker drawls out.

"I'm here," I say, rushing into the room.

"Danielle, you look stunning," Parker exclaims, his hands reaching for me. He palms my hand and turns it over, kissing the top of it gently.

"You look handsome, Parker," I say in return. He has his short, brown hair gelled back, and he's dressed in a grey suit which hugs his shoulders well.

"Where are you taking her?" Bobby asks, standing closely, his eyes stabbing Parker. Bobby's muscled body takes over the room, making Parker look small in comparison. Looking at Parker, I'm not sure he has any muscle now.

"Um," Parker hesitates. I can tell he is just as pleased with Bobby as I am. I raise an eyebrow at Bobby, my look of death trying to tell him to cut the fatherly bullshit out.

"I'm taking her to the Short Vine," Parker states, tugging me toward the door, his tone heavy with irritation.

Bobby scoffs as he sits back on the leather couch. "Of course you are," Bobby says, his tone unreadable.

I can see Parker puff out in anger.

"Let's go," I tell him. If I don't get us out of here, I know for a fact Bobby will cause problems.

"Yes. Let's," Parker says, eyeing Bobby with a raised eyebrow.

"Have a good night," Bobby sings, his blue eyes trailing Parker as we walk out the door.

As we make it out front to the pretty black car, I can literally feel the anger vibrating off Parker.

"Are those the type of people you hang out with?" Parker asks, his tone dripping with disgust. I stop before reaching for the door handle and look at him. 'Those people' he's talking about are my family, but I can see why he thinks Bobby is some kind of animal. I once used to think the same thing.

"They aren't bad once you get to know them," I say with a kind smile.

Parker smiles and opens the car door for me.

I climb into the expensive leather seat, it surrounds my body like a glove as Parker shuts the passenger door. A console sits between the driver's seat and my own, filled with a shifter and lots of controls. Seconds later, Parker climbs behind the wheel. His chocolate eyes take me in from head to toe, making my cheeks warm.

"Beautiful," Parker says, shaking his head like he can't believe it.

When we arrive at the restaurant, I feel out of place instantly. Just by looking at the place on the outside, it looks elegant and classy. There are vines sweeping over the patio where couples are eating outside, hiding them from the public's eye. The door is glowing with little light bulbs, which surround its entry, giving off just enough light to see the sand-stoned walkway. When we enter, the lighting is dim and there are racks of crystal and wine bottles elegantly placed for display with a bar set off to the right and women and men surrounding it. We are seated right away by a young lady dressed in a black cocktail dress with gold bangles. She doesn't speak; she just smiles and eyes Parker like dessert. She shows us our table and flashes Parker a knowing smile.

"You come here a lot?" I ask, watching the girl look over her shoulder at Parker as she returns to her podium.

"Uh, sometimes," Parker says, stumbling on his words. The table is classy with a white tablecloth and a little tea light in the middle, giving off a romantic energy. A waiter dressed to impress in a black tux hands us menus before bowing and walking away. This place is overkill and makes me feel extremely underdressed. I start tapping my foot, feeling anxious and uncomfortable, and open the menu. My eyes widen and I nearly have a heart attack at the prices. Parker gives a light chuckle at the expression on my face. "Order whatever you would like, Danielle." I smile lightly and look for the cheapest thing on the menu; money doesn't impress me. After we have ordered and are sipping on some very tasty wine, I look up at Parker who is staring at me intently. I swallow the gulp of dark wine and smile nervously.

"You are very beautiful, Danielle. Has anyone told you that?" Parker asks. I swirl the wine in my glass, looking at the dark-purple tides slam alongside the crystal.

"Yes they have," I whisper. Shadow comes to mind, taking me from the expensive dinner meant to impress me to mine and Shadow's first date. He made sandwiches and brought me to the beach; I love the beach. It was way better than this. I shake my head of Shadow and drink the rest of my wine.

During dinner, I learn Parker has a successful career as a lawyer, his car is his baby, and that he's recently divorced. Finally, after paying the check, we head back to his fancy car. As I reach for the door, Parker grabs my hand with force, pulling it away from the door handle.

"Let me," he says smoothly, his body so close to mine I can feel the heat coming off him. He opens the door but holds it so I can't enter.

"Are you in a rush to get away from me?" he whispers into my ear.

I don't say anything because I can't. My heart is beating so fast, and my palms are beginning to sweat. His eyes are hooded and marked with lust, telling me he wants me for dessert. He tucks his thumb under my chin and brings my head up and I try to pull from his grasp, but he tightens his grip on my chin painfully. He presses his lips to mine softly before letting me go and opening the passenger door.

"Holy shit," I mutter. I thought this wasn't supposed to be a date, but it really feels as if it is. This is too fast.

♦ ♦ ♦

He drives through traffic, precisely following all the traffic laws. He reaches his perfectly manicured hand over and laces it around mine.

"I can see something is holding you back from me, Danielle, and that's perfectly all right. I will wait," he says, giving my hand a light squeeze before placing it back on the wheel.

"You don't know anything about me," I retort, looking out the window. *How can a guy wait for someone he knows nothing about?*

"I look forward to knowing you better," he says, chuckling. I take my eyes from the window and look at him, a little shocked.

He takes his eyes from the road and looks at me, his chocolate eyes staring deeply into mine.

"You have the greenest eyes I have ever seen, Danielle," Parker declares sincerely as he takes in my face. I pull my gaze from his and look out the window. When Shadow witnessed my green eyes for the first time, he was shocked. Having vibrant colored eyes like my father, giving away that his president and I were related, scared the shit out of Shadow. The memory makes me smile.

We pull up outside Bobby and Shadow's apartment, the sexy car that purrs as you accelerate coming to a low hum before he turns the engine off.

"I had a great time tonight, Danielle. I haven't been out much since my divorce. I would love for you to join me for lunch. Give me the opportunity to get to know you better," he says, rubbing the side of my face with his soft fingers. I turn my head and look into his dark eyes. This hurts, being here with another guy, one who is anything but Shadow. Where Shadow is rough, Parker is smooth. Shadow has a colorful vocabulary, where Parker's is very mannered and educated. They are black and white. I look out the window and up at the apartment before looking back at Parker. It's lunch; what could it hurt? Having lunch with Parker, I know I don't have to worry about being dragged to some isolated location and having my mouth sewn shut for being a rat. He's safe.

"Ya, sure."

"How about tomorrow?" Parker asks eagerly.

"Sure," I respond, opening the car door.

I get out and hear Parker leaving the car, as well. I turn a little, surprised; I thought the night was over.

"Would you like me to walk you to your door?" he asks, walking closely to me.

"No. I'll be fine," I tell him, taking a step toward the sidewalk.

Parker suddenly grabs my hand and pulls me toward him. His face inches from mine, he leans forward slowly and kisses my lips tenderly. His touch is so soft, I'm not sure if he is actually kissing me, so I open my eyes.

"Goodnight, Danielle," he says sweetly.

"Goodnight, Parker," I reply stunned.

I make my way up to the apartment, the entire night playing on repeat in my mind. Parker is some prince charming. He's kind and sweet, yet I don't find myself head over heels for him. His touch is too soft, like he's afraid I'll break, and his money doesn't impress me.

I open the door and walk into the apartment, which smells of pizza and beer. I find the smell inviting rather than the smell of expensive wine and leather I just encountered. Bobby walks into the room, coming from the balcony.

"That's not how you kiss a woman," he says, with a smirk.

Oh, shit.

"How was the date with Pretty Boy?" Bobby asks, plopping down on the couch.

"Eh, fine," I answer, taking my heels off.

"You don't sound too impressed," Bobby suggests.

"I don't know. He's handsome and sweet; maybe too sweet. I don't know why I'm not crazy about him; he would be a total catch. Maybe I just need to go into it slowly. This whole thing with Shadow is going to take time to overcome," I say, sitting down next to Bobby.

Bobby snorts. "That's going to take you a lifetime, Firefly."

I grab the beer from his hand and take a sip with a questioning look on my face.

"You won't ever fall for that guy; he's a sissy. I saw the look on your face when he kissed you. You want someone to grab you by your hair and kiss you like they mean it," Bobby speculates, snatching the beer from my hands. I refuse to believe that, even if it may be true.

I stand up and grab the beer from Bobby's hand forcefully, nearly spilling it on his lap. "No, I was just shocked is all." I was shocked, but I didn't enjoy the kiss. There was no spark, no craving of hope that Parker would take it farther.

"Whatever you have to tell yourself," Bobby hollers as I walk down the hall.

Shadow

WALKING OUT OF MY ROOM THIS MORNING, I NOTICE THE CLUB IS littered with red cups and the smell of stale beer is overwhelmingly sickening. I partied alone, debating if I should go see Dani or not. I didn't go; she wouldn't want to see me. I have so much aggression built up, my beast craving the spill of blood, and my confusion with Dani doesn't help. My emotions and thoughts have been so out of control here lately. I can literally feel my ends fraying for the control I so desperately crave. I head toward the garage to lift weights, get my blood pumping.

I lay on my back and lift, the weights so heavy I feel the burn in my biceps instantly. Having pain somewhere other than my chest is welcoming. After about four sets, I hear boots thudding my way against the thick pavement.

I look over and see Bobby sit on some cinder blocks and lift weights with his left arm.

"Heard Dani got the job. You guys go celebrate or some shit?" I question as I continue to lift, the thought I should have been there to celebrate with her overbearing the pain in my biceps. Hell, it was me who got her the fucking job; as soon as I got back to the clubhouse after the strip club I called in a favor. I told Mila I would bail her mother out of jail and put her in rehab if she gave Dani a job. Mila and I go way back, and she herself has some drug tendencies but it's not as severe as her mother's addiction. I haven't fucked Mila, either; she's too much of a bitch for my taste. We just went to school together. Well, for the time I did go to school anyway.

"Yeah. Firefly is wild," Bobby says, laughing. I clench my teeth in anger; I trust Bobby but I don't like him around Dani.

"Good for her," I clip.

Bobby eyes me from the side. "You still on that trip about her being a threat, huh?"

"Nothing's changed for me to believe otherwise," I wheeze, out of breath as I lift the weights. I want Dani, but it's as if I have OCD and won't allow myself to have her until I know she's telling the truth.

"I knew you were going to fuck this up. That girl ain't going to be one of those who sits around and waits for you to figure your shit out," Bobby informs upon standing, his tone giving away how irritated he is.

"What the fuck are you talking about?" I ask, setting the weights in its original spot.

"Dani went on a date," Bobby replies with a smile, his tone of annoyance gone.

I stand, immediately pissed. "What?"

"You heard me. She met some guy at that ballet job, and he picked her up last night. Fucker is loaded with money and is fancy as shit," Bobby quips, rubbing his hands through his hair.

My jaw shoots with pain. It's clenched to the point I'm about to crush my teeth.

"Why'd you let her go on a date?" I demand. Dani is a threat to the club; she should be going to work and home, nowhere else.

"I didn't know I was supposed to tie her to the bed and hold her captive. I'm sorry," Bobby says sarcastically, pissing me off more.

"She's a threat to the club; she shouldn't be going anywhere!" I yell. "She could talk," I remind him.

Bobby scoffs like I've just said the most ridiculous thing.

"Well, she's going to lunch with him today," Bobby continues with a smirk. "Besides, considering you've already thrown her to the side, I think its best she gets as far away from you as possible." Bobby puffs his chest out, readying himself for my anger. "I told her it was a good idea," he shrugs.

I squeeze my fists closed with anger. How the hell is he going to encourage her to leave me?

"From the looks of that kiss last night, I'd rethink—"

Before I let him finish his sentence, I bash my fist into the side of his jaw as hard as I can muster. My force makes him stumble back, and my fist begins to radiate with pain.

"Fuck!" Bobby yells, grabbing his jaw, moving it side to side. "What the hell, man?"

I can't take the thought of Dani with someone else; she can't move on. I can't handle the idea that someone kissed her, and most of all, I can't accept the thought that Bobby encouraged her.

I thrust my fist into his gut, making him double over coughing. The anger of the situation has me thinking irrationally. I turn away from him, throw both my hands on my head, and take a steady breath.

"Who is this prick?" I ask Bobby.

"His name is Parker. He drives an Aston Martin and is supposed to pick her up for lunch today," Bobby wheezes.

"Why did you let her go? Why didn't you tell me before?" I question.

"You made it clear you didn't want Dani!" Bobby hollers, hunched over.

"Has anyone else come near her, laid a fucking finger on her?" I question, my voice wavering with anger.

Bobby looks towards the ground, his hesitation making me nervous, and pissing me off more.

"What aren't you telling me?" I ask.

"It was nothing, but I helped Dani put lotion on her burnt back and my hand slid against her tit."

My body rises with uncontrollable anger and my heart skips a beat trying to keep up with the amount of fury pulsing through me.

"I feel terrible about it, man. I shouldn't have crossed that line, I think of Dani like a sister." Bobby looks down at the ground shaking his head.

I can't help but throw a punch right into his guilt ridden face, his head snapping back as he takes the blow. I grab him by the head and loop my arm around his neck into a head lock, my arm constricting around his neck.

"I never un-laid claim to her as my ol' lady," I yell. Law is, an ol' lady is yours unless you un-lay claim to her. She doesn't have a say in the matter; nobody does.

Bobby suddenly kicks me behind the knees, making my legs buckle and causing me to fall hard on my ass. I stand, ready to kill the fucker, but am stopped short from his fist slamming into the side of my eye. My vision goes bright white for a second as a ringing screams in my ear from the impact. I use the back of my hand to wipe the blood gushing from my eyebrow and glare at Bobby.

Bobby stands, huffing.

"What the fuck are you thinking, Shadow?" he asks, out of breath. "You're out fucking around on her, claiming she's an enemy, but won't let her go." He shrugs in confusion.

I look at the ground. His words are true, but if I can't have Dani, nobody can.

"I get that you pulled away because you might have had to choose the club over Dani, if she was in fact a threat—"

"I did choose the club over Dani," I interrupt, my actions at doing so weighing heavy on my conscience.

"But this underlying-trust bullshit you got going on has got to go, brother," Bobby finishes.

I look away, knowing he's right, and I hate him even more for it. I love Dani, and I hate that I love her at the same time. I squint my eyes, the pain from my cut eyebrow starting to rise.

"She still loves you, ya know," Bobby advises, eyeing me from the side.

I scoff at his remark. Fuck love.

"The only reason she's with this guy is because he's a rebound. She seems repulsed by him." Bobby's admission makes me see red, but the thought Dani might still have some kind of feelings for me is replacing my anger with hope. Maybe she is trying to move on but can't. I can relate.

"Why would I care?" I ask, trying to get a hold of myself. Bobby looks at me with a cocky smile, knowing I do care and it's pissing me off. I growl in frustration. I can't get over the idea Dani has tried to move on; it hurts more than anything I have ever felt before. I would rather be with Dani and have her tear my heart out by ratting on me than live in this pain without her. I can't live with the idea of running into her on the street somewhere with another man. I know deep inside, in this exact moment, I would turn against the club to protect Dani if needed, making me feel like a traitor to my own brotherhood. If I have to choose Dani over the club, it could get me killed.

"You're fucking lucky I don't have my pistol, or I would shoot you in the dick," I say, pointing to his crotch.

"Why's that?" Bobby asks, his tone exasperated.

"You betrayed me," I mutter.

"You fucked up, and you know it. Dani didn't have anything to do with her mother and yet you cast her to the side," he declares, squaring his shoulders. "She deserves to move forward. It's not her fault you're so fucked up you can't see a good thing when it's standing in front of you!" he yells.

Fuck him. If I had my gun, I would really have fucking shot him.

I watch Parker pick up Dani from the apartment for lunch. The entire time, I'm gripping the handlebars of my motorcycle with such force my knuckles are white. I swear to God, if he kisses her, I'll shoot him. I park across from the sandwich shop where he takes Dani to lunch, I'm waiting for them to leave. I pull my phone out and look at the time; they've been in there for thirty minutes. How long does it take to eat a fucking sub sandwich?

I look up and see them leaving, finally. He's dressed in a suit, and his hair is swept to the back. He looks like someone who should be with Dani; there is no denying she deserves better than me. Dani looks beautiful, as always, wearing ripped jeans and a sexy, red top. My body vibrates with hostility just seeing them together. He reaches over and grabs Dani's hand. I can see her body stiffen and her face go pale. The idea of her uncomfortable with his guy makes me smile. She's not moving on. She's just trying to trick her mind into thinking she is. Parker reaches over and opens the car door for Dani, letting her slide in. What a pussy! I would have at least slapped her ass before she got in.

He rounds the car and adjusts his junk, wearing a smug look on his face. He doesn't seem very mannered at the moment; he's faking this whole gentlemen act. He climbs into the car and slowly pulls onto the road. I start my bike and follow. *What does Dani see in this prick?* I stay a few car lengths back so I'm not noticed and watch him drop Dani at the apartment. I can't see inside the car because I'm so far back, but that's probably a good thing. Usually when you drop a date off, you kiss them goodbye. I stare at the black car, waiting for her to get out. I groan heavily and look up at the sky. Stalking an ex-girlfriend, what a new low for me.

Dani leaves the car and nearly runs toward the front door of the apartment building. "Here we go," I mutter. I start my bike and follow Parker onto the road. I would go inside and shake Dani like a rag doll, asking what the fuck she's thinking, but I'm intrigued by this Parker. He darts off onto the highway and off the exit ramp; there is nothing on this side of town but bars and strip clubs. Not something I peg for Mr. Fancy. He parks in the Dirty Barrels parking lot and gets out. I sit on my bike and watch, interested what his kind would be doing at such a cheap bar. I figured him more for a cocktails and Bloody Mary kind of fucker.

After ten minutes has passed, he comes out with a brunette, who staggers and sways as she walks toward the parking lot. He points to his car and the drunk girl lights up. She walks faster toward it and starts to run her hand over the hood. He comes up behind her and grabs on her backside, making the girl arch her ass into him. He grabs her wrists and jerks her toward the passenger car door, opens it and pushes her into the back seat with force before climbing in. I sigh and look off into the distance. This asshole is not who Dani thinks he is, and I'll be damned if I let him near her.

After ten minutes of the car rocking, the door opens and the girl is pushed out. She stumbles onto the dirty parking lot, rolling on her back; she's really drunk. Parker gets out, pulling his pants the rest of the way up before using his foot to roughly roll the girl a few feet from his car. He then climbs in his car and takes off, throwing dirt and gravel on the girl. I shake my head and put my helmet back on before following. He heads toward the nice side of town, where the houses are big and you're paying for who your neighbors are rather than the quality of a house. When he pulls into a driveway, I pull over and watch him enter a circle drive. His house is huge and can be seen from the road; there is no denying he's got money.

◆ ◆ ◆

I wait by the car, leaning against it with my legs crossed in front. I'm going to ensure he never sees Dani again.

About an hour after he went in, Parker leaves his house and walks toward the car I'm waiting by.

"Get off my car, asshole," he yells, pointing his briefcase at me.

I look behind me at the car then back at him. "You mean this car?" I taunt.

"Yes, that car," he says, his tone irritated. I smirk and walk forward, my steps ones of a deadly promise.

"If you don't leave my property now, I'm calling the police," he snarls. His forehead starts to sweat, causing his hair to curl around his forehead. As soon as he's within reach, I grab him by the back of his head and pull him close.

"The police can't save you, pretty boy," I grit out, my teeth clenched with anger. I tighten my grip on the back of his neck and walk him to his car with force. With a violent thrust, I plow his face into the side mirror. His face breaks the mirror completely off, making him howl in pain. His body crashes to the ground, his face bloody and his nose probably broken.

"What do you want from me? You want money? I can get you money!" he pleads, holding his bleeding nose. I tilt my head to the side and laugh. Then kick him in the gut as hard as I can. He grunts in pain and starts coughing.

"I think you would do well to stay away from what's mine," I sneer, pulling him up by his gelled hair. His mangled face looks up at me as I threaten him. I throw him across the hood of his car, the weight of his body denting it as he tumbles off the hood. I walk around, not finished.

"She came on to me, asked if we could fool around in the back of my car," he justifies, talking about the girl he messed with earlier.

"I'm not talking about that girl, but you should be kicked in the head for that. Were you going to treat Dani like that?" I snap.

"Dani?" he questions. His eyes take on a confused look before brightening. "You mean Danielle." He looks at the ground and shakes his head. "I should have known," he mumbles. "No, that's why I found some nobody at a bar." He pauses and wipes the blood from his face with a handkerchief. "I wouldn't hurt Danielle." Dani's name in his mouth has me pouring with hatred for this fucker.

"Tisk, tisk. You should know, she's Devil's Dust property," I inform him. I grab him by his collar and drag him to his feet. "You will stay away from her and never talk to her again," I demand.

"Danielle is big enough to decide for herself who she wants to be with," Parker states, his voice calm. I tried to be nice in giving him the option to leave her alone.

I grab him by his shirt and pull him close. "Wrong answer, asshole."

I pull my fist back and slam it into his eye, marking his face with the impact of my hand.

"Okay. Okay. I won't talk to her again. Let's just go back and think things through," he says pathetically. He's a liar. First chance he gets, he'll be back sniffing on Dani's trail like a predator.

I pull his face close to mine. "There's no going back," I whisper.

I grab him by the throat and slam his head into the passenger-side window, the force shattering the glass as he falls to the ground, unconscious. I pull my gun from my holster and aim it at the back of his head. As my finger touches the trigger, I hear a shrill scream come from his house. I look over and see a frantic old woman dressed as a maid eyeing me with fear.

Shit. I put my gun back in its holster and hastily walk back to my bike. I've gotten sloppy; Dani has made me unfocused and careless at what I do best. I look behind me before pulling off and see the little old lady running out to Parker's limp body.

Dani

A week has gone by, and I haven't seen Parker. He also hasn't picked his daughter up from ballet or called me.

I grab my bag and leave work. A prospect named Tom usually shows up to take me to work and picks me up after. I'm not sure how he even knows my schedule; I don't know if he even speaks. He is always waiting outside on his bike with sunglasses and a helmet on, wearing a Devil's cut and blue jeans.

"Thanks, Tom!" I yell over my shoulder, entering the apartment after a long day of teaching girls to dance en pointe. When I enter the apartment, I see Bobby sitting on the couch watching T.V.

"Oh, hello," I squeak, shocked by Bobby's presence. I haven't seen him in about a week, either.

"Hey," he answers, lifting from his relaxed position.

"You've been gone," I say, pulling my keys from the door.

"Yeah, been on a run," he replies.

I set down the bag containing my leotard and head for the fridge.

"Shadow knows," Bobby tells me calmly.

"Knows what?" I ask, but I already know. Bobby opened his damn mouth about Parker and me. I bet that's the reason why I haven't seen him around.

"He knows about you and Pretty Boy," he informs me.

This catches my attention, I walk back into the living room and sit beside him.

"How'd he take it?" I ask.

"Not well; trust me," Bobby smirks.

"So, what happened?" My tone urges him to tell me more. He looks at me, holding my gaze for a moment before standing from the couch.

"You guys really need to work shit out. Just fucking talk to him." He grabs his cut from the couch and leaves.

I fall back against the couch with a sigh. The last time I talked to Shadow it didn't go too well. This world is not for me; I can't handle the life of being an ol' lady. Any place where the love of your life takes the side of men who may kill you and cheat on their women on a daily basis is not something I have in store for myself.

◆ ◆ ◆

It's late at night and I just finished soaking my sore feet on ice while watching sappy love stories. They seem to be the only thing on anymore. I start turning lights off and head to bed when the door opens. I pause from turning off the last lamp in the apartment. Shadow walks through the door, making my mouth part with fear. He's wearing ripped jeans; a snug white shirt; and of course, his cut, making him look badass. I gulp at the sight of him.

His eyes lock with mine, the torment in them holding me still. He scowls, his eyes narrowing with anger, reminding me Bobby told him about Parker and me. With that, I forget the lamp and start toward the bedroom quickly. Fear rides up my spine, hoping I can get to it and lock the door before Shadow can reach me. He leaps across the coffee table and grabs me by the hair, making me yelp in pain. Then he pulls my head back toward his face, the smell of grease and cologne arousing me as the hairs on my neck lift in fear.

"Heard you were with someone else. Thinking about leaving me, Firefly?" He speaks softly into my ear, but his tone is anything but gentle.

"Like you haven't messed around on me?" I seethe, my teeth clenched. My choice of words is not helping my situation. Shadow jerks my hair tighter with anger, making me whimper.

"Parker won't be bothering you anymore, trust me," Shadow declares, his words sharp and fierce. I try to turn in his grasp to see his face, to see if he is serious, but he pulls me close.

"You're mine, Dani" he whispers, the smell of alcohol strong on his breath. His words anger me; I refuse to let him own me and use me only when he sees fit.

"Like hell." I raise my voice as my fingers try to pry his hands from my hair. I wanted to be Shadow's, to be his everything. I came at him hard when we first met. There was no denying our connection but after recent events, I'm not so sure of anything anymore.

"You're my property until I say so," he says roughly. I can hear his teeth grit with anger as I defy him.

"Fuck. You." I annunciate each word hatefully.

Shadow laughs maliciously.

"Did that already." He says it like I was nothing, hurting me more.

I scoff at his remark, trying to act like his words don't affect me.

"Don't try and act like you don't want me," he taunts, nipping my ear roughly.

I huff and try to pull from his grip, but it's no use; he's too strong.

"Maybe I should remind you what it's like to be with a real man," he says, trailing his tongue up the edge of my ear, leaving a moist trail. His other hand plays with the elastic of my white-lace panties, causing them to wet with arousal. His alpha-male ways have me blistering with rage, but more than anything, I want him to throw me onto the floor and lay claim to my body, which has me even angrier. *Why can't I escape the ravenous hold Shadow has on me? Don't I deserve better?* I deserve some Prince Charming you read about in books growing up.

He roughly cups my breast with his free hand, making me sigh. His touch is like an old flame, and it ignites my arousal without my submission. My body hums with fear but warms with his touch.

I bite my cheek and hold my breath, trying to rein in my sigh and moan of lust.

"You and I both know you'll never escape my hell." Shadow pushes his groin into my ass, making me moan slightly.

I swallow the lump forming in my throat from my heavy breathing. "I'll find a way," I whisper.

"I wouldn't count on it," Shadow hisses, the sound of his rough voice makes me clench my thighs together tightly.

" It won't be with Parker. I can assure you that," he scoffs. "Prince Charming likes to find drunk girls at bars and push them in backseats of his car. I'm not entirely sure if that poor girl was consenting or not," he says in my ear. My body, warm from Shadow's touch, now cools. Parker wouldn't do something like that; Shadow is lying.

"You lie," I snarl under my breath.

"Believe what you like." He shrugs, pulling my head to the side by my hair. "But believe this, you are mine." His tone is promising and threatening, yet comforting.

Giving in, Shadow pushes me forward.

"How many other men have you been with?" he questions, walking into the kitchen with his shoulders squared and body puffed out. His blue eyes shimmer in the dark room as he passes the lamp, giving him a look of a fearsome animal ready to dismantle its prey.

"Excuse me?" I hedge, humiliated.

"You heard me. You sleep with that guy?" He digs his talons into me.

"None of your fucking business," I retort.

"Oh, but it is." He grins a smile so devilish it makes my body shiver.

My head turns when knocking sounds at the door. Curious who would be knocking at this late hour, I walk over and open it. Two half-naked chicks stand at the door with a distasteful expression on their faces. One is a blonde with her hair braided into pigtails, wearing a peacock-colored skirt with a green tube top. The other is a curly redhead with a pink skirt and pink, low-cut tank top.

I turn and cock my head to the side. "Friends of yours?" I ask Shadow, my voice tongue in cheek.

"Shadow, baby," one of the girls coos walking into the apartment, uninvited.

"Girls!" Shadow says excitedly, his eyes never leaving mine. I don't even try to hide the hurt in my eyes. Instead, I stare into his vindictive blue eyes and show him the damage he is causing. I look at the girls, eyeing me as if I'm the one out of place. I give Shadow one last look before making my way toward my room.

Once in, I slam the door and slide to the floor. I hear the girls giggle and laughing as I try to hide my sobs with the back of my hand. The sound of myself makes me ill. *Why does Shadow make me so damn weak?*

I deserve this. I was warned of the life the club lived. I created this Hell which is now my own.

I stare at Bobby's door, the door that bars the girl I *want* to be with but am conflicted to be with. Hearing she was with another man has me thinking unthinkable things. I want to kill someone; I want to brand Dani so everyone in the world knows she's mine. Yet somehow, I still feel the need to keep her at arm's length. I shake my head, pissed I did this to myself. I had a code, rules I lived by religiously to make sure I never felt like this but Dani slipped her way in with her innocence and underlying defiance, making me feel like I could be normal, could trust and love someone. I scoff at myself. Trust. Love. Listen to me; I sound fucking weak. I close my eyes and drag my hands through my hair. Weak is what I have become, though. Dani's love is like a plague, killing me slowly, making me powerless. Making me think irrationally, giving me false hope of what could be. It's poison.

"You okay, baby?"

I open my eyes to see two sluts standing in my living room, eyeballing me with concern. I wanted to hurt Dani, wanted to hurt her like she did me when I heard she was moving on. But after seeing the pain in her eyes, seeing her break down further than she thought she could ever fall, I felt regret. I feel like a jackass. I grit my teeth. I feel this way because I'm in love with Dani. If I was thinking clearly, I would drag these girls in the back and fuck them, watch them fuck each other and then fuck them again, making them scream my name. But I can't.

I stand, stomp my way toward the couch and hand one of the girls their purse. "Get out," I bark, the sight of them angering me.

"But we just got here," one says, trying to sound flirty. It might have been sexy at the bar, but now it's repulsive. These girls couldn't hold a flame to Dani; they're just trash.

I point to the door. "And now you're leaving. Get. The. Fuck. Out!" I shout.

"You're an ass, you know that?" one sneers, slinging her huge-ass purse over her shoulder. She isn't telling me anything I don't already know, though.

I grab my beer, which I probably don't need and walk back down the hall slowly, standing against the wall across from the door that holds a broken Dani. I slide down the wall in defeat, my emotions for this woman killing me from the inside out. I'm damned in destroying us, and I'm incapable of preserving a normal relationship. I'm like a little boy handling a butterfly too roughly, knocking the vibrant-colored dust which makes it unique loose then pulling its wings off one by one, keeping it from being free and making it a prisoner of flight. I reach into my pocket and pull out Dani's iPod. I don't know why I kept it. I could buy my own, put better tasting music on it even, but for some reason, every night I find myself listening to it. I put the ear buds in and turn it to "Torn To Pieces" by Pop Evil. The song is more fitting, describing my life so accurately.

6

Dani

I OPEN THE DOOR TO FIND SHADOW ASLEEP ON THE FLOOR ACROSS THE hall this morning. He looks sweet and at peace when he's asleep. Looking at him in his cut, tattoos peeking out beneath his shirt, I realize why I can't have a Prince Charming; I've fallen in love with the villain. Living life on the edge and breaking all the rules, I want to find redemption in us. Our love was never meant to happen but awoke by chance. Only time will tell if hope gets us anywhere or if it's just a word they teach people who are giving up.

Looking him over, the iPod in his hand catches my eye—*my* iPod. That asshole, I've been looking everywhere for that thing. I gently grab it and look it over then look back at Shadow, watching him sleep. His face is soft when he's asleep. I don't understand him and I don't understand us. I heard him yell for those girls to leave last night, but why? He clearly brought them here to make me jealous, to watch my pain. I look down at my iPod and find Justin Timberlake's "Not A Bad Thing" and put it on repeat. I sit it back down beside his hand and head toward the kitchen. I want him to know loving me isn't a harsh reality; it's an earth shattering high. As hard as it is to accept, Shadow will always be a part of me. He brought out a side of me out that was chained and kept prisoner. I was set free when I met Shadow, released from the throes of detained lies and flown into the dark truth of what lies beneath my surface.

I'm putting my bowl up from breakfast when I hear Shadow groaning as he wakes up from down the hall. He walks in and instantly my body is alive from his presence. He leans against the counter and eyes me with his stormy, blue eyes. I look away, trying to fight the internal battle my body is having with my mind.

"I didn't sleep with them," he says roughly, his voice still sleepy. He's talking about those two girls last night. I knew he didn't sleep with them, but I won't say that.

"Congratulations, you saved yourself an STD or two," I reply condescendingly.

Shadow smirks, but his eyes are held with sorrow. Sorrow from what, us? From me trying to move on with my life?

We sit silently, our bodies screaming to throw ourselves at each other, wanting to make up for the damage we have caused.

"I just wanted to get out, get away from the idea of being a prisoner. Parker seemed nice," I babble, breaking the silence. There was no way I would have ended up with Parker; being next to Shadow and the way he makes my body come alive confirms that. "I just wanted to talk to someone who didn't see me as an enemy," I whisper. Shadow flinches at my words as if I just reached over and slapped him.

He rubs his hands up and down his face as he groans in frustration. His reaction shows me I did exactly that, though. I hurt him. He hurt me, too.

"What are we doing, Shadow?" I ask, planting my hands on the counter. "I'm tired of this charade. If you want me, then be with me.

If not..."

Shadow looks up at me, his eyes hard and angry.

"You are my ol' lady until I say so," he hisses, his words clipped. I stare into his damaged eyes; images of us together before the raid swirl in the depths of them.

He shakes his head from our silent stare off and abruptly heads toward the door.

"Shadow!" I yell.

He stops and stares at me, our gazes of confusion and hurt trying to silently speak to one another before he shuts the door.

◆ ◆ ◆

"Very good, girls," I compliment, trying to encourage the little girls attempting to learn to dance en pointe. I look at the clock and see it's past six pm, quitting time.

"All right, let's call it quits for today and I will see you girls next week," I remark cheerfully and head toward the door. I'm glad it's time to end the day; my feet are killing me, and I'm pretty sure I split a toenail. My feet are truly taking a beating. I change out of my leotard and put on some loose-fitting shorts and a white tank top. When I peel off my ballet shoes, one of my toes is sticky with dry blood.

Shit.

I hobble to the bathroom and clean my foot before trying to stuff it in my shoe. Putting my shoes on is more difficult than I imagined with pain radiating up my leg as I squeeze my foot in. I hobble out and lock the doors behind me. Tom is usually waiting for me right outside the doors, but I don't see him tonight; he must be running late. I sit down and wait, because standing is too painful. A car door shuts, catching my attention from across the parking lot. I can barely see the car since it's hidden in the depths of the night, concealing its presence.

I squint at the shadowy figure walking toward me, trying to

make out who it is.

"I figured I would find you playing ballerina," my mother says, her tone harsh. I stand immediately and freeze.

"What the hell are you doing here?" I demand, stepping back and gripping my bag tighter to my body. The streetlights shine across her as she walks forward; she's dressed to impress, as usual. She has on black slacks with a white, button-up blouse, her hair in some trendy up-do. She looks like she hasn't lost a wink of sleep, even after everything she pulled on the club and myself. Go figure. Heartless bitch.

She looks at the traffic on the highway off in the distance. "I thought I would try and talk some sense into you one last time before I head to New York."

"You're wasting your time. Leave," I order, pointing at the black car she arrived in.

She laughs, pissing me off. She's stupid if she thinks I'm not serious.

"You don't know what you're doing, Dani," she states, her tone condescending.

"Do you know what kind of hell you left behind after you pulled the crap you did?" I ask angrily.

"You're dumber than I thought going back to that club. I'm surprised they haven't killed you." She snorts her last comment. "They will never trust you," she says, placing her hands on her hips. I shrug at her attempt to scare me.

"Get your shit and let's go back to New York, Dani. Where you belong," she insists, stepping toward me. I backtrack towards the door.

"I'm not going anywhere." The only reason she wants me to go with her is for the next time she tries to break my father.

She blasts forward and grips my arm to the point of bruising, her nails digging deep into my flesh.

"Yes, you are. You're going back to New York whether you like it or not," she demands, dragging me across the parking lot.

I rip my arm from her grip only to have her nails cut my skin. She reaches for my arm again but misses her target when I push her hard. Her feet catch, making her trip, but she catches her balance before falling and looks at me with fire in her eyes.

"You little bitch!" she screams, slapping me hard across the face. My head rings with pain from the harsh contact. She grabs my arm again and starts hauling me toward her car. My reasoning scatters and my body vibrates with sudden rage. I grab her arm and pull her toward me roughly before I clench my fist and hit her as hard as I can in her eye. She yells in pain, letting go of my arm.

"You want to play rough?" she jeers, holding her eye. Before I can process what she says, she kicks me hard in the stomach, making me fall to the ground out of breath. She leans down in my face. "You are just like your father. Weak," she spits, her tone laced with disgust while she grabs my arm hard. Thinking quickly, I grab her elbow and pull her down to the ground with one hard tug. She reaches back and grabs my hair, pulling it hard. I try to pull away, attempting to get to my bag, which is feet away. She straddles my back, pulling my hair hard as I crawl toward my bag, but my breasts scratch against the broken parking lot, making it painful. I claw at the ground, trying to pull myself with the weight of my mother on top of me when a chunk of the asphalt breaks free beneath my fingertips. I grip it tightly and thrust it backwards toward my mother's head. It connects with her scalp hard, making her cry in pain as she lets go and grabs at her head. I scramble forward, knocking her off me in the process, and grab my bag. I pull the drawstrings and reach in, fishing for the gun Bobby gave me. I look over my shoulder and see her racing toward me, blood running down her face, so I turn the safety off and point it at her head in a split second.

"Dani, wait," she commands slowly. Her eyebrow is bleeding where I hit her, and she has a huge gash at the top of her forehead from the rock I slammed into her head.

"I hate you," I state calmly, my tone threatening.

She steps back, her eyes looking right into mine.

"You have fucked my life up enough. Go back to New York and never come back here again," I demand, still pointing the gun at her.

"Dani, you are not one of them." She reaches for my arm holding the gun, but my finger pulls the trigger back without a second thought and a bullet lodges into the ground next to her feet. She looks down at where the bullet hit and then back at me.

"The next one goes in your head," I warn her, but I'm not sure if my aim will justify my threat. "This," I wave the gun between both of us, "is over."

She bites her bottom lip and smirks. Then my mother slowly walks back to her car and slams the door as she climbs in before pulling out of the parking lot. She'll be back, I know it.

I let out a breath when her car is completely out of sight. Bobby's words sling themselves in my thoughts.

'Never aim at someone unless you have every intent of killing them.' I bite my cheek, trying to hold the sob, which desperately wants to escape at the thought that I wanted to kill my own flesh and blood makes me feel ill. I blow out a steady breath, trying to get a hold of my emotions, I put the safety back on the gun. I grab my bag off the ground and stuff the gun back into it.

"You better hop on; cops will be here soon."

I whip my head around and see Shadow on his bike next to the building.

"How long have you been there?" I ask, not thinking to look there when I walked outside.

"Long enough to know someone surely called that gunshot in," he replies, holding a helmet out for me to grab. "Get on."

I grab the helmet and swing my leg around the back of his bike. My arms cling to his waist like old times and my body molds to his perfectly, warming at the touch of his against mine, and I can't help but find comfort in the smell of his leather cut. I hate how perfect this feels, because I know we are anything but perfect together. My body begins to tremble from the letdown of adrenaline, making it hard to hold on as we drive down the highway.

◆◆◆

Arriving back at the apartment, Shadow pulls up to his designated parking garage after cutting the motor to his motorcycle. I climb off the back and as soon as my feet hit the ground, my weight sets, making them tremble with pain. I hand Shadow my helmet and start to hobble to the door.

"What's wrong?" Shadow asks, eyeing my unstable walking.

"Nothing," I lie.

Without another word, Shadow scoops me up like a bride.

"What the hell are you doing?" I slap at his shoulder, trying to pry myself from his grip.

"Carrying you, what's it look like?" he states, walking into the elevator.

"I can walk by myself," I tell him, clenching my jaw.

"Not very well," he chuckles.

I sigh in defeat and let him carry me into the apartment.

As soon as we walk in, he plants me gently on my feet.

"You going to tell me why you can't walk?" he asks, nodding toward my feet. "You twist your ankle cat-fighting with your mother?"

I look down at my feet. "They are just sore is all. I haven't danced in a while and they're not adjusting well."

"How is the job going?" he questions. I can't help the look of surprise on my face. The fact that Shadow wants to do the chitchat thing has my mind in a complete whirlwind.

"It's…" I stumble on my words, "it's great. I love it," I eventually reply, being genuinely honest.

"I figured you would," he says, looking down with a smirk as his hand slides through his hair in that sexy way he does it.

"You got me the job." I'm stating a fact rather than questioning it.

Shadow gives a noncommittal lift of his shoulders and strides across the living room toward the kitchen. He opens the fridge and dips down, pulling out a beer. Then he shrugs out of his cut and slings it on the back of the couch, revealing his black shirt snug on his torso. The look of him makes my body heat to dangerous levels.

He looks at me with eyes that hold the look of lust and danger with the way he furrows his eyebrows and parts his plumped lips.

The weight of his stare has me feeling vulnerable, so I walk toward the couch, breaking eye contact.

I pull my shoes off slowly and notice my sock is soaked in blood.

"Shit," I whisper as I slowly peel the sock off my foot.

"Damn, Dani," Shadow remarks, walking toward me.

"Yeah, it feels as bad as it looks," I admit, eyeing the cracked toenail.

Shadow sets his beer on the coffee table and walks into the kitchen. I hear cabinet doors slamming and the faucet turn on briefly before he stalks back to where I'm sitting. He sits on the coffee table directly in front of me and starts to gently dab at my bloody toe.

"I can do it," I tell him, reaching for the towel.

He pulls it out of reach. "I got it," he says, dabbing at my foot again.

Why is he being so sweet?

"It looks like shit. Maybe you should take a week off and let it heal," he suggests, his tone laced with sincerity. His hand rubs the heel of my foot and the tension releases instantly, making me involuntarily moan. Shadow's head snaps up at the unintentional lustful sound leaving my mouth. I snap my lips shut and gaze at the hungry blue eyes looking back at me. His hand travels up my calf, rubbing along the way, and man if it doesn't feel fantastic. I can feel my body coming alive under his magic touch, my legs wanting to open wider and invite him in. I clench my thighs shut to help smother the growing desire between them. I want Shadow. I have never not wanted him. The idea I could move on without him makes me laugh on the inside. Shadow has ruined me for anyone to follow.

Shadows eyes slowly study my face, and he licks his lips slowly before dropping my leg gently. The loss of his touch makes my skin burn. He stands and turns his back on me. I can see his body rise with the steady breath he takes. I close my eyes and take a deep breath myself.

"I'm just going to go to bed," I state flatly as I start hobbling toward the bedroom. This overwhelming attraction toward Shadow is breaking my heart more than I can handle. Not to mention the menstrual cramps digging deep into my abdomen.

"Dani," Shadow calls, desperation in his voice. I open the bedroom door and step in. When I turn around and look back. Shadow's standing there holding the bloody rag with desperation written on his face.

"Night, Shadow," I say sweetly before shutting the door.

SHADOW

I drop the wet rag and stagger down the hall, sliding against the wall until my ass hits the floor. I look at the closed door, the same door I stared at last night for hours. I saw Dani dancing with those little girls tonight; she looked so angelic, so innocent. The smile she had, the energy she wore—she was truly lost in her own world.

I watched her mother pull up and wait for her, and then I saw the whole altercation. I didn't stop it or step in because I knew my question of whether Dani was a threat or not would be answered as soon as she stepped out of that dance studio. I didn't expect Dani to try and kill her mother, though. I had to pull away from her when she returned to the club, not knowing if I could go against my club one hundred percent. I wouldn't be the one holding a smoking gun that took the life out of the one I loved—the only girl I have ever loved, at that.

Knowing she was not involved, knowing it was all her mother now, I don't know what's stopping me from storming in that bedroom and claiming Dani's body as mine once again. Maybe it's the fact that I don't know if she wants to be with me anymore. I run my hands over my face. Who blames her for not wanting to be with me? What kind of man claims he loves a woman but doesn't take her side, doesn't trust her? I should have grabbed Dani and ran far away with her, protected her.

I reach in my pocket and pull out her iPod, putting the plugs in my ears as Justin Timberlake's "Not A Bad Thing" starts playing. I look down at the iPod dumbfounded. I know for a fact I wasn't anywhere near this song. I stare at the door holding my Firefly, hope rising within me that maybe she put the song on just for me to listen to. Either way, I will make this up to Dani somehow. I should have trusted her. I should have listened to her, but I didn't. I took the path of mistrust and damaged us both. Now I'll have to earn her trust once again.

◆ ◆ ◆

I'm sitting at the table, in the chapel where we have all our meetings. I've been here all morning, waiting for everyone to drag their lazy asses in so I can tell them what went down between Dani and her mother last night. I haven't even been to sleep. On top of that, all I can think about is Dani.

"Shadow, you're in early," Bull comments, sitting in his chair with a cup of coffee, the other guys following close behind.

"I have some important information," I say, sitting up in my chair.

"I would hope so. You called me for a meeting at three in the morning, son," Bull remarks, sipping on his coffee.

"You look like shit!" Hawk quips, his old wrinkly eyes staring right at me.

THE SCARS THAT DEFINE US

"Ya, I didn't sleep much," I say, frustrated. Who gives a fuck what I look like? I just said I have important news.

"All right, spill it," Bull implores, lighting a cigarette.

"Last night, I went to pick Dani up, and her mother stopped by for a visit." Everyone starts to talk amongst themselves.

"I fucking told you," Locks says, pointing at me with a cigarette in his hand.

"Go on," Bull urges, sitting up straighter in his chair.

"She wanted Dani to turn on us, come to her senses," I explain.

"What'd she say?" Bobby interrupts. I look away from Bull to glare at Bobby. Fucker is still on my shit list.

"Dani told her no and when her mom wouldn't let up, Dani tried to shoot her. Told her to go back to New York and if she came back, she would kill her." I release the breath I was holding from the moment all the shit went down last night.

"Well, I'll be," Bull exclaims, rubbing the scruff on his cheeks.

"That don't prove shit," Locks says, slamming his fist on the table.

Bull rolls his eyes but before he can lay into Locks, a petite knock came at the doors.

"What!" Bull roars.

Babs steps in with an ear-to-ear grin.

"Hey, boys. I just wanted to remind you that the Fourth of July party is next weekend, so don't forget." She smiles one last smile and closes the door.

"Are you kidding me?" Locks says, gesturing toward the door. Women are not allowed to interrupt a meeting unless it's important, but it's no surprise Babs gets away with it. I wouldn't be shocked if she was messing with Bull the way he sees her above all other females, but what do I know. I can't assess my own relationship right now, let alone someone else's.

Bull starts to laughs. "Damn women." He turns back to the table. "Make sure Dani is at that party. She is cleared of any potential threats to the club, so let's get her back in here and start making her feel like family," he commands, putting his cigarette out.

"What the hell, Prez?" Locks questions, looking at Bull like he's stupid. "You ain't thinking clearly. That boy is in love with her. He'll say anything!" Locks yells to everyone at the table, his hand pointing at me. His tone is pissing me off, and I grit my teeth.

"She didn't do a goddamn thing wrong, Locks. We did, by not trusting her. You better get that foot outta your ass and start showing her some damn respect right fucking now!" Bull hollers, his voice rumbling through the room.

Locks gets up, slamming his chair against the wall. "Screw this shit," he roars before leaving the room.

"I'll go check on him," Old Guy says, following him.

"I swear you got a bunch of pussies in this club. A bunch of women throwing temper tantrums," Hawk gruffs, gaining a sigh from Bull.

I wake up grateful I have the day off; my feet hurt beyond belief. I slowly open the door to see if Shadow is asleep across the hall again but see an empty spot. In the inside I'm pouting, but in my mind I'm grateful. The less of Shadow the better until I can make my mind up about him. I make my way into the kitchen and come to a complete halt. Atop the counter sets a wooden wicker basket full of foot creams, ice packs, pain reliever and right in the midst, my iPod. I can't help the smile, which creeps across my face at the gesture. I pick up the iPod and see a certain song paused, so I place the ear buds in my ears and hear "The Reason" by Hoobastank. I smile as I think of Shadow and me. God, how I miss him, and from this basket and this song, I think he misses me, too.

I spend most of my day sitting on the couch watching TV, using the care package Shadow left me to recuperate my feet. Not to mention, I've listened to the song Shadow left me on repeat nearly twenty times. Not eating much for breakfast or lunch, I decide to give the TV a rest and go make an actual meal.

I make my way to the kitchen as the door to the apartment opens and Shadow walks in. He's carrying a pizza box in one arm and a two-liter of Pepsi tucked under the other.

"I brought dinner. Sit down," he demands, placing the pizza box on the counter next to the Pepsi.

"That's okay. I'll make my own dinner," I respond, bringing a pan down from the cabinet. It's sweet he brought me dinner, but the last thing I need is for him to feel I depend on him.

"No, you won't," he replies, grabbing the pan and putting it back in its original place.

I huff at his controlling behavior. Jerk the pan back down and place it on the stovetop.

"Yes. I think I will," I say, raising my voice.

Shadow lowers his head and growls. His eyes hood with anger as he grabs me by the hips, throwing me over his shoulder.

"Shadow, put me down!" I yell, my hands slapping at his back.

He plops me down on the couch and points at me. "Don't get up or I'll just carry your ass back in here. I brought you dinner so you could stay off your feet," he states, opening the pizza box.

I groan in frustration and sit back on the couch.

He grabs a slice right out of the box and hands it to me. "Eat," he demands.

"No plate?" I question.

Shadow looks at me as if I have lost my mind. "Plate? It's finger food."

I shrug and take a bite of the pizza. I never knew pizza was a finger food. My mother always made me get a plate for whatever we were eating, even if it was chips, which we had to put in a bowl.

"How are the feet?" he asks, chomping on his own slice of pizza.

I look down at them and notice they look better than they did.

"Better. Thank you," I reply gratefully, avoiding eye contact. This is so awkward; there is so much which needs to be said but hasn't.

"Why are you doing all this?" I wonder, finishing my slice of pizza.

"All of what?" Shadow asks, rubbing his greasy hands on his jeans.

"You want to play that game?" I stand up, peeved he won't talk to me. I groan with frustration and walk toward the kitchen to get a cup but don't make it past Shadow.

"Dani," Shadow says, grabbing my forearm and stopping me. I look at him, waiting for him to explain why we have been broken and uncivilized toward one another. His face stares down at my legs before he slowly raises his gaze upwards.

He lets go of my arm and sighs, "I don't even know where to start to make things right between us."

My heart thuds against my chest, and my breathing quickens. I don't know what to say to that. He just admitted he wanted things to become right between us. If I'm being honest, I don't want to move on from the club or Shadow. As asinine as it sounds, I'm in love with the Devil and I can't escape the hold he has on me, even if it crushes me.

"Try," I urge, sitting back down on the couch.

Shadow sits on the coffee table, resting his elbows on his knees and sighing deeply, his back lifting as he inhales.

"The club has been my life before I ever knew you. They took me in and became my family when I had none," he says, taking a long breath. "If the club didn't believe you," he pauses, "who knows what the order would have been. I couldn't handle the thought of the club hurting you, and I couldn't accept the thought that I might have chosen to go against my club to save you. Worst of all, who knows if I would have been handed the orders."

His words suck the breath from my lungs. I knew the club might have found me guilty for being involved with the FBI, and I knew actions against me could occur. I just never knew how close to reality that possibility was until now. I stand and start walking, pacing as I take in what he just said.

"At first, I thought you were in on it with your mother, but then you came back. Even getting past my trust issues, the thought of harming you was suffocating." He says it with such sorrow, his eyes squinted causing wrinkles to form at the corners. I can't help the rage building inside me.

"My dad would never let anything happen to me," I whisper, emotion heavy in my voice. I blink away the tears pooling in my eyes, making it hard to see.

"Dani," Shadow pauses, "he would have been the one to give the order."

I fall to the floor, the weight of the situation too much for me to handle.

Shadow falls to his knees in front of me. "Dani," he coos softly.

"After last night, I assured the club you are not a threat. The club fucked up not trusting you, and everyone wants to show their apology by welcoming you back in. I fucked up," he whispers. "I should have trusted you, but the hold you have over me had me scared to death to let you back in. That feeling when you were taken away as a witness was terrifying. I have never felt so broken in my life."

All I can do is sob, trying to fight the tears of fear. He talks about how hard it is to trust people, but how can I trust he won't change his mind and kill me in my sleep?

"This is our world, Dani," he says, his tone sounding like it's supposed to make everything okay. Like this is normal.

"I don't know if I can live in this world. How do I know I can trust you?" I ask, wiping the tears from my face.

"If you want to leave, we'll pack up right now and leave," he replies, brushing a tear from my face.

My head snaps up, catching the *we* in his statement. *He would leave the club and everything he has behind just for me?* The sliver of hope that Shadow and I might be able to redeem what's left of us causes my hopes to rise.

Shadow's blue eyes pierce mine. "You're crazy if you think I'm going to let you go that easy," he informs me, his face serious.

He leans in and kisses my bottom lip softly. "I told you in the beginning you would hate me more than like me, but I'll be damned if I ever let you go again," he whispers against my lips.

My mouth parts with disbelief, his words hitting my heart in all the right places.

"I broke a club law going out with that guy, didn't I?" As soon as the question leaves my mouth, I regret it. Shadows face clenches and turns red.

"Yeah, well, I haven't been an angel," he states, justifying my actions. I cringe at his words. I don't want to know who he has slept with. Not right now, anyway.

"Doesn't mean I'm not fucking pissed about it, but we both fucked up," he says, running his hands through his hair.

"We are so messed up," I mutter. What couple has a conversation like this?

"No arguing there," Shadow remarks, leaning against the wall.

I lay my head against the wall, as well, and turn to look at his handsome profile, wondering why he sat on his bike last night and let things escalate between my mother and me.

"Last night, with my mom..." I start, wiping my tears from my cheeks.

"What about it?" he asks.

"You saw what was going on, so why didn't you try and stop it? Or better yet, why didn't you try and stop me from killing a federal agent?" I question, raising my voice.

Shadow grins and looks at me, as if I get what he smiling about.

"What?" I ask.

"The way you were holding that gun, there was no way you would hit anything," he chuckles, making me laugh along with him.

"Yeah, well, Bobby was supposed to teach me how to shoot," I state matter-of-factly.

"Bobby won't be teaching you anything," he sneers coldly. "I'll teach you." He stands up and looks down at me, a question playing on his lips.

"What?" I ask.

"If you didn't suck at aiming and could do it all over again, would you have killed your mom?" he wonders, staring at me with his eyebrows furrowed.

I think about everything: the way my mother hated me growing up, her never being around, and my never being enough for her. She only kept me around to destroy the club, never loving me, never caring. When I found love, found my place in the world, she tried to ruin it all.

I look up at Shadow, the answer clear. "Absolutely."

7

Shadow

I PULL MY CAR INTO THE PARKING LOT BEHIND A BURNT-DOWN GAS station, grab my rifle case, and sling it over my back for the hike over the grassy bluff. My feet crunch on the dead grass with every step I take; the sun has been hot and brutal this summer, killing everything in its path. The long-sleeve shirt I'm wearing to cover my tattoos begins to stick to my body with the perspiration building from the walk; this fucking heat is ridiculous. I finally make it to the top of the hill and lay my bag on the ground. I look across the highway and spot the dingy hotel about four hundred yards away. One thing I'm good at is killing, and this one I'll do with pleasure. I set the bipod for my sniper and load the rifle with jacketed hollow-points then grab the binoculars to get a better look at the hotel and scope out the surrounding area.

Ever since Dani told me she wanted her mother dead a few days ago, I figured I would do the honor in granting her that wish. Not only that, but I have no doubt in my mind Dani would kill her mother the next time she saw her. That is not something I want for Dani. She may have a dark streak, but I'm not sure she could handle the weight of killing her mother. Plus, she would make a mess of the situation, leaving DNA or witnesses.

I'm thankful Bobby saved me the pain of killing my mother. I still wish it was me who ended her life, but in a sense I don't. Since she's dead, I forget the nasty crawling whore she was and remember the times when she was actually a mother, before the drugs, booze, and neglect started. I shake my head of the memories and eye the hotel—it sure is a shitty place. I laugh. I bet Lady thought she was safe in a deserted hotel off the grid. Either that or she's so dumb she thought she would get out of town alive with no retaliation from the club. I look into the scope for her room number—she has been staying in room nine. I know because I stalked her down the last two days, watched where she's been and who she's talked to. Mostly she's been hanging outside the club and my apartment, circling Dani like a shark. I know in my gut she's going to fuck with Dani, use her to her advantage. I can't allow that to happen, considering it's a miracle the club didn't take Dani out last time. If something goes wrong again, I'm not so convinced she'll walk out of it alive.

I look away from the scope and sigh. *Am I killing for Dani or the club?* I'm not sure how either would take it. I'm with Locks that Bull has put family over the club, so killing Lady (who used to be his ol' lady) may not go over too well with him. Likewise, telling Dani I killed her mother would piss her off because I didn't let her do it. I adjust myself behind the rifle and look down the scope. She doesn't understand that killing her mother would kill a piece of her. My body has been having withdrawals from the lack of control I have had lately, trembling for the urge to take charge and pull the trigger. I spot Lady, sitting on the bed brushing her hair; it looks like she's getting ready to leave. My finger finds the trigger as I hear footsteps crunching the grass from behind me, making my blood rush to my ears. Someone has spotted me. I look over my shoulder and see by the moonlight someone is walking my way. I reach into my waistband and pull out my pistol. Looks like I'm taking out two people tonight. As soon as the person steps into the light where I can see them, I cock my weapon, aiming it right at them.

"The fuck?" Bobby exclaims, lifting his hands in the air.

"God damn it, Bobby!" I whisper; the fucker has my heart racing.

"You've been acting sneaky the last two days, so I followed you here," he explains, squatting.

"I could have shot you," I chastise in a low whisper.

"Who you taking out?" he asks, grabbing the binoculars from the rifle bag off the ground and ignoring my anger.

I wait for it, the ridicule he's bound to bark at me when he spots Lady. Her room is the only one lit up and open for the world to see.

He sweeps the hotel over before coming to a stop.

He pulls the binoculars down and looks at me with accusing eyes. His jaw is pulled tight and his brow is furrowed inward.

"Bull order this?" he asks.

I look over the highway at the hotel. "No."

I wait for him to try to talk me out of it. It won't work, though. Lady needs to go for multiple reasons. The biggest is she's cancerous to Dani's wellbeing, and she'll never let us be together while she's alive.

"Dani?" he questions, wanting to know if I told Dani my plans to murder her mother.

"No, she doesn't know," I reply defiantly, lifting my chin, ready to battle this out with him.

Bobby sighs loudly and lies on his belly, getting comfortable.

"What are you doing?" I ask, my voice low so nobody hears me.

"Helping you keep watch, what's it look like?" he says, eyeing the hotel room.

Bobby and I have done this together plenty of times, mostly for club hits though. He's never came with me on a side job. I never needed a wingman but I wouldn't turn him away if he wanted to join. He gets it, and he doesn't judge.

"Too bad she's not naked. I bet she's got nice tits," he jokes, staring contently into the binoculars.

I lie back down and position myself behind the rifle, taking steady breaths as my finger finds the trigger again.

I watch Lady stand and move toward the door.

"She's headed to the door," Bobby whispers.

"Got it," I confirm.

She pulls the door open, trying to hold it with her foot, but its force keeps pushing her small frame back. I release my steady breath and press lightly on the trigger.

"Wait—"

I jump from Bobby's voice as I pull the trigger. The rifle recoils back into my shoulder as I continue to stare down the scope. Lady is jolted backwards and falls to the ground. I notice her foot moving near the door. She's still alive.

"Damn it, Bobby. You made me miss my shot!" I yell, standing up.

"I thought someone was walking in the parking lot, but it was a damn cat. Sorry, man," Bobby apologizes, standing up.

I take apart my rifle as Bobby keeps watch. I put it back into the bag, zip it, and throw it over my shoulder before heading toward the car quickly.

I start to walk faster toward my car, the grass crunching loudly as I make way. I pass Bobby's bike parked right next to the stolen car. I throw my gun case in the backseat and grab my bag then grab an extra mask and gloves and throw them at Bobby to put on. I reach in, grab the silencer, and screw it onto the end of the barrel of my pistol then climb behind the wheel as Bobby rides passenger. We drive across the overpass to the crappy hotel, hoping nobody recognizes the stolen car. Luckily, it's late and not many cars are passing the area. I pull my mask over my face and tighten my gloves on my hands before getting out and walking toward the room concealing Lady. Her foot is caught in the door, leaving it open slightly. I kick her foot in as I enter the room, and the door slams shut after Bobby enters. Lady is lying on her back with a gunshot wound to the chest and is gasping for air. I can't help but smile.

I walk up to her and hover in her line of sight, aimed at the ceiling. I pull my mask up to my hairline and smile. Her dull eyes widen with fear.

"I bet I was the last mother fucker you thought you'd ever see again," I sneer, with a wolfish grin.

She tries to talk but nothing but gurgling comes out, spluttering blood down her chin. I squat down, pull my gun from my waistband, and place it against her bloody lips. "Shhhh," I whisper. The gun against her mouth muffles her strangled cries.

"You can't hurt Dani anymore," I say softly. She begins to whimper and tries to pull away from me, but she's too weak to make much of an effort.

I stand up, point the gun at her head, and pull the trigger. The bullet rips into her skull, throwing brain matter all over me.

"There are her keys," Bobby points, bending to pick her keys up from the floor, which are thrown haphazardly across the carpet. I place my gun back in my waistband and grab her body, throwing her over my shoulder easily and walking to the door. I try to pull the door open but it has a spring causing it to want to slam closed, making it near impossible to keep open.

"Are you going to get the fucking door?" I ask Bobby, who's looking at the mug shots of the club members thrown about the bed.

"Shit. Sorry, brother," he apologizes, rushing toward the door. It's amazing he's not a prospect still.

He pulls the door open as I squeeze through.

"It's spring-loaded," Bobby explains, pushing the door back and forth, fascinated by the silver spring at the top of the door.

"Nice to know," I remark, struggling with Lady's limp body.

"Trunk," I remind him. He aims the keys in hand and presses the trunk button on the key fob. It pops open with a flash of its lights. When I said I didn't mind having Bobby around for these kinds of late-night outings, I take it back. I throw Lady's lifeless body into the back of her trunk and slam it shut. I reenter the room and cut out the stained carpet which held her blood. Beneath it is concrete, so I pull out the small bottle of bleach in my cargo pants and pour it all over the concrete and surrounding carpet, hoping to eliminate any trace of blood. I'm sure if someone saw the square missing they would know what happened, though. Still, no evidence, no jail time.

"Let's go before someone sees us," I say, opening the door. I walk casually to the stolen car and get in while Bobby gets in Lady's car.

We drive off the exit ramp in search of an abandoned area.

About an hour out, I turn under a bridge. There hasn't been anyone in sight for the last thirty minutes, and I haven't spotted any traffic on the bridge.

I pull under it and see the headlights of Lady's black car bouncing in the rear view mirror, pulling up behind me.

"Nice fucking ride," Bobby says, slamming the door to the black BMW.

He grabs the bottom of his shirt, pulls it over his head, and throws it over his shoulder. He pops open the gas tank and stuffs the shirt in. He then reaches into his pants pocket and pulls out a lighter, lighting the tip of the shirt on fire before running away.

"This feels good," Bobby states, digging in his pockets.

"What?" I ask.

"You and me, back to our old ways," he says, smiling a goofy ass grin.

I continue to stare at the growing flame. "There is no us, and we aren't back to anything," I snap coldly.

I feel the air pick up tension as Bobby realizes I have not forgiven him so easily for not having my back with Dani, even if he was right. Not to mention, him putting his hands on her.

"Shadow, I just want what's best for Firefly." He says it like he means it and I believe he does, but I couldn't care less. His transgression festers within me until I can find a way of revenge.

"Unless you want to wind up in the trunk, too, this conversation is over," I declare, looking at him.

"Fine, it's over," Bobby spits. "But, seriously," he continues, cocking his head to the side, not giving up on the subject.

"Bobby!" I yell, hoping my rise in voice will shut him up.

"Fine," he says with a breath.

The car explodes, throwing a rim in our direction and shrapnel everywhere.

"Fuck, that never gets old," Bobby laughs.

He puts a joint in his mouth and walks up to the burning car, leaning into the flame trying to light it.

"You're going to burn your face off," I chuckle.

"Nah," he says, stepping back and puffing out smoke.

"Let's get out of here," I say, heading back to the stolen car.

Waking up this morning, I smell of cleaning products and fire. It's been a week since I told Dani everything, which was the hardest thing I think I have ever done. Seeing her break down made me realize just how fragile she is, and it made me want to shelter and protect her from danger. If she wanted to pack up and leave, I would have. I already fucked up picking the club and my brothers over her. From now on, she comes first.

She's worked twice this week, and both times I have picked her up and dropped her off. We have watched T.V. and talked about senseless shit. Yet all I can think about is throwing Dani over the counter and fucking her, claiming what's mine once again, reminding her she is mine for eternity until I say otherwise, but the severity of our situation has me questioning if she wants me. Don't get me wrong if I wanted Dani, I could easily take her whether she wanted it or not; she is my ol' lady, after all, but it wouldn't be us. It wouldn't be Firefly, unless I know she trusts me. I don't want half of Dani—I want all of her. I want her to scream who she belongs to, ruin her for any man who might stand behind me. Given my nature, there is a strong possibility I will fuck this relationship up again. Knowing Dani's angelic nature in our world, there *will* be men standing behind me. Regardless of what Bobby says, his ass would be in line to take Dani as his; he would be stupid not to.

Snapping me from my thoughts, Dani comes in with a towel wrapped around her midsection, singing some chick song as she moseys in the shopping bags on the counter. The towel is riding high as she bends over the counter, showing the rounds of her ass, her hair dripping down her back. I can't help the groan that rumbles through my chest.

Dani spins around and grips the towel at her breast.

"Shit. I didn't know you were back," she gasps with surprise.

"Yeah, just got back," I reply, adjusting my cock, her skin tanned from laying out and screaming for my mouth to devour it.

Dani looks down at herself. "I'll go get changed," she says meekly, before taking off.

She scampers off down the hall, and it takes everything in me not to follow her like a horny teenager. I want to see that body of hers again. With that thought, my dick twitches, making me growl in frustration. Things have been getting a little better between Dani and me, I can still feel some of the tension in the air between us, and I'm not sure if it's because I admitted I chose the club over her, or if it's sexual.

"So, what are the plans for the weekend?" she asks, plopping down on the couch next to me, her smell of perfection reminding me of what I want and can't have. She's wearing a peach-colored, loose top which hangs off her shoulder with shorts that were once jeans, cut too short.

"Um," the words catch in my throat as I eye-fuck her, "tonight, I thought we could just chill. In two days, there is a Fourth of July party at the beach," I inform her, trying to look at anything but her, but it's not working.

"Oh, yeah, what time is it?" she questions, picking up the remote from the coffee table. As she bends over to grab it, her shirt hangs loose, giving me a glimpse of her perky breasts. My cock swells at the sight.

I look up and see her eyes catch mine, a slight smirk crossing her face as she leans back on the couch and flips through the channels. She's teasing me.

"It starts at noon, but I don't usually go till night," I say, trying to think of anything but sex.

"Why's that?" she asks, still staring at the screen.

"That's when the sinners come out." I look at Dani's stunned expression, her vivid green eyes wide with surprise, and I wink.

◆ ◆ ◆

I slide my empty beer across the bar toward Babs. I had to escape Dani; her sexy tits have been screaming for my mouth to take them all day, and my hands twitched with the urge to grab them. It's weird not having someone else's trust and actually giving a shit about it.

"We got a problem," Bull states, walking into the clubhouse. I watch a flustered Bull lean against the bar. He grabs the side of the counter with both hands and arches his back so he's looking at the floor.

"What's going on?" Bobby asks popping the cap off his beer with the side of the bar's counter.

"Locks just called me. He said his bike caught on fire," Bull confides, glancing up at us, his face looking tired and worn out.

"Holy shit. He okay?" Bobby wonders, mid-sip of his beer.

"Yeah, he was inside the smoke shop when it caught fire," Bull confirms with a raised eyebrow.

"Did someone set it on fire?" Bobby questions. I turn to look at Bull, curious myself. Seems we have done nothing but piss people off here lately; wouldn't surprise me if that list grew.

"Let's get over there and check it out," Bull orders, pushing off the counter. "Tom Cat, drive the truck over there," he yells at our newest prospect. Let's just say, our last one, Charlie, didn't make the cut after he let Dani get kidnapped.

◆ ◆ ◆

We pull up to the smoke shop where Locks buys his tobacco; he rolls his own cigarettes so he's always here buying supply. When we pull into the parking lot, there are motorcycle parts from one end to the other. Sitting in the middle is what's left of the bike with dissipating smoke surrounding it. It's a disaster, and it looks more like it was blown up than caught on fire. You can see a wheel against the store, which was blown from the bike, and I have to weave through the shrapnel pieces everywhere. Just feet from the trashed bike is Locks. He's sitting down against a light pole which resides in the parking lot, one leg bent while the other is out straight. He looks completely relaxed for someone who just had his pride and joy ripped from their hands.

"That is not a casual bike fire, my friends. That is one hundred percent fuck you," Bobby laughs.

"That's what I was afraid of." Bull shakes his head, throwing his leg over his hog.

"What the fuck happened?" I ask, stepping over part of an exhaust pipe.

"I dunno. The damn thing has been leaking fuel, been meaning to get it fixed." Locks tosses a piece of gravel.

"You leave it running?" Bull asks, surveying the burnt lump of bike.

Locks looks up at Bull. "No, but the engine was hot."

"Nah, I'm thinking this is a message," Bobby concludes, kicking at the charred asphalt.

"I agree. Did you piss anyone off?" I wonder.

"No. I haven't," Locks snaps, his eyes furrowing with anger in my direction. "However, I have a strong idea someone heard we had the FBI on our ass, and not to mention we let a fucking rat into our club. That may not sit too well with other clubs," Locks spits as he stands.

Bull looks over at Locks and glares, and I find myself glaring at him, too. I can't help but feel protective of Dani, and hearing Locks talk shit about her has me furious. Dani is not a threat; she has earned her trust. Apparently not everyone thinks so, though. I can feel my fingers tighten as the urge to plow my fist in Locks' mouth for talking ill about Dani circulates through them. I'm starting to question his commitment to the brotherhood here lately.

"It's a warning," Bobby states, glaring at Locks.

Bobby is right. This was no accident. This was on purpose, and whoever did this sent it as a warning. They'll be back again, and by surprise.

We hear sirens sound close behind us, and turning we find a black and white cop car parked feet away. I didn't even hear the damn thing pull up; fuckers are sneaky.

"Shit," Bobby mutters.

"Well, hello, boys."

Skeeter slams the door shut to the cop car and places his hand on his holster. He's got short, black hair which always looks like he put way too much shit in it, and a stupid-ass mustache over his top lip. He's tall and really fast. I know because I've had to run from him a couple times. Cops are a shady breed, but when you get a dirty cop, it goes darker than a shade.

Skeeter used to be in our pockets about a year back, but he got greedy. His price of pay-off got ridiculous, and on top of that, he started asking for a percent of our sales. I offered to take the fucker off the grid, but Bull said it was bad for business. Instead, we moved all our merchandise and stayed clean from any illegal running for a few months. When Skeeter learned we weren't taking to his demands, he did exactly what we thought he would do, he cried to his cop buddies. Told them we were running guns and dealing drugs and he knew exactly where it all was being held. After a search warrant turned up nothing, Skeeter lost connections in the law enforcement and unfortunately, it put us on his shit list.

"What do we have here?" Skeeter asks, eyeing the scene.

Another cop exits the passenger side of the cruiser. He's bald, pale and freckled and looks young and frightened by the sight of a bunch of bikers gathered together.

"Gas leak, it's handled," Bull states, stepping in front of Skeeter.

"It will be handled when I say it's handled. Now, step aside," Skeeter orders arrogantly as he points for Bull to step away as he turns back to the cop-in-training. "Officer Manny, keep an eye on this one."

"You guys multiply like cockroaches," Bobby jokes, making me laugh.

Skeeter whips his head in Bobby's direction. "Watch it, boy."

Bobby huffs and crosses his arms.

Skeeter walks up to what's left of the bike and squats down.

"Gas leak, you say? Must'a been a hell of a leak."

"Yup," Locks agrees.

"Like I said, it's handled," Bull states again, crossing his arms in front of his chest.

"You guys drive these streets with no regard to others' safety, going way too fast, disobeying traffic laws. It's no wonder one of these death contraptions caught fire." Skeeter talks while spitting chew from the side of his mouth. I watch the nasty spit fling near Bull's boot, and the disrespect has me seething. I step up ready to go head-to-head, but Bobby pulls on my shoulder, holding me back.

"It would be a day to mark on the calendar if all your shitty motorcycles caught on fire." Skeeter chuckles as leftover chew dribbles down his chin.

"Are we done here?" Bobby asks, squaring his shoulders in anger.

Skeeter scoffs as he takes in the scene. "This your bike, Locks?" he questions.

"Yes," Locks replies, rubbing the back of his neck.

"I'm going to have to write you a ticket." Skeeter pulls a notebook from his back pocket.

"For what?" Bull asks with disbelief.

"Unsafe operation of a motor vehicle," comes Skeeter's reply while writing on his ticket book.

"Are you fucking kidding me?" I grit out. Surely he can come up with something better than that.

"You want to go for a ride to the station?" Skeeter asks, puffing his chest out.

I step up to the challenge, ready to throw a punch.

"I think you just assaulted an officer," Skeeter lies, pulling out a pair of chrome cuffs from his waistband. "You saw it, didn't you, Officer Manny?" I look over and see a pale Manny looking scared to death at the situation unfolding.

"Bullshit," Bobby snaps, stepping up, ready to take Skeeter down for trying to arrest me. If Skeeter's going to lie and claim I assaulted him, he's going to get what he wished for.

"All right, let's calm it down," Bull orders, sliding his hand between Skeeter and me.

"Locks, take the fucking ticket. We'll get the mess cleaned up, Skeeter. No need to arrest anyone," Bull tries to reason.

"I don't like your tone. You better watch it, boy. I think you forgot whose town you're in," Skeeter states, cocking his eyebrow. My teeth grit in anger, a couple nights in jail for assaulting a police officer, Skeeter in particular, doesn't sound too bad at the moment.

He rips the paper from the pad and throws it in Locks' direction.

"Enjoy the rest of your day," Skeeter practically sings before walking back to his cruiser.

"Fucking prick," I rumble in anger.

"Are you trying to get thrown in prison?" Bull questions.

I shrug and mutter, "It would be worth it."

"Locks, I had Tom bring the truck, so ride back to the club with him. I'll call a couple of guys and get this cleaned up," Bull promises, climbing on his bike.

"I have to ride in that fucking thing?" Locks asks, pointing at the SUV. He hates vehicles; I've seen him ride his motorcycle in every kind of weather just to keep from being in a vehicle.

"Unless you want to ride bitch?" Bull laughs.

Locks strides over to the SUV and climbs in, shaking his head and cursing. I don't know what happened to his bike, but I know it didn't catch fire by a gas leak. He takes care of that thing too well to let something like that go unmended.

◆ ◆ ◆

After we head back to the club, I'm ready for another beer. Only when I find Locks sitting at the bar getting drinks at the clubhouse, I can't handle the temptation to throttle him and need to go somewhere else. I haven't forgotten how he disrespected Dani so easily.

"What'll it be, babe?" the bartender asks, her red hair tangled and sticking to her sweaty forehead. When just us boys are looking to get out and get some fresh beer, we hit up this hole-in-the-wall bar. I don't even know if it has a name aside from Bar.

"My usual," I reply, cracking a peanut in half.

"Get me one, too, babe," Bobby slings her way, sliding onto a stool next to me.

"You followed me again." I observe rather than ask, tossing the peanut in my mouth.

"Yeah, I want to clear the air between us," he states, taking his beer from the bartender.

"Not anything to talk about," I say, grabbing my beer, as well.

"Bullshit there's not."

I look up at the TV and see the missing person add for Parker flash between commercials. I grin, they'll never find Parker. I may or may not have paid him a visit in the night recently. I never leave a job unfinished.

"Hey, I'm Heather." I look over and see a short, blonde-haired girl sliding up Bobby's side. She has on ripped fishnet stockings with a red skirt and a black corset.

"Well, hey, doll," Bobby grins, sliding his hand down over her skirted ass and giving it a squeeze.

"Heather, let's go. We got business." Another girl wearing the same outfit yells from the door.

"Shit, I gotta go," Heather says, pulling from Bobby's hold and walking toward the door.

I can't help but hold judgment at Bobby, my disgusted gaze telling him just that. That girl would be nasty even if I was shitfaced drunk.

"What? Anything goes with hoes," Bobby chuckles.

"That's repulsive. Do you not have any standards?" I ask, popping a peanut in my mouth.

"I wouldn't have slept with her," Bobby tells me, his tone serious while he cracks a peanut. "But I'm not going to be a dick to her either," he continues with sincerity.

"Right," I sneer. I can't help but be pissed at Bobby, since he encouraged Dani to move on without me and put his hands on her.

"Hey, asshole!" Bobby and I look over our shoulder's to see three men standing at the door, the one in front pointing at Bobby. He has on baggy jeans and a sleeveless shirt, his head bald and shiny. Of the two behind him, one has a flannel shirt with the sleeves ripped off and the other is wearing a white shirt with holes all over it. All walks of life in this bar.

"Me?" Bobby questions, pointing to himself.

"You mess with my girls, you pay up," the bald man roars, slapping his chest with a loud roar.

"I didn't mess with anything, and you better watch who you're talking to," Bobby retorts, pointing at the man.

"That's not what my girl said, so you calling her a liar?" The bald man's walking up to Bobby.

Suddenly, Bobby is ripped from his bar stool and thrown on the ground. The bald man straddles him and punches Bobby square in the face. I turn leisurely on my stool to get a better view of the action. Nobody seems to even notice the fight; everybody just goes about their business, drinking, dancing, and playing pool. A fight in this place isn't uncommon. Bobby takes the hit and throws his own punch, making the guy fall off him. Then Bobby rolls over and punches the guy in the face again; he might actually have this fight. The bald guy spits blood to the side and grins at Bobby maliciously. The two guys who followed the bald one suddenly grab Bobby by the elbows, one on each side, and haul him off the guy in charge. He rises to his feet and wipes the blood from his lip before delivering a punch to Bobby's gut without warning. Bobby grunts in pain as the man throws another.

"Little help here, man," Bobby moans.

I crack a peanut and watch the two guys holding Bobby while the bald one punches him again. Yeah, I should help him, and any other time I would. I would make sure all three of these assholes lost their teeth. But seeing how Bobby's a traitor and I haven't actually plotted my revenge on him, this will do.

I cock a smile and toss a peanut in.

"Should have had my back with Dani. What you did wasn't the brotherly thing to do; touching what wasn't yours, brother," I sneer.

The guy throws another punch to Bobby's stomach before the two hounds let go of his elbows, letting him fall to his knees.

"Pay up!" one of them yells, placing his hand out palm up in Bobby's face.

Bobby coughs and grabs his wallet in his back pocket, pulling free a few twenties and tossing them onto the floor. The bald guy grabs the cash and stuffs it in his pocket before stalking out of the bar.

"What the fuck, man?" Bobby asks, sliding onto the bar stool slowly, holding his stomach and coughing as he takes a small sip from his beer.

"You deserved it," I shrug.

"You owe me sixty dollars," he says, holding his midsection in pain.

I turn and look at Bobby. His mouth is split and bleeding and he's hunched over, grabbing his stomach. It makes me smile to see him in such pain.

8

Dani

I WAKE UP ALONE THIS MORNING. I SPENT THE WHOLE DAY WITH Shadow yesterday. Laid up in the apartment, we sat around munching on food and watching TV. I found out he's ticklish under his armpits, and in return he found out I'm ticklish everywhere. It was nice to not think about the weight of the club or our trust issues. It was just us and nothing on the outside interfering with that. Today, I went grocery shopping, and I stopped by the dance studio to see the older girls audition for Swan Lake.

I walk into the apartment as the sun begins to set, hoping to see Shadow, but it's empty. I pop some popcorn and plop on the couch to paint my toes. After surfing the channels and coming up with nothing, I turn it off, bored out of my mind. My phone vibrates on the counter, catching my attention, and I pick it up without looking at the caller ID. Right now, I would talk to a sales person I'm so bored.

"Hey, girlie!" Cherry chirps on the other end of the line.

"Uh, hey," I respond, surprised to receive a call from her.

"You doing anything tonight? Me and a couple of the girls are going to a club where my brother is DJing."

"That sounds great," I reply, excited.

"Great, we'll be there soon," she says, hanging up the phone.

I clap my hands in eagerness and run off toward the bedroom, heading to the closet and grabbing a black, strapless number which falls mid-thigh. It's sexy and provocative, and I can't wait to wear it. I throw my hair up into a loose up-do; apply a smoky eye shadow, light lip gloss, and a spritz of perfume to top it off. There's knocking at the door as I'm putting on some black heels; my sore feet don't even seem to mind the squeeze.

"Wow, you look hot!" Cherry says, eyeing me as I open the door. She's wearing a purple dress shorter than mine which ties behind her neck, and her eye shadow matching it. She's also wearing her property patch over her dress, which makes her look fierce. I follow her down to the parking lot as she hops into a red Bug. When I climb into the passenger side, Babs and Molly are sitting in the back smiling at me.

"Hey, girl," Babs smiles.

"I didn't expect you for a club-hopper," I joke at Babs.

"Ugh, Locks' has been gone for days, I'm bored as hell," she replies, rolling her eyes.

Cherry speeds off from the curb, making the girls in the back squeal. She bobs and weaves in and out of traffic. How she got her license I don't know; she had to have worn something like she's wearing now because the girl is death on wheels. We pull up to a building shining in bright gold lighting around the doors.

"The Rogue?" I question, reading the club's sign.

"Yeah, it's supposed to be the big thing right now," Cherry answers, getting out of the car.

"My brother Tyler is ecstatic to DJ here," she continues, twisting her face in humor. "It's not all bad. We get free drinks and get in free." She points to a line of people waiting to get in.

We walk up to the bouncer, who is wearing a black suit, his head shaved. He's huge and looks like someone you would see playing professional football or wrestling.

"Name?" the bouncer asks, looking at the crowd. He doesn't even glance at the girls and me. He doesn't have a clipboard or anything; he must have the guest list memorized.

"Name is Cherry. I'm with Twistin Tyler," she yells, the music blaring from the club doors making it hard to talk over.

He looks away from the club and eyes us up.

"You going to let us in or what?" Cherry sasses, placing her hand on her hip. The brawny bouncer moves to the side, opening a path to the doors, which lead into the thumping club.

"Dick," she says, passing him.

"Yo, take over for me." The bouncer yells at a guy wearing a matching black suit, he looks just as intimidating.

Walking into the club, it's crazy, like nothing I have ever seen before. There are balconies with sheer curtains for private parties and booths surrounding the walls with gold lamps sitting on the tables. The lighting is dim, except colors of gold from spotlights above swirling around the people on the dance floor. A large bar sits next to the DJ station at the far end of the club, and my eyes go wide at what's sitting on the bar. It has a silver cage resting on top with a girl in a shiny, gold bikini dancing in it.

We follow Cherry over to a booth next to the DJ station. "Hey, I'm going to go tell my brother I'm here real quick and then we'll dance," she says, skipping off. I slide into the center of the booth, making room for the girls.

"Ha. I ain't dancing, but I'll drink," Babs tells us, pointing toward the bar.

"I'll join you," Molly says, leaving me at the booth by myself.

I tap my fingers against the tabletop as I watch Molly and Babs order drinks when suddenly a tall, blue beverage is placed in my line of sight.

"This is from Mr. Ross," the girl states. She's wearing a gold shiny dress, and her black wavy hair sways down her back.

"Who?" I ask, confused.

"Mr. Ross," she answers, pointing to a booth across the way. I push myself up to look over the crowd and see a man wearing a white button down shirt wave slightly. He has dark hair and seems to be middle aged. I've never met him before.

I look at the drink. Aren't you suppose to reject drinks from strangers at a bar, or do I watch too many CSI shows?

"Uh, no thanks," I reply, pushing the drink away.

The girl looks at me surprised then shrugs, taking the drink away.

Molly and Babs come back to the booth with drinks in their hands, laughing about something.

"So, I hear you went on a date with some rich guy," Babs says, taking a small sip from her shot glass and shimmying back into the booth.

"Yeah, I did. He was a gentleman. Well, at least I thought he was." I give a weak smile. I still find it hard to believe Parker would treat a woman ill, but Shadow insisted he saw it with his own eyes.

Babs laughs in hysteria. "I bet Shadow fucked that guy up."

"That boy must have had serious balls messing with a Devil's property," Molly says with a grin. I groan with frustration. Only the Devil himself knows what happened to Parker, and I'm not about to ask him.

"Let's dance; he's playing my song next," Cherry orders, grabbing my hand and pulling me out of the booth. She drags me through sweaty bodies into a small opening on the dance floor. The club roars lyrics from "Turn Down For What" by DJ Snake & Lil Jon, and Cherry starts throwing her arms up with the beat. She bends her knees and shakes her hips, dancing like nobody's watching. I, on the other hand, just stand there, not sure what to do. I've never been to a club; my mother never allowed it.

"Just let loose. Nobody is watching you!" Cherry yells above the music.

I start to bob my head to the music, trying to follow her advice.

Suddenly, Cherry grabs me by the hips and grinds herself onto my pelvis.

"Like this," she says, showing me how to move my body seductively.

She grabs me around my neck, and her floral perfume suffocates me. Her body rolls against mine as if we were in a lovers' embrace. I take her lead and start to twist my body against hers just like she showed me.

"You got it," she smirks.

I smile back and grab her hips, feeling like I got the hang of things as I grind myself against her hip while she continues to dance.

Feeling the confidence override my insecurities I let go of her and just let loose. I pump my hands in front of me as I shake my ass. The beat is so loud it vibrates through my chest and down my legs. I tangle my fingers into my hair and toss my head back and forth to the music.

"Animals" by Martin Garraix instantly plays next, and I close my eyes and continue to dance. I feel free and sexy. This is exactly what I needed, to just get out and have fun with some girl companions. Hands grasp around my hips and slam me into a hard body, and I suddenly smell weed and alcohol. My body stiffens, and my eyes flare open. I pull away from the foreign body pressed firmly against my backside and spin around to see the guy from across the club, Mr. Ross.

He slides his hands over my ass roughly and slams my body against his.

"I don't want to dance. Thanks." I squirm, trying to pry myself from his grasp unsuccessfully.

"I ordered you a drink, and you declined. That wasn't very nice," he states against my ear, his grip rough and unsought.

"Fuck you and your drink," I spit, pushing him away. I look around for Cherry frantically but don't see her anywhere. I dive across the crowded dance floor, weaving through to make my way back to the booth,

"You pussy! Take it!" Babs shouts at Molly, handing her a shot glass as I slide into the booth.

Feeling a little paranoid, I stare out into the crowd looking for Mr. Ross.

"Yuck, you're all sweaty," Molly says, poking my arm with a finger.

"Yeah, I got a little carried away," I apologize, trying to smile.

"Hey, there you are! I got a great song coming up next," Cherry tells me, grabbing my hand and pulling me from the booth. "Come on. You can rest when you're dead!"

Cherry notices my hesitation and stops to look at me. "You all right?"

"There was this creepy guy out there. He gave me a weird vibe," I admit, looking at the girls, wondering if I'm being ridiculous or not.

"What guy? I'll fuck him up," Babs threatens.

"You just have to be firm with them. Then they'll leave you alone," Cherry advises, tugging me forward. "It happens all the time," she yells over her shoulder.

I follow Cherry onto the dance floor—actually, I'm dragged. I look for Mr. Ross because something about him scares me. He doesn't seem like some normal guy trying to get lucky, his dark eyes, and solemn tone make me uneasy.

"No Hands" by Waka Flocka Flame starts to sing and Cherry starts to jump up and down with excitement. I look around me, unsure; I feel like he's watching me.

"You're fine," she says, slapping my shoulder. I suddenly feel silly; this happens all the time at clubs and men are a little too eager hitting on women. I need to let loose and have fun. I throw my hands up and start singing the lyrics as Cherry yells them back at me.

Cherry starts shimmying her shoulders as another blonde girl walks up and starts dancing with her. I forget all about the creepy guy and start dancing and singing with them. I suddenly smell alcohol and weed strongly again; I smell Mr. Ross. I stop dancing and look around me, but all I see is a mass of sweaty people dancing. My body coats with a slick, cold sweat as my heart pounds with fear.

"Looking for me?" a voice behind me whispers in my ear. My blood runs cold as my body stills. He digs his fingers into my arms so hard I feel like they'll penetrate.

"What do you want from me?" I ask, unsure if he even heard me from the loud music. My instinct to fight rises from my fear; I'm strong and will not allow myself to falter. I start looking for a weapon, my high heel the only thing coming to mind.

The guy chuckles. "Just have a drink with me. Just one and—" He stops talking and the music instantly screeches to a halt.

Cherry turns toward me and her face goes pale as if she's seen a ghost. I hear a girl scream off in the distance as the crowd begins to shuffle. I slowly turn and see what Cherry is staring at, why the music has stopped, and why everyone has the look of fear written on their faces. A group of rugged bikers push their way through the crowd—The Devil's Dust, to be exact—and Shadow's leading them. His jaw is clenched, his face red with anger.

Shadow points at Mr. Ross as he strides forward. The asshole puts his hands up in surrender and opens his mouth to speak, but before he can get a word out, Shadow grabs him by the shirt and throws him on his back. Mr. Ross lands on the dirty dance floor with a loud thud, and everyone gasps and even more people start rushing out of the club.

"I hear you put your hands where they don't belong!" Shadow growls.

He straddles Mr. Ross and drives his fist right into his mouth, making blood spurt when his hands makes contact. Shadow leans up and slams his boot into the guy's ribs, making Mr. Ross yell in pain.

Bobby walks forward and pulls on Shadow's shoulder, grabbing him from the dark place he's fallen to and back to reality. I can't help but notice Bobby has a split lip as he's pulling Shadow off the guy. *What the hell happened to Bobby?*

Shadow huffs and rubs the back of his neck, trying to regain his composure before looking at me. His eyebrows furrow, giving that little line he always gets when I'm angering him.

He steps over Mr. Ross who's laying on the ground in pain, grabbing me by the arm with one hand and the waist with the other, throwing me over his shoulders. As I'm jostled upward, I feel a heel slide off my foot.

"Have you lost your mind?" I yell at Shadow. This is the most humiliating thing I have ever been through.

Shadow finally sets me down as soon as we are outside the club, his bike parked right next to the door along with everyone else's.

"Get your ass on the bike, Dani," he demands, handing me a helmet.

"I am not getting on that with you," I hiss, pissed at him.

"Dani!" Cherry yells, coming out of the club doors, my black heel in hand.

"Thanks," I say, grabbing the heel from her, my face turning red with humiliation.

"Why aren't you wearing your fucking property patch?" Shadow asks me as he looks at Cherry, her property patch hard to miss.

"Are you fucking kidding me right now?" I snap. He can't be serious. I haven't worn that property patch since I caught him with another girl.

Shadow huffs at my response. "Get on the bike, or I'll *put* you on the fucking bike."

I know he will, and I've had enough embarrassment for the

night. I place my heel on my foot and snatch the helmet from him.

"How am I supposed to ride in this damn dress?" I throw my hands out, gesturing toward my outfit.

"Get. The. Fuck. On," Shadow grits as he starts his bike.

I growl in anger, slam the helmet on my head and get on the damn bike.

The ride back to the house is quick and angry.

As soon as we are in the apartment, I lean down, pull my left high heel off my foot, and throw it at Shadow. Missing him entirely, the shoe slams against the wall right behind him as he looks at me surprised. "Are you seriously throwing fucking shoes at me?"

I reach down, pull off my right heel, and throw it at him, too. It bounces off his leg before falling to the floor. "I have never been so humiliated in my life!" I scream, walking toward the bedroom.

"But getting groped by a douchebag isn't?" he yells, following me down the hall.

I scowl at him. "I can handle myself."

I admit I was freaking out when the Ross guy grabbed me. My only thought was to stab him in the eye with my high heel, but I could have handled him if things escalated.

"Yeah, clearly. If that were the truth, the bouncer wouldn't have called your father," Shadow says.

I whip around in shock.

"The fucking bouncer? Is there anyone in this town who doesn't kiss the club's ass?" Of course, Cherry wearing her property patch was a dead giveaway. I guess with Cherry wearing her cut and I being there with her, the bouncer didn't want to leave anything to chance so he called my dad.

Shadow laughs. "Not really."

I start reaching for the zipper in the back of my dress, but I can't unzip it to save my life.

"Let me," Shadow offers, walking behind me and grasping the zipper.

I turn and face the mirror in front of me, my eyes staring at his in the reflection.

He slowly pulls the zipper down to the mounds of my ass cheeks, his fingers tickling my spine and his eyes never leaving mine. I slightly twist my body, letting the dress fall to the floor, pooling around my feet. My black strapless bra and panties are the only thing I'm wearing. Shadow's eyes leave mine, overlooking my body's reflection in the mirror. His eyes become hooded with desire and he inhales sharply. My lips part in anticipation, hoping he'll touch me more. He slides one of his calloused fingers down my spine, the simple touch making me mew. After the abandonment of our relationship, the reconnection makes my body vibrate with want.

Shadow thrusts the front of his body against my back and wraps his hand around the front of me, grabbing my neck, he gently pulls my head up to look at our reflection in the mirror.

"Mine," he whispers in my ear, his hot, sticky breath not making me any less horny. He bites my neck, his teeth scraping the sensitive flesh while a moan escapes my lips as my eyes catch his. Throttling my senses, I arch my back into him, wanting more. His hard gaze softens before he squeezes his eyes shut like he's in pain. He pulls away, leaving me panting for more. Then he looks me over one last time before he leaves me in a frenzy of emotions. I don't get it; he says I'm his, but he won't treat me as his. Not like he used to, anyway. I look at the mirror and see my cheeks flushed and lips swollen with anticipation. I look a hot mess.

◆ ◆ ◆

I sleep well past morning and into the afternoon. Following a long shower, I look through the closet, searching for something provocative but not obvious. Shadow wanted to go further last night, but something stopped him. I gulp the thought down and start flinging through my clothes. I grab a black, silk nightie, which goes to my thighs, and choose not to wear panties. Okay, so maybe it's a little obvious, but I need answers. Now that everything is out in the air, I want to move forward.

I look in the mirror on the back of the dresser and tousle my long, dark hair. I pinch my cheeks for color and walk out of the bedroom in search of Shadow. He's sitting on the couch with his legs propped on the coffee table. I smell food and notice a bucket of chicken on the counter.

I grab a plate and pretend to accidently drop it, the plate clattering to the floor and catching his attention. I position myself to where my ass is facing Shadow and slowly bend down to pick it up, my silk nightie rising in the process, letting my bare ass peek from underneath.

I hear Shadow rise from the couch and before I stand straight, his hands grip my hips harshly. He pulls my ass hard against his groin and moves my hair to the side of my neck to rest on my shoulder.

"I know what you're doing," he growls in my ear. His hand slides slowly underneath my nightie and skids its way across my hip and down over the apex of my thighs, making my head fall back with pleasure.

"What do you mean?" I whisper, my breathing becoming fitful.

"You know exactly what I mean. You have been baiting me for days," he replies, pushing his hard length against my rear, the feeling divine.

"I really don't know what you're talking about," I lie on a whisper, hoping he moves his hand a little lower.

"Right," Shadow says sarcastically, letting me go.

Our eyes hold for a moment as he releases a steady breath.

"I got a call to make a run tonight. I don't know when I'll be back." He grabs a chicken leg from the bucket and tears into it. Then he looks me up and down like he's programming me to memory before walking to the door and leaving.

"Damn it," I mutter.

After having to relieve myself last night from the sexual torture between Shadow and me, I finally fell asleep. Waking up today, I realize it's the Fourth of July. I am anxious to get out of the house, so I call Tom to come pick me up and take me to the party the club is throwing.

I grab my black-leather bikini, hoping I will see Shadow. I know this is his favorite bikini, and I'm hoping it will be the last straw in his abstinence.

After arriving at the beach and changing, I walk out onto the hot sand and immediately spot my dad. His presence isn't as endearing knowing he might have had violent orders to ensure my silence of the club's activity. The fact that he might have sent Shadow is the worst.

"Dani, Darlin'," my dad coos as he walks my way. He throws his burly arm around my shoulders and gives me a big hug, the smell of booze stronger than his aftershave.

He suddenly pulls back and eyes my bikini. "You can't wear that," he declares, pointing at me.

"What?" I look down at myself.

"Go change," he says seriously, pointing toward the bathrooms across the beach.

"Oh, leave the girl alone," Babs tells him, walking up behind my dad.

"Do you see the shit she's wearing, or not wearing for that matter?" he points out, his tone sounding frustrated.

"She looks fine, Bull. It's a beach party," she replies, placing her hands on hips.

My dad sighs in defeat and walks off, shaking his head in dismay.

THE SCARS THAT DEFINE US

"How ya doing, Doll?" Babs says, smacking her gum.

"I'm all right," I smile.

"That's good. You better get used to your dad trying to make you wear a paper bag," she laughs. "Enjoy yourself, ya hear?" she yells over her shoulder as she walks over to the table full of food.

I throw my towel down and lay out on it, listening to the kids scream and play in the water and the ol' ladies laughing with each other in the background.

"Hey." My father sits down next to me.

"Hey, Dad," I say, sitting up.

"I haven't had a chance to get over to the apartment and see you. Shit's been crazy at the club," he apologizes, taking a swig from a beer can.

"I understand," I smile.

"Damn proud of you, though." He smiles back at me. "You got out there and got yourself a job you enjoy, making something of yourself." He lifts the can really high, getting the last drop of the beer to fall into his mouth. "I'm sorry, Dani," he says glumly. I look under my lashes at him, watching his face line with regret and sorrow. "I'm sorry about the way things were handled when you returned. I had my doubts about it, but because I'm the president, I have to set an example."

I look out at the setting sun, the question I want to ask playing in my head.

"What if I had been guilty of conspiring with my mother or you couldn't prove I wasn't? Would you have had me killed?" I question, narrowing my eyes.

He sighs deeply, looking behind him before leaning into me.

"I knew you weren't a threat when you came back, regardless if you were in on it with your momma or not," he replies, kissing my head. "But the club has rules, and I have to go through with the rules myself. I knew your innocence would rise soon enough; I just needed you out of the club until that happened, for your protection," he continues, lifting my chin to look at him. "Your innocence shows you have this club's back, and this club will forever be in your debt, Dani." He looks at me bright-eyed and smiles.

I think about this for a second, knowing the world I used to live in was harsh and vile. It didn't matter how many times I proved myself to it; it was relentless, always coming back to bite you in the ass. Knowing I proved myself to the Devil's Dust and hearing they will always have my back is a relief.

"And there is no way I would have let anyone harm you," he states quietly. My eyes widen, not expecting to hear that. "If it came down to it, I would have stuffed your pockets with cash and told you to run. The club is supposed to come first, I know, but last time I put the club before my family, I lost your momma. Something I'll never get back." He crumples the empty beer can in his hand. "Don't get me wrong: I'll die for this club, and this brotherhood is all I got." He tangles his big hand in my hair, looking at me with a sincere gaze. "But there's no way I could let someone hurt you," he tells me, his tone serious, and his brows furrowed with force.

"And I knew Shadow wouldn't hurt you, not physically, anyways. That boy is twisted something bad over you," he says with a chuckle as he stands up, leaning down to kiss me on my forehead gently.

"You have fun, Darlin'," he finishes, walking over to Babs and the group.

◆ ◆ ◆

"You're a little burnt." I open my eyes to see Tom, only he looks different now that he's not hiding under a helmet and sunglasses. I can see his hair, which is brown and short, and his eyes are light brown and inviting. The only thing he's wearing is blue board shorts. He has tan skin and is a little soft in the torso rather than built. I sit up and realize it's dark. I have been here sunbathing and listening to everyone for longer than I thought.

"You have hair," I comment, ruffling the top of Tom's head.

"Yeah, I do," he says, eyeing my hand with a smirk as he hands me a cold beer. "Brought you a beer."

"Thanks," I reply, grabbing the cold can from him. I open it and drink a small sip.

I look out and notice all the kids are gone. My eyes fall on Shadow across the beach, standing around a small bonfire. His smoldering gaze penetrates me.

"Where are all the kids?" I ask.

"Sun goes down, family time is over," Tom smirks. "That's what I was told anyway," he says.

"Even for the Fourth of July? That's when all the exciting parts happen." I raise my eyebrow.

"Yup, they go home," he states, sipping his beer loudly.

I look across the bonfire and see my dad slap Shadow on the back, laughing as if Shadow had just told a joke, making me smirk. He's like the father Shadow never had.

I stand up and head toward the bonfire, which looks as if it had just been started.

"Thanks for the beer," I yell at Tom as I walk away. I can feel Shadow staring at me, the blue tormented eyes causing goose bumps to rise against my spine. I look at where he was standing and spot Candy in a bright-pink swimsuit walking toward him. My claws immediately come out, wanting to scratch that bitch's face off.

"Dani!" Someone yells, catching my attention. I look over and see Doc tripping her way over to me.

Bobby comes up behind her, wrapping his arm around her waist trying to steady her.

"Yeah, Doc has had a little too much to drink," he explains, eyeing over my shoulder. I look to see what Bobby is looking at and see Shadow walking toward us.

"How much have you drank?" I ask, looking back at Doc. She flips her long, blonde hair over her shoulder and giggles like I just asked the funniest question.

"Seems Bobby likes drunk girls," Shadow says coldly from behind me.

Doc giggles and nods her head in agreement.

"Let's go," Bobby orders Doc as his eyes narrow with anger at Shadow.

I watch Bobby help a stumbling Doc toward the parking lot. I sympathize with her. Bobby can be more than encouraging with his alcoholic beverages; no girl could say no to him if they wanted to.

"What did you and Tom have to talk about?" Shadow asks, taking a swig of his beer bottle casually.

I look up at him. "Why, jealous?"

Shadow grits his jaw as his finger slides down my back, his touch shooting sparks through me. My body wants him more than I have ever wanted anything, the depriving release becoming unbearable.

"You don't want to tempt me, Dani," he warns, skipping his hand down and grabbing my ass firmly.

I sigh from the contact; my body wants more of him but Shadow won't budge. He walks away from me, and looking back, he smirks, making my bikini bottoms melt.

Feeling the urge to pee, I start making my way toward the bathroom; on my way, I hear loud moaning and panting. I look into the darkness where the noise is coming from, the bright moon lighting up the night for me to just barely see. I spot Locks sitting on the ground with his pants pulled to his ankles, a bottomless Candy grinding on top of him. He brings Candy closer, biting on her shoulder when his gaze catches mine. I quickly avert my eyes to the ground and keep going. Seeing him cheat on Babs has me sick to my stomach. *Where in the hell is Babs? Surely she stayed?*

After doing my business in a sandy, wet bathroom, I leave and am immediately snatched to the side of the building. My mouth opens, ready to scream, but is slapped shut with a muscled hand.

My eyes go wide with fear and I notice Shadow, whose face is full of humor laughing at me.

"Asshole!" I yell, slapping his arm in anger.

Shadow growls and pulls me closer.

"Your temper has a way of turning me on," he whispers against my collarbone.

He runs his nose up my neck, making my head fall back against the brick bathhouse. He slides his hands down my frame until they reach my ass where he digs his fingers into my flesh. The feeling of his rough grasp makes me moan and my body sparks alive, wanting more.

"Man, I miss this," he moans, tightening his grasp on my backside with one cheek in each of his large hands. My breathing becomes heavy with lust, I bring my mouth toward Shadow and smash my lips to his, demanding contact. He immediately nips my lip with his teeth and slips his tongue into my mouth, devouring my senses. That feeling I get when I'm with Shadow slams forward, the feeling that nothing else matters. He's the air that fills my lungs, and every time he pulls away, I am deprived of that refreshing breath which keeps me alive.

My hands trail down his bare, chiseled chest to his red board shorts, his excitement for me pressing against the fabric. A loud bang erupts in the sky, and colors of red, blue, white, and zinging gold illuminate around us, our bodies tangled in a Fourth of July display. Shadow trails his finger down my stomach over my belly button and plays with the elastic of my bikini bottoms. My body vibrates with desire, craving for him to go further.

"Mine in leather is very tempting," Shadow whispers into my mouth as he continues to kiss me. I smile against his lips; my plan to bring Shadow to his knees with the leather bikini is working.

Ear-piercing whistles sound off in the distance, catching our attention. He breaks away from our kiss and looks at the fireworks lighting up the night sky before he releases his grip on me and pulls away.

I sigh in frustration, pissed he's refraining going any further with me when he clearly wants to.

"Why are you resisting?" I pant, my voice heavy with lust.

Shadow smirks as he runs his hands through his black, ruffled hair. "Your body may want me, but I'm greedy. I need all of you, Dani," he replies somberly. "Including your heart."

I swallow the lump building in my throat; I've always loved Shadow, even when he broke my heart. If I hated anyone, it was myself for not being able to hate him.

"I've always loved you, Shadow," I whisper candidly, emotion muffling my voice.

Shadow walks up close, grabbing the nape of my neck and forcing me to look up at him. "How can you love me? How can you love me when I deserted you when you needed me?" he asks, his tone deep and angry, giving me the impression he doesn't feel worthy of my love.

What am I supposed to say to that? He's right. I should hate him, should plot my savage revenge which flows like a raging river, but I do love him. I'm so damaged that I can look past the manic beast before me and see the caring man he wants to be. Most of all, I can relate to his darkness, our desperation so thick we'll do anything to feel something beyond the poisonous pain which consumes our lives.

"Do you still love me?" I ask.

Shadow looks out at the fireworks blooming into the night's sky, his eyes squinting as he's deep in thought. He turns and looks at me with a serious face, a wrinkle right between his eyes. "I never stopped."

My heart skips a beat as his words register.

"I love you the same way you love me. No matter what we do to break each other, we are irreparable without each other," I whisper.

He brushes a calloused finger over my bottom lip then runs it along my cheek as his mouth lifts slightly in the corner hiding, a smile. "It's late. You want me to take you home?" he asks, as if we weren't just having a deep conversation.

"I can get Tom to take me. You can stay and have fun," I reply, pushing off the wall.

Shadow snorts. "That won't be happening."

I turn to argue but am interrupted. "Have you guys seen Babs?" my dad asks. He looks at Shadow and me and narrows his eyes with anger. Shadow and I hidden behind the bathhouse probably doesn't look great.

"No, why?" I ask, concerned.

"She left for more food an hour ago and nobody has heard from her," he responds, pulling his phone out, clearly trying to call her. The hairs on my arm rise with alert. Something feels off and I know it can't be good.

"Sorry, brother. I haven't," Shadow says, grabbing my hand. "I'm taking Dani home."

9

Shadow

AFTER A LONG COLD SHOWER, I LAY IN BED THINKING ABOUT DANI IN that fucking black-leather swimsuit. Not helping myself with those thoughts, I end up in another cold shower. I knew the remedy to my boner lay in the other room, and the thought of her even there pisses me off. I climb out of bed and head over to Bobby's room. Opening the door, I notice the lights off and Dani asleep in bed. Her shirt is tattered, way too big for her, and it's twisted up, showing off her stomach and a peek at her right breast, her pink nipple barely showing. I throw my head back and moan at the throbbing piercing in my dick. I want Dani, and I want her badly. But it won't be tonight when she's half-asleep; I want her full attention. I want to know she's mine willingly, and I want to know she trusts me.

I pull her shirt over her pink-laced panties—not helping with my blue balls at the moment—and lift her from the bed. She snuggles against my chest and moans my name. My name on her lips is bliss.

I lay her down in my bed and pull her close, her body fitting mine like a glove. I nuzzle her hair and smell her scent of peaches, wondering how I could ever think of possibly harming her. Looking back, I know I couldn't have pulled the trigger on Dani. I want to believe I would do it for my brothers if they had asked, but considering how messed-up I am over her, I know I could never hurt her.

◆ ◆ ◆

"Wake up," I whisper, pulling the sheets off Dani. She stretches and moans, her shirt falling off her breast again, reminding me of what I want and can't have.

"Wait. How'd I get in here?" she asks, pulling the sheet up to cover herself.

I smirk at her reaction. I could fuck with her head, but I won't.

"Don't worry, you'd know if we fucked," I say winking, gaining an eye roll from her. "Get dressed," I demand.

"Why?" she asks, looking for the clock.

"Because I'm teaching you how to shoot a gun properly today." She looks at me dumbfounded, making me roll my lips to keep from laughing.

◆ ◆ ◆

Dani couldn't make it any harder on a man. She walked out of the room with her hair in braided pigtails, wearing a black tight tank with ripped shorts. The ride to the gun range was more than uncomfortable with my dick so hard I thought it would pierce the gas tank.

"Don't I need ear plugs or something?" she asks, looking out at the targets.

"Are you going to pull your earplugs out and put them in before you shoot your attacker?" I counter, loading the gun.

"No," she replies, rolling her eyes. I reach over and slap her ass, making her squeal from the contact.

"Ouch!" she yells, rubbing her ass cheek.

"Roll your eyes again," I threaten.

"I don't think I want to," she says, smiling.

"Okay, show me how to hold a gun," I order, handing her the gun.

She grabs the gun and points toward the target, locking both arms straight at the elbow, her legs so wide I could crawl between them.

"Wrong!"

"Well, we established that I don't know what the hell I'm doing," she smarts, lowering the gun and frowning those beautiful lips at me. I bite my lip to keep from smiling at her sassy attitude.

"Your legs need to be the width of your shoulders," I explain, kicking her feet in. I walk up close behind her and unlock her right arm slightly. Then I bend her left elbow and adjust her right hand to grip the gun. Her left hand supports the grip, and her index finger on her right hand is next to the trigger.

"Pull the trigger with your right finger when—"

A loud bang resonates through the area, interrupting me.

"Shit!"

"You said to pull the trigger," she smiles, lifting her eyebrow in a mischievous way.

"I was going to say pull the trigger when you were ready. You didn't even aim," I say, pointing toward the target.

She rolls her eyes at me and turns toward the target. Gritting my teeth, I slap her ass harder than before.

"Ouch!" she yells, turning toward me.

"Gun or no gun, you don't roll your eyes at me," I reply. I place myself behind her and help her hold the gun again. "Steady your breathing, and when you're ready to pull the trigger release on an exhale," I whisper in her ear.

I feel her body inhale as she studies the target, and with a loud bang she releases her breath.

"Did I hit it?" she asks.

I squint my eyes and look out at the target. "I can't tell. Shoot a couple more times and we'll go look," I tell her, standing back.

She places her feet like I told her, grips the gun like a pro, squints her eye and begins shooting.

"Holy Hell," I say to myself.

"What?" she asks, not taking her eyes off the target to look at me.

"The sight before me would make a nun weep," I respond honestly.

Her mouth turns into a smirk as she aims. Like she's been doing it her whole life, she shoots till the clip is empty. My ears ring from the loud bangs, but damn if I wouldn't reload that clip in a heartbeat to watch her shoot again. She turns toward me and smiles, knocking me from my thoughts.

"Let's go see how you did," I say, walking out into the field.

"Wow," I whisper, looking at the target. She only missed the bull's eye once. I have never seen a woman shoot so well. "God, you're fucking incredible," I whisper, astonished by the woman before me.

Not being able to withhold my urges anymore, I grab the gun from her and toss it on the ground beside us, watching as her body swells with acknowledgment of my desire for her. I grab her by the waist and push us to the ground.

She shoves her hands into my hair and locks them tightly. Man, I missed her hands in my hair; I missed her, period. My lips kiss her neck, pecking, nipping and sucking; her taste is a drug, a curse, my weakness. Her nails dig in my back as she rocks her hips into me. I pull the ties from her hair, releasing her pigtails; I want to feel her silky hair in my hands. She moans as our lips caress each other, our tongues reclaiming what was once theirs.

"Take me, Shadow," she orders.

"Do you trust me, Dani?" I whisper against her lips. I need to know she trusts I will protect her at all costs, I won't make that same mistake again.

She pulls back and looks at me, her green eyes tormenting me with her hesitation.

"I do," she replies softly, her green eyes heavy with desire.

I grab her by the hips and unbutton her shorts, pushing them and her panties to her ankles, our actions hurried with anticipation. I wanted to go slower and take my time when I took Dani, but having her beneath me I can't help the urge to be inside her. She pushes my jeans and briefs down in a rush. I kick my boots off and pull my jeans the rest of the way free, my eyes never leaving her gorgeous body. She pulls her panties and shorts tangled around her ankles off, and like a fire needing the heat, her body smashes into mine, her lips kissing me everywhere they land. She grabs the hem of my shirt and pulls it up and I lift my arms, helping her take it off. I grasp her shirt roughly and pull it off her not so gently, not being able to wait any longer. I lay a hand on her back and gently lay her back on the grass as she spreads her legs, inviting me in. Without a second thought, I plunge my more-than-ready cock deep inside her. She arches her back and moans loudly with pleasure, our bodies finally connecting, giving us a high we have both longed for. My head falls back at the wet warmth, which surrounds my hardness. I've missed her. I've missed this. No woman could ever compare to Dani; she is it for me.

I begin to thrust myself into her slowly, wanting to savor everything she has to offer. I sit up and place my hands on her knees, looking down at the girl who has me changing in ways I don't even understand. I've never understood forgiveness, never cared if someone trusted me, never needed to, until her.

Her green eyes open with lust and they're captivating, reminding me why I fell for her in the first place.

I lower myself down, place my forearms beside her head, and begin kissing her. She drags her nails across my back as she deepens the kiss, her tongue gliding against mine.

"I've missed you, Shadow," she whispers into my mouth.

Feeling my balls tightening from the pleasure, I pick up the pace, lowering my hand and grabbing the back of her thigh, pulling her onto me more. I go from slow to urgent, slamming into her, her perky breasts bouncing out of her black bra from the urgent thrusts. She arches her back and starts moaning, the walls of her pussy clenching my cock. Her mouth opens, and closes as she gasps for air when the peak of her orgasm begins to surface.

Not wanting to, I pull out, depriving her of what she needs to fall over the edge. I'm not fully satisfied that she knows she is mine, and I won't continue until I'm convinced.

She snaps her head upright, pissed off, she pulls herself onto her elbows and scowls at me.

"What the hell?" she growls, irritated and out of breath.

"Who do you belong to, Dani?" I grab her by the hair roughly and pull her face close to mine.

She looks at me shocked, her eyes wide and mouth parted.

"Who do you belong to?" I repeat, clenching my hand in her hair harder.

"You," she whimpers.

"This," I grab her wetness with my hand and slip two fingers in, making her moan. "Who does it belong to?" I ask, sliding my fingers in and out.

"Oh, God," she whispers loudly, throwing her head back in ecstasy. I stop and wait for her reply. "You," she says, trying to ride my hand.

"That's right," I agree, pulling my finger from her and slamming my cock back in its place, the contact making her moan, it's the sexiest sound I've ever heard.

She wraps her legs around my hips and meets my thrusts with her own, the tightening in my balls returning as I continue to slide in and out of her.

"I've always loved you," she moans, her voice soft with pleasure. I feel her walls squeeze my dick like a vise as her light moan heightens to a full-out animalistic growl. With that, my knees begin to tremble as my balls tug and I come. I come so fucking hard. I feel like my dick may explode. I growl at the empowering feeling of release and collapse onto her chest, our bodies heaving from the exertion and emotional rollercoaster we put each other on.

I lift myself from her body and roll over onto the dead grass.

We lay there out of breath, staring at the blue sky and passing clouds, when my phone rings.

"Shit." I dart up, looking for my jeans. I find them inside out and thrust my hand into the pocket to pull out my phone.

"What's up?" I question, trying to steady my breathing.

"It's Babs," Bull says.

"What about her?" I ask a little irritated at his vagueness.

"She's in the hospital." I look at Dani who senses something is wrong by the look on her face.

"What happened?" I question, still looking at Dani.

"Hit and run. Get your ass to the club, now," he commands before hanging up.

The ride to the clubhouse is quick and hurried. I can feel the tension building in Shadow's arms the closer we get. Apparently, Babs is in the hospital from a hit and run. I can't believe it; this world is turning to crap. Shadow reaches back and places his hand on my leg, claiming me as his. I can't help the smile which runs across my face. Feeling this connection once again with Shadow is the best Heaven Hell has to offer.

We pull into the club and hop off the bike. Looking around, I notice a lot of bikes and cars all parked randomly across the yard.

"Let's get in there," Shadow says, pushing me by the small of my back.

Walking in the club's doors, I spot the girls by the bar. I notice Cherry crying and sniffling on a bar stool as Vera sits on the other side, smoking a cigarette. Vera's not crying but you can sense her unease by the look on her face. She has this scowl that narrows her whole face downward.

"I'll be out in a bit," Shadow states, giving my butt cheek a slap as he kisses me passionately, not caring the whole club sees his display of affection. I hate how I feel on cloud nine as a terrible situation is unfolding in front of us.

"Looks like you and lover boy are back to good graces," Vera smarts as she blows cigarette smoke into the air.

I just give her a kind smile and sit next to Cherry. She is slumped forward with her hands in her strawberry-colored hair, which is acting as a curtain, shielding her face from everyone.

"It's so awful," Cherry whines, turning toward me. Her eyes are red and puffy while mascara is smeared down her face.

I rub her back and give a half-smile. "She's going to be okay," I reassure her.

"She's in a fucking coma. How is she going to be okay?" Vera spits.

"She's in a coma?" I ask shocked, hearing that information for the first time.

"They found her in the street with bags of chips everywhere in a mangled mess. She's got a heartbeat, but is in a coma," Vera explains, lighting a cigarette with a cigarette.

"Shit," I say, thinking about poor Babs.

"You know who did this," Cherry declares, looking at Vera.

"Shut the fuck up, Cherry. You don't know shit," Vera demands, slamming one of the cigarettes in an ashtray.

Cherry slumps forward again and begins to sob. I give Vera a confused look as she stares back at me with an angry one.

"Who?" I ask, curious who Cherry thinks did this to Babs.

"Nobody," Vera snaps.

SHADOW

"So, we don't know who hit her?" I ask Locks across the table and everyone looks at him, waiting for his reply.

He looks at the floor. "I don't know, probably just some drunk not paying attention," he responds casually. I can't help the look of uncertainty on my face. Why isn't he freaking out, screaming for the blood of the person who did this to his ol' lady?

"What did the cops say?" Bull asks, tapping his fingers on the table.

"Oh, you know, the same bullshit they tell everyone," Locks replies, rubbing his beard.

"Which is what?" I push, irritated.

Locks looks at me, his blonde and white speckled mustache twitching with irritation. "That they will do their best."

"Who found her?" Bobby asks.

"Some passerby," Bull answers.

"Any video surveillance around the area?" Old Guy wonders.

"Yes. But it only shows a white car speeding like a bat out of Hell. Can't see anything but a white blur," Locks rambles, his voice wobbly with excitement.

Bobby looks at me across the table, his eyebrow raised.

"Right. Well, I'm going to go over and see her." Bull stands, patting Locks on the shoulder. "We'll get to the bottom of this, Locks."

Maybe I'm being irrational, but I feel there is something Locks is not telling us.

The door slams open and the men's boots stomp out.

"Come on," Shadow calls, giving my shoulders a light squeeze. I gently rub Cherry's back before slipping off my stool. Shadow grabs my hand and pulls me down the hall to his room, away from the crowd.

He shuts the door behind us and runs his hands over his face in irritation. I cross my arms over my body as I look at the bathroom; the last time I was in here, a slut stood in there. I close my eyes, feeling the light tension of the ache, which used to reside in my chest cavity try and resurface.

"What's wrong?" Shadow asks.

"I don't know if I can be in here," I reply honestly, looking back at the bathroom.

Shadow scoffs.

"Why, because I had a girl in here?" he demands arrogantly.

"Yes, that's exactly why," I respond, uncrossing my arms and feeling defensive.

He falls on his back. "Unbelievable," he whispers. He sits up on his elbows and scowls at me. "You're upset I brought you in here, because I may or may not have fucked another woman in here?"

"Yes, I don't need you to rub it in my face, believe me." I raise my eyebrows; now I'm pissed.

He growls in frustration and pats the bed beside him for me to sit. I comply hesitantly, and he grabs me by the hips and pulls me on top of him. Straddling him, I place my hands down on his chest to keep me from toppling over.

"Let's just leave the past in the past. Looking back doesn't do anything for the future. Especially for us," he says, trailing his fingers up and down my arm. His touch raises little goose bumps on my olive skin, and I relish the feel of his touch.

"How many women did you sleep with?" I ask. I can't leave it in the past until I know what I'm leaving behind.

"None," he says flatly. My eyes nearly bug out in shock. I surely thought he had reverted to his old ways, sleeping with countless women.

"None?" I repeat in question.

"What, shocked?" he sneers, sitting on his elbows and looking up at me. "I couldn't get your innocence, your face, or those fucking eyes out of my head." He shakes his head like hearing it out loud sounds crazy. "No one can ever compare to you," he explains, pulling me to lay on top of him.

I lay on his chest, listening to his heartbeat beneath me. *Why does he feel I'm so innocent, so angelic, worthy of never doing anything wrong?* Living in the Devil's Dust lifestyle has taught me one thing: I'm no angel. Far from it even. I broke a club law by going on that date, did drugs, tried to kill my mother, and I've nearly beaten a guy to death.

"Shadow?" I ask, for his attention.

"Yeah?" he questions, his voice rumbling within his chest against the side of my face.

"I'm not as innocent as you think," I state, looking at the wall.

Shadow laughs. "I know. That's why our relationship is ideal."

"I can't believe what happened to Babs. And damn Locks," I whisper.

"What about him?" Shadow asks. I look up, surprised he even heard me.

"Nothing," I say, sitting up.

Shadow grabs me by the nape of the neck, forcing me to look at his angry blue eyes.

"Don't keep fucking secrets from me, Dani." His voice is cold and angry, not making me feel better about any of the secrets I have. But what's the worst that could happen? Besides, sleeping around on ol' ladies is normal around here.

"It's nothing that doesn't already happen around here, but when everyone was worried about where Babs was, Locks was busy messing around with Candy."

"Are you sure?" he asks, sitting up on his elbows.

"Yes."

I remember seeing Locks' eyes catch mine; they were eerie and unfriendly.

Shadow shakes his head in understanding.

"I understand why you're pissed, but you need to keep out of it," he orders with as much sincerity as he can, but it still hits a nerve.

"President's daughter or not, you can't go around making waves like that. I'll handle it," he finishes, running his hands through my hair.

"I'm going to go in and see her," Dani says, kissing my cheek.

"Yeah, go ahead," I encourage, staying back waiting in the hallway. Hospitals make me uneasy.

I look up and see Locks typing on his phone with a smile on his face. He's pissing me off. "What the fuck you smiling about?" I ask, lifting off the wall.

He looks up at me for a second before tucking his phone in his pocket.

"What the fuck is your problem?" Locks asks.

"You are my fucking problem," I spit, my tone angry and clipped. I walk up and get in his face, my blood pounding through my body so hard it pulses in my temples.

"And why's that?" he replies, puffing his chest out.

"What the fuck where you doing when Babs went missing?"

"I was—"

"Tell me why we are all concerned about her, while you're over here fucking smiling on your phone instead of in there with her?" I question, gaining attention from the nurse's station. "Who were you fucking when your wife was nearly killed?" I roar. I am so angry. I can feel the veins in my neck pop out. Babs has been like a mother to me since I joined this club, and it's time she deserved some respect from this asshole.

"What the fuck is going on out here?" Bull asks, leaving the hospital room with Dani following him.

"Whatever your fucking little girlfriend told you is a fucking lie!" Locks shouts. "Or did you forget she's the enemy when you were fucking her?" he continues, his tone patronizing. Without a second thought, I bash my fist into his face. Who the fuck does he think he's talking to? Bobby comes up and grabs me from behind as Bull grabs Locks.

"You got your fucking priorities messed up, brother. This is what that bitch is trying to do, break up the club!" Locks yells as he wipes blood from his split lip.

"Let it go brother," Bobby whispers in my ear.

He pushes me out the hospital doors before I can turn around and put Locks in the fucking ground.

"We sure know how to make an appearance, don't we?" Bobby chuckles, but I'm not laughing. "What the fuck was that about?" Bobby asks.

"He's fucking hiding something," I announce, flexing my fingers from the pain climbing my knuckles. The bruising is already forming from hitting Locks.

"Ya, I picked up on that," Bobby affirms.

"You think Bull noticed?" I ask.

"I did," Bull responds, stepping out of the hospital.

Bobby and I both look in his direction.

"Until I figure it out, you need to keep your cool," Bull commands, pointing to me.

I scoff at him. "Where's Dani?" I can't get her face of anger when Locks cursed her out of my mind.

"She's in the bathroom," Bull says. "Something ain't right with Babs' hit and run. A piece of the puzzle is missing."

"Prick," Dani mutters under her breath, cursing Locks as she leaves the hospital. Her spitfire attitude brings a smirk to my face.

"Why don't you stay at the club, just for a few days?" Bull asks her.

"Yeah, sure," she agrees, squinting her eyes against the sun.

Dani

AFTER STOPPING AT THE APARTMENT TO PICK UP SOME OF MY clothes, we arrive back at the clubhouse, but it's practically a ghost town. With Babs' accident, nobody is in the mood for company. It goes to show Babs is truly the glue to this family.

"I got to go check on some shit. I'll be back," Shadow states, dropping my suitcase on the bed. I know better than to ask, so I just nod.

"Don't leave the club," he orders, giving my head a light kiss before leaving. All of this feels so surreal; I never thought for a second Shadow and I would end up back here.

I put away my things and clean myself up in the bathroom. Still waiting for Shadow to return, I head to the kitchen for something to eat. The place is eerily quiet and makes me nervous.

I grab some pasta Babs must have made recently and throw it in the microwave to warm it up before going back to my room. I eat my pasta and lay on the bed, looking up at the chipped ceiling, wondering what all its seen in its years.

◆ ◆ ◆

At some point, I must have fallen asleep last night, and I wake up to the sun shining brightly this morning. The club has gained more people, but not many. My dad grabbed a bottle of booze and retreated to his room last time I saw him. He seems to be more affected by Babs' accident than anyone. I notice Old Guy chasing some girl who is not his ol' lady down the hall into a room, and Hawk has stared at the same newspaper for over an hour. I saunter off to my room and lay on the bed, waiting for Shadow's return.

"I see you managed to crawl your way back in," Candy smarts, her voice irritating. I roll over and notice her leaning against the doorframe.

I sit up on the bed slowly and take in her usual slutty attire. Her blonde hair is let down in waves and she's wearing a pink dress which is way too short and showing too much cleavage.

"What do you want?" I ask annoyed.

"You know the only reason you're back in is because you're daddy's little princess? Otherwise, the man you're fucking would have put a bullet in your head," she replies with a smirk. My temper rising, I jump to my feet.

"You know nothing," I spit.

She laughs, the sound of it making me angrier. I stalk toward her.

"I know you're fucking Locks," I say in defense.

"Yeah, so what?" she questions, chuckling. *Does she have no remorse for being with him the night of Babs' accident?* I feel my fist itching to dismantle her pretty little face.

"You going to rat me out to Babs? I hear that's what you do best: ratting." Griping Candy's throat, the action takes me by surprise, but I don't remove my hand nonetheless. Her eyes widen when my fingers begin to lightly apply pressure. I should feel her fear and let go, but all I feel is the rage drumming through my body and the pulse picking up in Candy's neck beneath my fingers. Like a beast feeding off the fear in her, I relish in it and thirst for more. My vision begins to blur with rage and my body temperature rises quickly, making beads of sweat form between my breasts. My top clings to my back as my grip clamps down. The look of fear carved on Candy's face becomes a look of a soul whose life has just flashed before its eyes. Her hands begin to claw at mine, leaving little red marks across my knuckles. Her face begins to redden, but I can't let go for the life of me. I want to, but my fingers won't obey.

"Dani!"

Snapping me from my fury-induced state, I look over and see Shadow standing next to me. The rage flees my system and my vision becomes clear. I turn back toward Candy and notice she is a hue of red and purple under my death grip. My breath hitches at what I'm doing, but I still don't release her. My hand is ripped from Candy's throat as I watch, her body collapsing to the floor like a slinky. She grabs at her throat and makes a horrible gasping sound.

"You could have killed me, bitch," Candy rasps, her voice scratchy and strained. She's right. I could have killed Candy; my actions were manic and unpredictable.

"Don't ever fucking come near me again," I threaten quietly. She looks up at me, her eyes spilling with tears, but I have no pity for her. She removes her hands from her throat and I instantly see bruising, making me feel queasy that I am capable of such a thing.

"Get the fuck out of here, Candy," Shadow bellows, pointing off into the distance. Candy crawls to her feet and scampers off, sobbing.

"What the fuck was that?" Shadow growls. I shake my head, unsure. I've been back at the club a month and I've nearly killed three people. If Shadow hadn't shown up, I know I would have killed her.

"I don't know what I've become," I whisper, shocked at my

behavior. I look down and notice my hands trembling from the shock. The images of smeared blood from the guy I beat flash across my palms and I close my eyes, trying to wash the images away. *Why couldn't I let go?*

Shadow backs me into the bedroom.

"You're the Devil's Dust." I look at him, unsure what that means. "You have Hell's fury inside you; it owns you and consumes your thoughts. There is no escaping it. The anger and darkness which is harbored within you will surprise you, making its presence when it sees fit," Shadow explains.

"Outside of Devil's Dust, where civilization casts people like us out because they don't understand us— that is your prison. In here with us, this is where you are free; this is your family where we are alike and have each other's back." Shadow cups his hands to the side of my face and brings his forehead to mine.

"I feel like a monster, like I'm out of control," I whisper. I feel the tears fall along my cheek and slide across my lips.

Shadow lifts my chin so I'm forced to look at him. "We are more alike than you'll ever know," he murmurs, looking into my eyes. I can see it, the beast which feeds off another's blood is telling the dark creature which resides within me—the one just starting to rise from the nest—that me and Shadow are not so different from each other.

My bottom lip begins to tremble at the thought that I am capable of taking another's life.

"What if I had killed her?" I question.

"You're not a killer. A fighter, yes, but not a killer." He runs his hands up and down my back.

"If you didn't show up, I could have killed her, Shadow," I insist, my voice stern.

"I'll teach you to control it," Shadow responds, nipping my trembling lip.

His connection is my comfort. I suck in his bottom lip and kiss him passionately. Shadow grabs me by the hips and plows my back against the wall as I fumble with the button on his jeans, so desperately needing the connection. Shadow pulls my shirt off and throws it to the side quickly, and then grabs my shorts. Helping him in a hurried daze, I pull them down along with my panties in one fast motion. I reach up and cup his cheek as I lock my lips with his feverously. Shadow grabs the hem of his shirt and pulls it over his head, breaking our kiss momentarily.

Within seconds, he brings his plush lips back to mine and grabs me by the hips. I wrap my legs around his waist as he spins us around and drops us on the bed. I feel his length, his proof of arousal; glide across my leg as he moves across me, leaving a trail of excitement behind. Shadow sits up and glides the head of himself against my opening, teasing me. I close my eyes and moan with frustration.

"Eyes," Shadow demands. I open them and see his piercing blue eyes lock with mine.

"Don't be gentle," I whisper. I reach up and thrust my fingers into his thick hair. I need pain. I need to know I'm alive and not a walking ghost without a soul, incapable of remorse.

"I wasn't planning on it," Shadow states fiercely, slamming himself into me so deep he's buried to the hilt. My back arches, and I sigh loudly with satisfaction.

Shadow slides his rock-hard chest over mine and pulls my hair roughly, moving my head to the side. He dives his mouth in and bites my shoulder, making my pleasure heighten to new levels.

Doing the things I have done, the inhuman, savage acts, which should cause a normal person to feel pain, like almost killing someone—they haven't affected me that way. Not until the worst is over, anyway. Otherwise, I would have let go of Candy, and I didn't. I know I wouldn't have if Shadow hadn't shown up.

I extend my arms as far as they will go and grab onto his firm butt cheeks, pushing him further inside me, wanting him to hit the back of my pussy. Feeling him slam as far as he can go causes me to whimper from the pain. Shadow tries to stall, but I urge him to continue by pushing his ass forward with my hands.

"Don't stop," I demand, my voice strangled from the lack of air entering my lungs.

Shadow sucks on my right tit hard, as he thrust into me relentlessly.

"Fuck yes," Shadow growls when my nails dig into his back.

His hips begin to go faster, and my breathing becomes fitful as I feel my inner core become warm. My toes begin to curl and my eyes clench shut when I feel the peak of my orgasm try and surface.

A slap sounds through the room, followed by a powerful burning sensation on the right side of my thigh.

"Keep your eyes open," Shadow grunts, my pain becoming his pleasure as I feel him begin to pulse inside me, his speed picking up when I begin to moan with each powerful thrust. A piercing warmth blooms from my thigh before a loud 'slap' echoes in the room from Shadow smacking my thigh once again. Pinpricking sensations of my release begin at my feet and extend to every nerve ending in my body as a bang explodes between my legs. My undoing Shadow's vice, he comes quickly, moaning deeply into the crook of my neck. He thrusts a few more times before collapsing beside me. I look over and see him smile at my spent energy and inability to move.

"Sex helps," I say with a grin.

"Yes, it does," he agrees with hooded eyes.

◆ ◆ ◆

Shadow takes me to work today. He seems more open with me since he has discovered I'm not so different from him. That last barrier of trust I feel like I couldn't break through, I have since crushed with my darkness. Now we have each other to pull through the depths of violence and maybe together we will figure out a way to have mercy on those who cross the line of the Devil's Dust.

"Hey, so next week is a fundraiser. I need you to bring a date and dress in something nice," Mila informs me, redoing her blonde hair into a tight bun.

"A fundraiser?" I question, taking off my slippers.

"Yeah. I partner with another ballet studio in town, and once a year we have a fundraiser together. The governor will be there along with many other high profiles, so you have to be there," she answers, shutting off the lights to the studio.

"Yeah, I'll figure something out," I say unsure. I finish changing, the whole time wondering how I'm going to swing bringing a date to this fundraiser. Shadow is not going to want to go.

I walk outside and see him picking his nails with a knife. When he looks up and sees me walking toward him, his face lights up.

"Someone's happy to see me," I chide.

"You got a nice rack, who wouldn't smile," Shadow says cockily.

I laugh and grab the helmet from him before swinging my leg over his motorcycle.

On the ride to the apartment, I think about how I'm going to ask a badass, outlaw biker to attend a ballet fundraiser, and to dress in a tux for that matter. My mind is a complete blank; I have no idea how that is going to happen. I am just going to have to go by myself.

I climb off the bike and hand him my helmet.

"What's on your mind?" he asks, grabbing my wrist as I begin to walk away.

I look at him dumbfounded. *How does he do that?*

"I have to go to a fundraiser next week," I finally say.

"So?" he responds flat.

"I'm supposed to bring a date." Shadow eyes me quizzically. "And it's a dress-to-impress event," I croak.

"Fuck. That," Shadow says, rushing past me.

"The governor is going to be there along with other important people." Shadow stops suddenly and looks at me with those gorgeous blue eyes. "I understand if you don't want to go, but I have to," I shrug. Shadow looks off into the distance, the wind blowing his black hair around, he places his hands on his hips.

"What, and let one of those rich tools try and pick you up again?" he asks, looking at me with the most drop-dead smile.

I smile foolishly along with him. "So, you'll go?"

Shadow grins even wider. "Yeah, I'll go."

Not being able to contain my excitement, I squeal with delight and jump at him. He catches me with his muscled arms and smashes his lips to mine.

"Only you could get me to dress in a fucking tux," he whispers against my lips.

"Wake the fuck up, Shadow!"

"Go away," I mumble into the pillow beneath my head.

The door is thrown open and slams against the wall.

"You're going to miss church again," Bobby whines.

I nearly fall out of bed trying to find my underwear, but ultimately, I find my pants and pull them on. Buttoning them up, Bobby throws a shirt laying on the floor at me. I grab my socks and pull them on, along with my boots without tying them. I lean over and give Dani a light kiss on the head as she sleeps, then I grab my cut and make my way towards the chapel. I remember Bull reaming my ass out for missing yesterday, he's not going to be happy I nearly missed today.

The last three days have been a mess. The other day, I nearly missed a run with the boys because Dani and I were at the beach too long. I missed church yesterday because Dani and I were up all night playing strip poker, and last night we were up all night fucking, something I'll never get tired of. Before Dani, there were nights I didn't sleep, instead, I was doing runs or partying. But she is, by far, my favorite reason for not sleeping. She has my focus elsewhere and is a huge distraction, but I can't say I hate it.

I push the doors open slowly, hoping I can slip in unnoticed when my foot trips over my shoelaces and I stumble in the chapel. *Shit.* I sit down in my chair and look around the table, all eyes are on me. My eyes stop scanning the brothers when I come across Bobby's face of humor. He points toward my cut as if something is wrong. I look down and notice I have it inside out, so I pull it off and put it on right.

"As I was saying," Bull continues, his eyes lifted with annoyance as he stares at me, "we have no leads on Babs' hit and run, and apparently Locks doesn't give a fuck." I look at Locks' place at the table and see he's missing. *He never misses church, what the hell?*

"I got a hold of the tape myself, Prez, and you can't see shit," Old Guy admits, scratching at his chest.

"Wonderful," Bull exhales with a heavy breath, rubbing his hands up and down his face. "Well, nothing suggests this is an attack on the club, but watch your backs just in case." He slams the gavel down, dismissing everyone.

"Shadow, stay," Bull roars. I look up and see Bobby laughing, clearly amused I'm about to get my ass chewed out.

Everyone leaves and I wait for my lecture.

"You're unfocused and sloppy, why?" Bull asks, staring right at me with green eyes. They are like Dani's but hers are more vibrant with youth. What do I say? I'm so fucking messed up in the head with your daughter I've become careless?

"It's my daughter, isn't it?" he counters, rubbing his scruff, which he's let grow out.

I don't respond.

"This is why I didn't want you with her." he sighs. "I need you focused and on your game, but I want to see my daughter happy, as well. Tell me, what I'm supposed to do?"

"It won't happen again," I lie, knowing full well it will.

"Right," Bull says with a raised eyebrow. He knows I'm lying. "Get focused, son," he mutters.

Dani

The next couple of days are filled with lots of sex; it's our way to make up for lost time. Our bodies crave each other, needing the human contact to remind us we're alive. I have seen Babs a few times but she just lays there. Sometimes she moans and I jump up in excitement that she may be awake, but she never is. Every day I have seen her, I've not seen Locks once, but Babs is a strong woman. She's the glue to a broken family that needs her strength to keep them together.

I walk into the kitchen and see Shadow leaning against a counter in nothing but his underwear. His feet are crossed at the ankles and he's eating out of a tub of chocolate ice cream.

I smirk as I walk to the fridge and grab some juice.

"You want me to make you something?" he asks, stuffing the tub back into the fridge. The thought of food has me feeling ill.

"Yuck. No, I'll stick with my juice," I say, sipping from the glass.

"I gotta go out of town a few days," he says softly.

"Really?" I set my glass into the sink.

"Yeah. I'm hoping to be back in time for the event thingy, but I can't make any promises," he admits, shaking his head. I can't even hide the disappointment on my face.

Shadow grabs me by the hips. "I will try like hell to make it back in time," he promises, kissing my forehead.

I put on a fake smile and lie as I lay my head on his chest. "It's okay. When do you leave?"

"Now."

I close my eyes and take a heavy breath. I guess I'll have to get used to him leaving at a moment's notice.

"What are your plans for the day?" he asks, tangling his fingers through my hair.

"Work, maybe go dress shopping," I reply. Even if he can't make it to the fundraiser, I still have to go.

"I don't want you shopping alone," he demands, his tone serious.

I roll my eyes at his over-protectiveness.

"I'm serious, Dani," he insists, lifting my chin with his thumb and forefinger.

"Fine. I'll take Cherry."

"Good." He smiles, smacking my lips with his. His tongue tastes of chocolate as it glides along mine with eagerness.

Shadow eyes me as he walks to the door.

"Oh, and wear your property patch, damn it!" he growls before shutting the door.

◆ ◆ ◆

Hey, wanna go dress shopping tonight? - Dani

Hell yes! - Cherry

I'm at work right now, but I get off in an hour. - Dani

I'll come pick you up. - Cherry

After an hour of teaching little toddlers how to dance ballet—which usually just ends up in them spinning really fast in a circle, not listening the whole time—I sit outside and wait for Cherry.

I hear loud music as her red Bug comes flying into the parking lot.

"Hop in, bitch!" she laughs, pulling her sunglasses down the rim of her nose.

I smirk and jump in the car as she turns down the music and eyes me.

"What?" I ask nervously.

"I see you're wearing your property patch," she smirks, her hand pointed at my leather jacket.

I look out the window, not sure what to say.

"I'm happy for you guys. I was rooting for you two," she admits, watching traffic.

I look to see if she is serious or being sarcastic but can't really tell.

"So, a dress, huh?" she asks.

"Yeah. I'm going to a fundraiser for my work."

"Is Shadow going?" she wonders.

"He was until he got put on a run today," I say with a sigh.

"Too bad. I would love to see a biker in a suit," she giggles.

"Man, I would have loved to have seen that," I agree, laughing.

Cherry pulls up to some little store on the main strip.

"I love this place." She climbs out of the car, staring at the storefront. "I think famous people shop here."

I quickly jump out and look at the classy little brick store.

"Come on," she calls, pulling the front door open.

Cherry eyes me from bust to waist and starts grabbing dresses off racks as we walk through the store.

"What about that one?" I ask, pointing to a flowing pink dress with flowers printed all over it.

"You're not going to church. You got to dress in something a little flirty," she scoffs, looking at the dress I just pointed at with disgust.

After her arms are completely full of dresses, we head to the dressing rooms.

I start looking through the dresses she picked out: a very short black one, lots of low-cut ones. Cherry has big boobs and would look killer in these, but I'm not so sure I would.

"I don't think any of these would look right on me," I protest, looking through the pile one last time.

"Here, try this one." She slaps a dress over the top of the door.

It's champagne-colored and has little lace flowers all over the front with see-through lace on the side. It is strapless and goes past my feet with a small train behind it.

"I love this one," I exclaim, looking for the price tag.

Its cost is a little high, but I have saved up some checks from work so who cares.

I grab some matching shoes and check out.

"Let's get some food. I'm starving," Cherry says, dashing across the street to a burger joint, heading to the sectioned-off patio.

I grab the menu, looking for something to order, when it's snapped from my hands.

"You have to get the Trucker Fries. It's delicious." She rolls her tongue across her lips for effect.

"Sounds good," I laugh.

My phone chimes, catching my attention.

Find a sexy dress? - Shadow

Very sexy. - Dani

Not too sexy, though. - Shadow

Earth-shattering. - Dani

You can't go then. - Shadow

I laugh.

Nice try. - Dani

"Man, I miss Phillip," Cherry confides, stirring the straw in her cup, her sad face reminding me Phillip went to jail and here I am smiling like an idiot at my phone, clearly giving away I was talking to Shadow. I shove my phone in my pocket, feeling like a bitch.

"Why did he go to jail?" I ask.

"I don't entirely know," she admits, arranging packets of sugar. "The club got into some shit on a run, he took the fall for Bull is all I know."

"Wow, that seems shitty," I reply.

"Phillip did what he had to. He protected his president and for that, Bull will forever have his back," she states, moving her hands for the waiter to put our food on the table.

"This life is rough, but it's a hell of a ride," she tells me with a Cheshire grin.

"How did you and Phillip meet?" I ask, taking a bite of my fries.

She laughs while looking out over the crowd.

"I used to be a wild child before I met Phillip. You and Shadow aren't the only ones who grew up with troubled childhoods." She stirs her salad with her fork as she speaks.

"I left my home when I was fourteen. My dad was an abusive drunk and my mother left when I was just a baby." She looks down at her fries as she continues. "I had to provide my own way of living, and let's just say, it wasn't honest." She looks up and smiles at me wolfishly. "One of the ways I would score money was pick-pocketing; I would wear next to nothing and pretend my car broke down on the highway. One day, Phillip showed up to help me with my car, and I snagged his wallet." She grins as she tosses her strawberry hair over her shoulder.

"You weren't afraid of him?" I ask, shocked. There would be no way in Hell I would think about stealing from a biker.

"Where I grew up, men like Phillip were your neighbor," she responds, her face not giving anything away that she might be joking.

"Anyway, he didn't get too far before he noticed I swiped it. Hell, I hadn't even pulled onto the highway before he came back asking for it. I tried to pretend like I didn't have it, but he bent me over the hood of my car and pulled it from my back pocket. Before he got on his bike and drove off, he asked me for my number." Her face lights up into a big happily-ever-after grin as she finishes her story, making me smile for her.

"Not your everyday story to tell your kids how you met, but it's ours," she finishes, taking a bite of her fries. She throws her hair over her shoulder and looks at me, waiting for my reply.

"I love it. It's not any of that pretend bullshit that happens in the movies or in fairytales you read as a kid. It's real and it's raw, exactly how love is supposed to be: unexpected and unpronounced."

She nods. "Exactly. We were two damaged souls who found each other."

11

Dani

THE REST OF THE week goes by at a crawl. Shadow texts when he can, but it's still lonely as hell.

What are you wearing? - Shadow.

A ripped Budweiser shirt and white panties. Sexy, right? - Dani

Sounds hot, show me. - Shadow.

I bite my lip in embarrassment as I adjust the phone and take a selfie.

I'll be using this later. - Shadow.

What are you wearing? - Dani

Seconds later, my phone chirps. I open it and see a naked Shadow against a white background.

I'll be using this later, as well. ;) - Dani

You better not; you will wait for me. - Shadow

We'll see about that.

Tonight is the fundraiser, and I am in no mood to go. I take a long shower and finally decide to get dressed. I thought if I took my time getting ready maybe Shadow would show up, but I'm going to be late if I stall any longer. I slide my dress on which hugs my curves and curl my dark hair. I pull on my matching champagne-colored heels and walk out the door. Not sure how I'm going to get to the fundraiser, I pull my phone from my clutch to call a cab; I really need to get myself a license. As I'm searching my phone, a long, sleek black limo pulls up. The driver, wearing a suit, gets out and opens the back door, his white gloves standing out amongst the night. I stand there staring oddly; it can't be for me.

"Lexington?" the driver asks in a thick accent.

I nod and proceed to the opened door. I slide into the limo and see a black rose sitting on the seat with a letter under it.

"You said only the most important people are showing up. You, being the most important, should arrive in class." - Shadow.

I can't help the giggly laugh which escapes me, but seeing the rose and letter make me miss Shadow even more.

The limo is luxurious with leather seats all around and gold running lights along the top. It has a little TV, which is turned off near the front, and beside me is a little mini bar. I've never been in a limo, not even for prom.

We arrive to the big event and I'm nervous. It's a huge building with a round glass dome in the center, and there are lights flashing from cameras and limos from one end to the other.

The driver pulls up to the red carpet and someone opens my door. I place my foot out and immediately cameras begin flashing at me. I don't know why they are taking my picture; I'm not famous. I shield my eyes with my arm, trying to get past the rush of people and praying I don't trip on my long dress, when someone loops their arm with mine and gently pulls me forward.

"Thank you. That was crazy," I laugh, straightening my dress. I look up at the person who rescued me to find a very handsome Shadow wearing a tux.

"You made it," I say with a smile.

"I made it," he replies, grinning. "You look fucking hot in that dress. It's not leather, but mine looks just as good in lace," he whispers in my ear, his voice still managing to be deep and sexy, causing my skin to heat with affection.

He looks hot himself, dressed in a black and white suit with a red tie.

"You don't look so bad yourself," I admit, trying to mask the lust in my tone.

"I know that look," Shadow says with a raised eyebrow.

I turn my head away, caught in my naughty schemes.

"Finally," Mila cries, walking our way. "Shadow, don't you look dashing?" She looks him over, sizing him up.

Shadow nods in the man-way he does.

"The governor is about to give his speech, so please find your table," Mila pleads, pushing us.

We step up to the double doors that enter into the dome, but a group of people who have stopped to talk to each other have blocked it, making it hard for anyone to get in. I look across the way and spot a black-haired woman, her face seeming familiar to me. She's wearing a tight, red dress, which trails behind her, and her dark hair falls to her shoulders. She throws her head back in laughter, and when she positions her head just right, her eyes catch mine. She squints before her eyes go wide. She knows me, but how do I know her? She mouths something to the guy standing beside her and walks toward Shadow and me.

"Shadow, what are you doing here?" she asks, crossing her arms and looking around as if she's uncomfortable.

"Chelsea?" Shadow asks in surprise. Chelsea, now I remember. She was the girl at the party a while back. I got drunk with Bobby to keep me from killing her. She was wearing leather and made me feel inadequate and that Shadow was out of my league. She was all over Shadow that night and I wanted to beat her ass, but Bobby told me if I made a scene, it would bring mine and Shadow's secret to light. She looks different now: she has on glamorous makeup, expensive jewelry and hair extensions, which make her black hair fall below her shoulders.

"What are you two doing here?" she whispers.

"What the hell are you doing here?" Shadow asks at the same time.

"There you are, Chelsea, my dear. Who are your friends?" An older gentleman pushes his way through the crowd and slides his arm around Chelsea's waist, claiming her.

He's older, much older than her. He has white, balding hair and wrinkles, and I would guess he's around fifty years old. He's wearing a suit, as well, with a watch that shines when the lights hit it.

"These are some guests I was just making idle chit-chat with, my dear." She turns to him, smiling big.

"Well, aren't you going to introduce me?" he urges with a smile.

"This is Shadow and Dani," Chelsea tells him, pointing to us. "Dani and Shadow, this is my husband, Sir Franklin."

"Married?" Shadow questions.

"Yes, for four years," Sir Franklin says, pulling Chelsea close and kissing her on the head. "Hard to believe I could manage to keep something so beautiful for so long." She looks down, her cheeks flushing with shame. A skinny man in a suit comes hustling up toward Sir Franklin and whispers into his ear. When he nods, the skinny man takes off.

"Nice to meet you both but if you will excuse me, I have to watch my brother give a speech now," he says, tugging on Chelsea's arm.

"You got to be fucking kidding me," Shadow mutters under his breath. Who knew Chelsea was out with outlaws, living a double life by cheating on her husband on weekends, while being a high-maintenance, glamorous, gold-digger by weekday?

I grasp Shadow's hand and go look for our table.

The room is filled with little tables from one end to the other, all draped in white tablecloths of elegance. There are little lights strung along the wall and tea lights on the tables.

I find our names written in cursive on little note cards on a table near the back and sit. I can't help but look over at Shadow; seeing him in a suit is the most erotic thing I have ever seen. His sleeves are tight where I know his toned biceps rest, and my hands twitch to tug at the tie around his neck.

"Thank you, ladies and gentlemen," the governor says, interrupting my sinister thoughts.

"It is an honor to be here tonight, to help make…"

I lose focus on what the governor is saying when I feel Shadow's hand slide up my thigh, my dress being too long not stopping him as he starts to rub between my thighs. I slide my hand under the table and run it up his pant leg in return. When my hand reaches his crotch, it's met with a hard bulge. My eyes slide from the governor to Shadow who arrogantly smirks. He grasps my hand hard, pulls me up from my chair, and heads for the doors.

"Where are we going?" I ask, my heels clicking against the tiled floor.

"We are going to the bathroom. The governor is boring me," Shadow informs me, pulling me faster.

He pulls me into the women's bathroom and shuts the door.

"Aren't you going to lock it?" I ask.

"Where's the fun in that?" Shadow smirks.

He grabs the bottom of my dress and starts to bunch it up around my hips as he lifts me on top of the cold, granite counter. He reaches for my underwear to find I'm not wearing any.

"No underwear?" Shadow asks, shocked. He narrows his eyes and smirks. "You bad girl." He slides his finger into my already-wet folds, making my legs vibrate from the pleasure building within them.

I grab him by his tie and pull his mouth to mine then bite his bottom lip and whisper against his plush lips. "I don't know if you've noticed, but I'm not much of a good girl."

I place my feet on the edge of the counter as Shadow pulls his hard length from the zipper of his pants. He grabs me by the waist and pulls my ass to the edge before thrusting himself deeply inside me.

I throw my head back, the feeling of him inside me and the thought that we could be caught is all very erotic.

He leans down and shoves his nose in the crook of my neck before biting hard. I moan at the piercing pain consuming the area as he continues to thrust his hips forward.

"Yes," I moan loudly. Shadow clamps his hand over my mouth with a grin. My ecstasy blurring my rationality of where I am.

I grab onto his hair for support as I feel his cock begin to contract. Knowing he's close, I focus on the feeling of him gliding in and out of me. Shadow begins to pick up the pace, making my back slam against the mirror placed along the wall. His force makes me lose my footing and my foot slips, causing my heel to fall off my foot.

Shadow grabs me roughly as he begins to growl with his release, the feeling of him letting go inside me pushing me over the edge seconds later. Trying to keep quiet from the overwhelming electricity coursing through my body, I clench my jaw tightly, waiting for the cool-down before I unlock my clenched teeth.

I pull myself from my slumped position on the counter. My hair has to be a tangled mess from where I was pressed against the mirror, and my dress is still raised to my stomach.

Shadow leans down, grabs my heel off the floor, and hands it to me.

I place it back on my foot as he tucks himself back in his pants.

I hop off the counter and straighten my dress as Shadow sticks his arm out. "Shall we?" he asks with a laugh.

I loop my arm with his and exit the bathroom. "Dani, can I get a word?" Chelsea asks, pushing off the wall beside the bathrooms. *How long was she out here? Did she follow us in the bathroom and see Shadow and me?*

He glances at me in question.

"I'll be right there," I tell him. I could use the bathroom anyway; I can feel the wetness of Shadow seeping down my thigh.

Shadow looks at Chelsea with disgust before walking toward our table.

"Can we?" Chelsea points to the bathroom.

I nod and follow her to the bathroom I was just in.

I look in the mirror and notice my flushed cheeks and smeared mascara. I look thoroughly fucked.

"I don't know why you're here, or what you think you know, but you don't say shit to my husband," she demands, slapping her hand down on the counter.

I stop trying to tame my curls and look at her. "You mean about your double life?"

She presses her lips together tightly. "You don't know shit about my life."

I sigh, knowing this chat isn't going to end well, and head toward the stall to clean myself up.

"I know enough to know you're a lying, cheating bitch. I don't need to know much more," I yell, hoping she hears me from the other side of the stall. She remains silent, and as I'm wondering if she's still there, I open the door to see a flustered Chelsea. She flexes her hands as if she wants to hit me, making me grin; I'm making her lose control. I walk to the counter and wipe away the little bit of mascara running beneath my eye.

"What I want to know, is if you would have gotten a property patch, would you be biker by weekend, wife who bakes cookies by day?" I mock.

She turns a vibrant red and slaps me across the face hard. My head whips to the side with burning crawling across my face. I raise my hand and slap her back as hard as I can, making her head fling to the side. She gasps, holding her face where I hit her with shock woven into her eyes.

"Hit me again and I'll tear every one of those extensions from your head," I threaten, lifting my chin.

"Just stay away from me," she demands, holding her cheek with her palm.

"You wanted to talk to me, remember? I will stay away from you as long as you stay away from my club." She raises an eyebrow as if she can't believe what she's hearing.

"You heard me. Go find another place where you can pretend like you don't hate your life. You show up at my club and you'll wish you hadn't, bitch," I seethe with anger.

She slaps the counter in anger before exiting the bathroom. I look in the mirror at my reflection, an image of danger and satisfaction looking back. I grin maliciously; the Devil's Dust looks good on me.

The sun is casting a glow across Dani's flawless skin and not being able to sleep, I watch her. My white button-up shirt is way too big for her, hiding her tiny frame within it. She looks adorable as hell this morning.

She's different since I met her. Once a naive little girl, now she's a woman as damaged as I am, her innocence and allure her weapon of choice. Who knows what this beautiful creature is capable of?

She was all I could think about on our run. With Bull gaining more connections, we had to meet in person to assure shit went down well with the new buyer. The boys stayed, getting gifts from the other club, which entailed drugs and pussy. I skipped out.

Dani begins to moan as she wakes, making my cock swell.

"How long have you been up?" she asks, her voice strangled with sleep.

"Not long," I lie. "Did you have fun last night?" I ask her, brushing the hair away from her eyes. The red mark from her face now gone. I was sitting outside the bathroom waiting for her when a raging Chelsea came out of the bathroom holding her face. I was worried something had happened to Dani so I ran into the bathroom, only to find Dani smiling with a matching red mark on her cheek, but of a lighter hue.

"What happened?" I had asked her.

"What had to happen to keep you and my club safe," she said fixing her hair. I knew then I was more in love with her than ever, and trusted her more than I ever thought I would.

"I'm sore," she laughs, taking me from my thoughts. Not only did I fuck her in the bathroom at the event, I then took her home and fucked her over the kitchen counter, heels and dress still on; she looked like an angel in that lace. I love to see her in leather, but I might have a thing for her in lace, too. It's one of both worlds, Heaven and Hell.

"You keep moaning like that, I'm going to fuck you again this morning," I threaten.

"I think I'm going to get dressed and go see Babs," she counters, sitting up.

"You've been there every day, babe. She may not wake up for a long time." I know she cares for Babs—we all do—and what happened was a shitty thing, but she can't keep doing this to herself; it's unhealthy.

"I'm going," she snaps.

I scowl at her, her tone of voice wrong.

"Maybe I should remind you who you're talking to," I chastise, rolling her over on her stomach. She peers those emerald eyes over her shoulder. I move the shirt from her ass and around her waist and give her ass a vicious slap.

She moans with the harsh contact and looks over her shoulder again, her green eyes daring.

"I said I'm going." Her voice is strong and challenging.

I give her ass another slap, this time a little harder. The print of my hand rising on her olive skin makes my dick race with the craving to release itself.

She bucks beneath me. "You're going where?" I ask.

She looks over her shoulder, her breath heavy with desire.

"I'm going to see Babs!" she yells. I slide my hand down the mounds of her ass and slide my finger into her. I give her ass another hard smack, making her head thrust backwards with a loud moan.

"You can't control me," she moans, her voice faltering. I slide my fingers out and position them over the opening to her ass. Her eyes haze over her shoulder with shock written over her face. I've never taken her here, but man, do I want to. I thrust my fingers in and out of her pussy slowly, feeling her grip down on my finger, so I know she's close.

I give her ass another slap to help stimulate her.

"Please, can I go?" she sighs, submitting to me.

I give her ass one last slap, watching her skin glow bright red. I slowly apply pressure with my finger at the opening of her ass, her pleasure rising as she moans louder. She throws her face into the mattress as she rides her orgasm, and I know she's satiated.

I walk into the hospital room and see Babs is awake. "You're awake?" I exclaim.

She smiles half-heartedly.

"How long have you been awake?" I ask, sitting next to her.

"I woke-" She pauses. Her voice sounds awful and it's hard to understand what she's saying. Her red hair is matted into a nest around her head, and her face is cut up. She has bruises of the ugliest color spotted all over her face and forehead. She looks terrible.

"Last night," she says, struggling with the words. My eyes fill with tears; her words are strangled with force.

"I see we have visitors this morning," a doctor says, walking into the room wearing blue scrubs.

"Can I have a word?" I ask him.

"Certainly," he says, stepping to the other side of the room.

"Why is she talking like that?" I question, trying to be quiet so I don't offend Babs.

"Well, she was hit by a car—"

"I feel like I've been hit by a Mac truck," Babs yells, interrupting the doctor.

I give a weak smile, walk to her side of the bed, and grab her hand for support.

"Well," the doctor continues, "she's been hit by a car, and when she fell, she hit her head. With some therapy, I feel she will make some recovery, but she still needs to undergo some testing and extensive observation before I can be certain of anything."

I nod in understanding. "Did you guys call her husband?" I ask, looking at a scared Babs. Her eyes are squinted, causing little wrinkles to form in the creases, her lips (usually in a smirk) are pierced with concern. I hate seeing her like this.

"We did," he says, placing a stethoscope on her chest. "He was the only one listed as an emergency contact."

I look back at Babs. "Has Locks been to see you?"

She shakes her head no. If I have ever wanted to kill anyone, it would be him right now.

"You can visit for a few moments but it's crucial she rests at this point," he tells me, writing on a clipboard.

"Let me know if you need anything," he says to Babs before

walking out of the room.

"Do you know who hit you?" I ask.

She shakes her head again.

"Do you need anything?" I don't want to leave since I just got here, but I know I have to go before I'm kicked out.

"No." Her words are slurred and hard to understand as she looks toward the hospital window. I walk over and give her head a kiss before reluctantly leaving.

How could Locks not show up? I get that things are not good between him and Babs, but what a shitty way to say "I want a divorce."

I bite my lip in anger and walk onto the elevator.

◆ ◆ ◆

Shadow and I lounge on the couch watching TV. I have my legs in his lap and my head on a pillow I dragged from the bedroom.

I take my eyes off the screen and look at Shadow, curious why he's not out with the boys or why Bobby hasn't come back to the apartment lately.

"You and Bobby still not talking?" I ask, but I already know the answer.

Shadow slowly moves his gaze from the TV to me, one eyebrow raised.

I feel like I wrecked Bobby and Shadow's friendship. Bobby has been there for Shadow for so long, way before I ever was and way more than I ever could. Bobby understands Shadow; there is no question they are family. I sit up, suddenly feeling sick.

"You can't keep doing this, Shadow," I tell him angrily. He's holding such a grudge on Bobby, but not me, and I don't understand why.

"Don't start with me, Dani," Shadow warns.

"Don't give me that shit," I snap. Shadow's face goes blank with the sound of my tone. "You can't act like an asshole to your brother, but not me." He moves my legs off his lap and stands.

"What did you want Bobby to do? Strap me to the bed so I couldn't leave. I thought you were done with me, and everybody treated me like shit. I thought a simple night out would be nice!" I yell, the situation pissing me off. I owe it to Bobby to stand up for him, considering he stood up for me when nobody else would.

Shadow rubs the back of his head with one hand while the other rests on his hip, his face red with anger and hostility.

"I know Bobby touched you, I know he put his hands where they didn't belong," Shadow hisses.

My teeth bite my lip in anger. What happened was inconsequential, Bobby and I would never cross that line.

"If you're going to hate Bobby, you have to hate me, too," I continue, stepping up to him, ready to go head-to-head.

"I'll never hate you, Dani. Believe me, I've tried. Hating you would make things so much easier." His tone is harsh and angry. He licks his pouty lips as he grabs the back of my neck and pulls me closer. "I don't want to talk about this anymore. Don't bring this up again, Dani." I open my eyes to two blue, tortured ones staring at me, waiting for my reply.

"Fine," I whisper, not having the energy to argue anymore.

"You don't look so well," he states, noticing my discomfort.

"Everything that's been going on, I'm just past the point of stressed," I respond.

"Let's go to bed, babe," he says, pushing me toward the bedroom.

I climb in bed and smother myself in the soft blanket as Shadow curls himself around me, nuzzling into my neck.

"I could never hate you, Dani," he whispers against the skin of my neck.

"I know," I agree, staring into the darkness.

◆ ◆ ◆

A week goes by and the stress has not let up any. Seeing Babs slip in and out of consciousness everyday hurts. After spending the day at the beach with Shadow, we head back to the clubhouse. He heads off to church and I plant my ass at the bar. It's not the same without Babs behind it; the club isn't the same. I look around, wondering if Candy is still here and if she's dumb enough to mess with me again, but I don't see any sign of her. I lift from the stool and head into the kitchen in search of something to snack on; maybe it will help my queasy stomach. I hear glass jars clink into each other, catching my attention as I look toward the fridge. It slams shut and I am face-to-face with Locks. He looks at me and sniffs as he stares daggers at me. I feel a sudden rage rise, vengeance for Babs.

"Been by to see Babs?" I ask, knowing the answer.

"You would do well to keep your mouth shut, bitch," he snarls.

My eyes widen in anger, shocked he would talk to me like that. "Excuse me?" I question.

He stomps toward me, his boots thudding against the dirty floor.

"You heard me. Your daddy might think your shit don't stink but I'm here to tell you it does. You should be six feet under, and everyone around here knows it."

"Fuck you!" I scream, pushing him in his chest.

He looks down at where I pushed him and suddenly backhands me, making me stumble into the counter. My hands grip the stainless-steel sink and the dirty dishes in the sink catch my attention, a knife in particular. I reach in and grip the dirty butcher knife then turn around and glare at Locks. He has a smug look on his face, proud he just hit me, and by the looks of him flexing his hand, he's ready to do it again. The feeling of rage, which surfaces when things get ugly, pushes forward, crawling over my rational thinking. I grip the knife and assess where I should stab him. No man will ever hit me. Just as I push off the sink ready to attack, the kitchen doors fling open and Shadow walks in. He takes in the scene with a raised brow. "What's going on?" he demands.

I look at Locks, whose attention is on Shadow.

"You need to keep that bitch on a leash!" Locks yells as he points at me.

"You fucking hit her?" Shadow asks pointedly.

Locks looks at me with a smirk. The cool-down from adrenaline raises the pain in my cheek where he hit me. I lift my hand to touch the tender spot and wince.

"Did he hit you?" Shadow questions me. If the heat rising from cheek indicates anything, I'm sure Shadow knows the answer.

Shadow strides forward with a crazed look in his eye. He grabs Locks by his leather cut with both hands and pulls him within a hair's length from his face.

"You just signed your own death certificate, brother," Shadow threatens.

Before Locks can react, Shadow head-butts him in the face, making Locks fall to his knees dazed and confused. Shadow paces back and forth in front of him, flexing his hands with anger. Locks tries to stand but Shadow throws an upper cut to his jaw and throws him back into the kitchen chairs.

"What the hell is going on in here?" my dad bellows, pushing through the doors to the kitchen with force. I set the knife back into the sink, hoping my father didn't see it.

"He put his hands on Dani, and I'm going to kill him," Shadow yells.

"He touch you, Dani?" my dad asks.

"I can take care of myself," I reply, straightening my shirt.

"Get the fuck out of here, Locks, before I fucking kill you myself," my dad orders, nodding toward the doors.

"Fine, but this club went to shit when that little bitch showed up. Remember that," Locks spits, his voice cracking as he pushes past everyone.

"What the fuck was that?" Shadow asks my dad. "He's going to fucking pay for hitting Dani." Shadow walks up to me, taking me by the chin and surveying my face. My right cheek feels hot and irritated from the hit.

"I understand that. Trust me. I want him dead for that just as much as you," my dad admits, rubbing the back of his head in frustration. "But until I figure out what the hell he's up to, I need him alive." He blows out a strangled breath and looks at my cheek. "You okay, doll?"

I nod in reply.

"Stay out of his way. You see him, you walk the other way," he demands.

I nod again, but really I want to grab that dirty knife and shove it into Locks' kidney. Show him what happens when he puts his hands on me.

"What do you think he has up his sleeve?" Shadow asks, letting my chin go.

"I don't know. Maybe he's in with another club. We need to keep an eye on our merchandise." My dad shakes his head, shrugging.

"Think he would sell it from under us?" Shadow asks, his tone high with shock.

"I don't know anything," my dad responds, taking a cigarette pack from his pocket. "Get her home, away from the club for now."

12

Shadow

I'M GOING TO GET IN THE SHOWER. I HAVE TO WORK TOMORROW," Dani calls, walking into the bathroom.

I'm lying on the bed, staring at the ceiling of the apartment. It hurts to look at Dani with her cheek a light pink from where Locks hit her. I should have killed that fucker before Bull had a chance to come in and spare him. When I close my eyes, I can see the look of defense written on Dani's face as she gripped that knife. Her instinct to fight has me a little relieved but not by much. I wouldn't have put it past Locks to shoot Dani if she stabbed him. I feel like I let her down; I didn't protect her, again.

"What are you thinking about?"

I look up and see Dani with wet hair and in a Devil's Dust shirt, her cheek reminding me what a piece of shit I am. She is beautiful, though, glowing even.

"You look like Heaven," I say, eyeing the droplets flinging off her hair and dripping down her neck.

She smiles. "It's not happening tonight. I don't feel well," she says, climbing on the bed.

"I noticed you didn't eat dinner," I comment, moving over so she can climb in bed. She hasn't been feeling herself for a while now, and she has me worried.

Maybe I should take her away from all of this for awhile. With her mother and the events of the club lately, it appears to have taken its toll on her. If we left this place, even for a little while, I could focus solely on her.

"I'll be fine. Just a lot going on," she counters, cuddling with one of the pillows. I climb off the bed, turn the lights off, and then return, shuffling behind her. I pull her ass closer, where it belongs, her smell of peaches surrounding me giving me a chub.

"Trust me when I say I'll kill that fucker if it's the last thing I do, Dani," I whisper into her ear. I don't have to say his name; she knows who I'm talking about.

"I know you will. I trust you," she whispers back.

I wake up to the smell of food cooking and I stretch out, trying to wake myself up and make my way into the kitchen. As I get closer, I can see the house is filled with smoke and the smell of burnt food lingers in the air.

"Someone is up early," I say, wiping the sleep from my eyes.

"Hey!" Shadow greets as grease pops him from the skillet. "Fuck, that hurt," he yelps, sucking on his finger and making me laugh.

"Well, I tried to make you breakfast, but all it's proved is that my ass can't cook," he admits, turning the faucet on and tossing the skillet with black food in the sink. "Let's go get breakfast," he says.

"We don't have to," I suggest, shrugging.

"Yes, we do. You need to eat," he declares, rounding the island only wearing black briefs, the sight making me want him for breakfast. He brushes the hair from my face before continuing, "We can eat anything you want: pancakes, eggs, you name it."

"To be honest, the sound of food makes me want to gag," I tell him, trying to hold down the vomit crawling up my throat.

He rubs his finger over my sore cheek, making me wince. I pull away, mad I didn't kill Locks myself for hitting me.

"I'll kill that asshole for hitting me," I mumble.

Shadow squints his eyes at me, as if he's waiting for me to say I'm joking.

"Not if I get to him first," he says, surprising me. I can't help but smile, and then a laugh escapes me.

"What's so funny?" he questions, tilting his head to the side.

"Here we are over burnt brunch, planning the death of someone you consider family."

He smirks. "Sounds like a typical Friday morning to me." He leans down and kisses my forehead before heading towards the bedroom. Get dressed; we'll go get food."

"But—"

"Now, Dani," he demands, cutting me off.

◆ ◆ ◆

After breakfast, which consisted of an English muffin, Shadow kept pushing me to eat; we head back to the apartment. I throw my purse on the end table and face-plant on the couch, exhausted.

"What do you want to do today?" Shadow asks, walking past me to the kitchen.

"Sleep," I mumble into the couch cushion.

He chuckles and sits down next to my head.

"For some reason, I cannot get enough sleep. I feel like a

hibernating bear," I complain.

"You sleep and I'll play video games," he offers, giving my ass a slap and turning on the game console.

I moan and turn over, burying my head into the couch before I pass out.

◆ ◆ ◆

"Dani."

I wake up and see Shadow standing over me.

"You're going to be late for work," he says, pointing to the clock on the wall.

I look over and notice it's four in the evening. "Shit!" I yell, jumping off the couch. I forgot I was filling in for one of the instructors today.

I grab my bag from beside the coffee table and open the door with Shadow following me closely.

The breeze from the sea feels good as we ride; it's refreshing and makes me feel more awake than I have in days. We arrive at the dance studio and I climb off the bike. "Thanks for the ride," I say appreciatively, giving him a kiss on the cheek.

"I'll be here later," he reminds me, revving the bike motor and taking off. I love it when he does that; the roar of the motor sounds sexy.

I walk into the dance studio, already apologizing.

"I know I'm late," I say, noticing only a couple little girls are in attendance instead of the usual group.

"Did the parents get tired of waiting?" I ask, pointing to the girls stretching.

"A lot called in. Seems the flu is going around," Mila says, sticking her tongue out in distaste.

"Yeah. I haven't been feeling too well myself," I admit, grabbing my leotard from my bag.

"Well, I'm going to work on the books and then I'll be out of your hair," she tells me, grabbing a book with 'Monthly Tuition' etched on it in black marker.

"Okay," I respond, heading to the changing room.

"Okay, girls, let's practice the five basic positions of ballet, starting with the first position," I command, clapping my hands, hoping the loud noise will motivated the girls.

"Miss Lexington?"

"Yes?" I respond to one of the little girls, noticing her complexion is a little pale.

She opens her mouth to speak but vomit spills out, chunks of food and liquid splatter onto the floor, followed by a foul odor. I have to look away and swallow slowly or I'll puke myself.

The other girls start gagging and ewwing. This is going to be a long day.

After calling Hayden's parents and cleaning up the mess, I decide to call the other girls' parents and inform them a bug is going around and to come pick their kids up. I don't want to clean up anymore puke, and I'm not feeling well myself, so it's a short night of work.

"Hey, I'm going to head out," Mila says.

"Okay, I'll be outta here, too, when the parents come pick up my last fairy," I tell her, pointing to the last little girl twirling in a circle.

Mila laughs. "Okay, have a good night."

Finally, after the last kid is picked up, I decide to text Shadow and let him know I'm off work early. I turn all the lights off and go to grab my paycheck only to find Mila forgot to set it out.

"Damn," I mutter.

I leave the dance studio and start to walk where Shadow has been parking lately.

I kick a stray rock as I make my way across the side of the lot and notice a bright beam of lights flare behind me.

I turn and am blinded, so I shield my eyes with my arm, trying to look under the bright lights making it hard to see anything. The car starts and tires screech with sudden speed. The hairs stand on my neck and my heart begins to race as the car flies toward me. I turn around and sprint, not knowing what else to do. My heart is pounding with fear as my mouth lets out a scared whimper. I look over my shoulder and notice the car is catching up. I drop my bag trying to lighten my load and give myself speed. The car speeds up and drives right next to me, I clench my eyes shut for a second, urging myself to try and run faster. When I open them, the car door suddenly opens and slams into me. The asphalt bites into my knees, tearing at my flesh unforgivingly as I'm hurled forward. I hear the car tires scream to a halt, making my heart skip a beat. I crawl on my hands and knees and let out a strangled cry at the raw flesh digging into the ground. I look behind me for the car to find a bunch of men climbing out. I look for my bag to grab my gun but remember I dropped it, so I push myself to stand but one of the guys kicks me back down, making me fall on my back painfully.

"This is for Darin!" one of the guy yells as a wooden bat flashes in front of me. The name Darin hits me like a bolt of lightning: the guy me and the girls beat to a bloody pulp and left for dead.

I shield my face and curl into the fetal position, knowing this is going to hurt. The bat slams into my arm hard. I scream as an earth-shattering pain riddles deep into my bone. My lungs run out of air to scream, leaving me gasping for more.

"Fucking punta!" one yells as the bat slams back into the same arm. If it wasn't broken before, it is now. My ears ring as my vision blurs from the pain and I bit my cheek to try to keep from screaming again. The only thing I want is to pass out, but it's no use; I can't help but scream in pain.

My head is jerked back with a sudden kick to the face. I feel my eyebrow split when the rubber sole makes contact. I close my eyes as blood begins to pool into them. My entire body aches, unbearable pain pulsing from one end to the other.

"Shut the hell up!" another yells as I continue to scream in pain.

They all begin to kick and slam their feet into me. All feeling starts to fade slowly, and I can sense myself becoming numb with the amount of pain my body is consuming.

"Hey, get the fuck away from her!" I hear a voice yell. "I've called the cops. They're on their way!" I try to open my eyes to see who is yelling but can't.

"Let's go," one of the guys yells. I hear footsteps fade, along with everything.

Shadow

"Royal Flush, boys," I laugh, laying my cards out for all of them to see.

"Fucking cheater," Locks says, slamming his cards down. I raise my eyebrow, wondering why I'm even listening to Bull's orders. Locks should be dead by now.

"He is a cheater," Bobby agrees, tossing his cards along the table. Bobby always thinks I cheat when I win; he has since we were kids.

My phone rings in my pocket, breaking my laughter. I straighten my legs so I can pull it out. It shows I missed a text from Dani as it continues to ring, and the caller ID reads the hospital.

"Hello?"

"Is this Adrian Kingsmen?" the lady asks.

Bobby laughs and Bull yells, making it hard to hear.

"Maybe, who's this?" I question her, turning my head to hear better.

"There has been an accident, and I was told by the doctor to contact you at this number," the lady replies calmly.

"What accident?" I ask.

"It's regarding patient, Danielle Lexington."

I jump from my seat, panic rising in my chest.

"What's wrong? Is she okay?" I'm moving frantically, my heart speeding up to a level consistent with doing cocaine.

"It's best if you just come in. Then we can give you more details, sir," she replies sweetly.

Hesitant, I hang up. Danielle's photo of her sleeping as my phone background catches my attention. My finger slides across the screen of my phone. I don't pray—never did any good before—but I find myself praying right now. *Can the Devil pray? Or does it get cast to the side with the rest of the sinners, gambling on a second chance?*

"Everything okay, son?" Bull stares my way, snapping me from my silent prayer, my hope there's a God and he's listening to me.

"Dani's in the hospital, some kind of accident," I answer him, taking my eyes off my phone's screen.

"What?" Bobby says, standing in panic.

"Let's go," Bull orders, throwing his cards on the table.

◆ ◆ ◆

I race toward the hospital, Bobby and Bull trying to keep up, but my bike is faster.

I park in the unloading zone, not giving a fuck about the law right now, and rush inside. I run toward the front desk and slap the counter to get the receptionist's attention.

"A lady called me, said Danielle Lexington had been in an accident."

The lady starts typing into her computer—slowly, I might add.

"Yes, she's in the emergency room down the hall."

Without any more details, I take off down the hall like a bat out of Hell.

Around the corner, I spot Mila in the waiting room, sitting in a chair crying.

"Mila, what the fuck happened?" I demand, walking toward her.

"I came back to the studio because I forgot Dani's check," she says, sobbing.

"What happened?" I repeat, urging her to get past the petty information.

"There was this car full of men, and they chased Dani with their car, so I called the police. When I came back out, they were beating the hell out of her with a bat," she cries, her words hard to understand.

"Holy shit," Bobby whispers from behind me.

"We've been targeted," Bull says gravely. This confirms Babs' hit was not some drunk. This was personal.

I look into each room, trying to find Dani.

"Sir?" A nurse calls after me after I've looked into the fifth room. I ignore her.

"Sir?" she calls again, her voice louder than before. I still ignore her.

I open the last door at the end of the hall and see Dani. Tears immediately fill my eyes, and I have to take a step back before I can go forward. Her face is matted with blood and there is a deep gash in her eyebrow.

"Sir, you can't be in here," the nurse says, standing in my view of Dani.

"Christ," I whisper in disbelief as tears tumble from my eyes. I will kill the person who did this to her.

"He's fine, Sandy." I turn and see Doc standing in the doorway, ushering the nurse to leave me alone.

"Is she okay?" I ask frantically.

"She's in a lot of pain. I gave her a low dose of pain reliever until I can run some tests," she tells me, tucking Dani in with a sheet.

"Her arm is broken, so we'll have to cast it, and she also needs stitches in her eyebrow. She needs more tests done to make sure there are no internal injuries as well," she informs, brushing the hair from her face.

"I haven't seen her in a while. How's she been?" Doc asks,

adjusting Dani's pillow.

I run my hands through my hair, frantically. "She's been feeling sick and not eating much. But she's been doing all right," I respond.

Doc furrows her eyebrows at me. "She get a fever at all?"

"No, not that I know of," I state, my eyes never leaving Dani's face.

"Has she been taking the pills I gave her?" Doc asks.

"What pills?" I ask, confused. I didn't know Dani was taking any pills.

"Right. Well, I'm going to do another blood test before continuing." Doc grabs the clipboard hanging on the wall and exits the room, leaving me with more questions than I arrived with.

Two guys in white lab coats come in carrying a container full of needles and tubes. They put a rubber band around Dani's arm and push a needle into the crook of her elbow, then pull a cap off and push a tube onto it, making blood squirt into the tube.

"What are these tests for?" I question, pointing toward the needles.

They ignore me, wrap her arm up with colored tape, and leave the room. I'm getting no answers, and it's starting to piss me off.

I look over at Bobby and Bull. "What the fuck?"

I sit down next to Dani and grab her good hand—the one that's not broken—and give it a light squeeze. I bring her limp hand to my mouth and give it a kiss. Whoever did this to her, they will pay.

She moans and shifts in her bed. I sit up, hoping she wakes.

"Dani?" I ask in a shaky voice.

"Shadow?" Her voice cracks.

"I'm here," I tell her, standing up and looking over her. I've never been more wrecked in my entire life than I am right now, worried that God might punish me for the life I've lived by taking Dani from me.

"Where am I?" she asks, looking around her room.

"You're in the hospital, doll," Bull informs her, stepping up to the bedside.

She blinks her eyes a couple times. "Oh, yeah," she says, in a whisper.

"Do you remember anything that happened?" Bobby asks.

She licks her dry lips and looks up at me. "Just that—" She pauses as a commotion outside the door grabs her attention.

"I'll look." I step away from her bed and look into the hall to see two police officers at the front desk.

"If she is awake, we would like to ask her some questions," one of the officers says to a nurse.

"She's just been through a traumatic experience; can't this wait?" Doc says, stepping up to the desk.

"I'm afraid not," one of the cops responds.

I step back into the room and go to Dani's side.

"The police are here. You tell them nothing. Do you understand?" I ask, trying to mask my harsh tone with as much force as I can.

She looks up at me in confusion.

"We take care of this our way. I'll kill the person who did this to you. That's a promise," I inform her, my tone not to be messed with. "Trust me," I whisper, hoping she knows I will take care of this.

She nods in agreement.

A knock sounds at the door, interrupting us.

"I'm sorry dear, but some gentlemen are here to ask you some questions," Doc says, walking into the room, the police following her.

"We need to speak to her alone," one of them says, pulling out a notepad as the other eyes me accusingly. By the look on his face, he probably thinks I did this to her. In a way, I did. I wasn't there to protect her.

Dani

"So, you don't remember what happened?" a police officer asks me with a raised eyebrow; he doesn't believe me. I have never been any good at lying. I try not to stare at the two of them, but they are an odd pair, one bald and fat with glasses, the other tall and skinny with freckles.

"No, I don't remember anything," I say, fiddling with the hospital bracelet around my wrist.

"Let's go through this one more time," the fat officer sighs, flipping his notepad over to a fresh sheet of paper.

"You left work and...?" he asks, twirling his hand and encouraging me to keep going where he left off.

"I woke up here," I lie.

The skinny officer moans in irritation. "Right, well, we can't help you or anyone else if you can't help us, Miss Lexington."

"You don't have any idea who might want to hurt you?" the one with a potbelly asks on a groan.

I look at them, irritated. "I told you what I know. Now, please leave!" I yell.

"I think questioning time is over, gentlemen. I can't have you getting her upset," Doc declares, entering the room quickly. She must have been just outside the door.

"All right then," the skinny one says, tucking his notepad in his shirt pocket.

They all head out as the boys enter.

"You did well, kid," my dad states, giving me a light kiss on the forehead.

"Dani, I took some test while you were under and would like to discuss something with you in private, if I may?" Doc asks, looking at the boys in question.

I look at Shadow and notice he's not pleased with Doc's request.

"No, it's okay. You can speak in front of everyone," I say, trying to sit up but wincing from the pain.

"I advise you to reconsider," she pushes, looking at the paper in her hands.

"Jessica," Bobby warns, using Doc's real name.

Doc glares at Bobby. "Fine. I took a pregnancy test in question of you taking your birth control or not," she tells me, looking at the paper.

"Birth control?" Shadow asks in shock.

"And?" I ask, fear pooling in my heart of what she's about to say.

"It came back positive." She hands me the paper with information printed on it which I can't understand.

"You're pregnant."

"Oh, fuck," Shadow gasps as he fumbles for a chair to sit in.

"Hot damn!" my dad shouts in excitement.

"Pregnant?" I question, still in shock.

"Yes, by a few weeks, from the levels of your hormones," she says, pointing at the sheet.

"How far along is she exactly?" Shadow asks, with concern.

"I'm not sure. I'll make a call and get her up to the OB floor, get an ultrasound and make sure the baby hasn't sustained any injuries," she promises before giving my arm a pat.

"Pregnant?" I repeat

"Pregnant," Doc confirms with a smile. The realization of the situation hits, making my head ache more than it already does. How could I be so naïve to think I wouldn't get pregnant? I got lucky not getting pregnant before, and I took advantage of that luck.

I sigh and let the paper fall from my hands. How stupid am I? How did I not think this would happen?

"Holy shit," Shadows mutters as he grabs my hand from the side of the bed.

◆◆◆

I am wheeled into a dark room on the third floor of the hospital moments later. The room is dimmed and on the yellow-painted wall is a medium-sized, flat-screen TV. In the corner of the small room there are a couple of chairs and on the other side of the bed the ultrasound machine.

A nurse with curly, short black hair places a white blanket around my waist and pulls the hospital gown up a little.

"I'm going to try this first, so I'll need you pull your knees up," the nurse warns as she grabs a long wand and puts a condom on it. I look at Shadow who is sitting right next to me. He's focused on the TV, his face lined with worry. My father and Bobby look towards the wall giving me privacy. I take a big gulp and pull my knees up. She darts the long wand through my open knees and slides it inside me.

I look at the screen, but all I see is black and white spots. She angles the wand and presses firmly. The nurse starts to click and push buttons as lines form across the spots on the screen.

"The baby looks good," the nurse says with a smile. I watch as she zooms in on a little black and white oval.

"That's the baby," she chirps, and the sight makes me suck in a breath.

"Well, I'll be," my dad comments with a big smile.

I glance at Shadow; his face is tight and staring intently at the screen. His eyebrows are furrowed and they're causing a little wrinkle right between his eyes.

"Looking at the measurements, you're a month along," she says, pulling the wand out of me. I instantly pull my knees together and pull the blanket down. The lady hands me a black and white picture of our baby. "Congratulations. I'll have someone take you back to your room in just a moment." She stands up and walks out.

"Holy shit," Shadow says again, his voice laced with shock and disbelief.

I look at him; his eyes are closed and his arm is brought up, rubbing the back of his neck.

My eyes begin to fill with tears.

"Fuck," Bobby says, staring at my stomach like something is going to jump out at him.

"We are going to go and give you guys some space," my dad tells us, pushing Bobby toward the door.

Shadow looks at the blank TV screen on the wall, his hands running back and forth through his hair frantically.

"I can't be a father," Shadow whispers.

"Well, you are," I say softly.

"Look at me, look at what I am!" Shadow roars, his loud voice making me jump.

He walks closer and leans into me. "I'm a fucking monster, a murderer. I live a life of hell. I don't deserve you, and I sure as hell don't deserve a child," he whispers, his tone somber.

"This is our child, Shadow, not the kid from down the road," I snap, my tone clipped and cold.

"You have been around me a couple of months and already have succumbed to my darkness. I've killed your innocence. How can you expect to keep a child safe around me?" Shadow wonders, his blue eyes looking right at me.

"My violent urges were always a part of me, Shadow. Whether I'm around you, or the club, or the angry guy down the street, they were bound to come out," I say, sitting up. "You have another side of you, just like I have another side to me. You will be a great father, you just have to give—"

"I need some time to think," Shadow interrupts.

"What?" I ask in disbelief.

Shadow leans in and kisses my forehead gently. "I need some time to process this, Dani," Shadow says gravely before rushing out.

13

Dani

I'M WHEELED INTO MY ROOM BY MYSELF AFTER SHADOW LEAVES.
"All right, so we will have to go about some medication for pain differently," Doc says, her voice tender and caring. I stare at the ultrasound picture the nurse gave me of the little black and white dot, my mind going everywhere, not solely focusing on one thing or the other.

"Everybody will get over it, and if not, they will when they see the baby," she continues sweetly.

I tear my eyes from the picture and give her a weak smile, not so sure of her optimism.

"Are you keeping it?" she questions. I look out the dark window of the hospital room, her question playing repeat in my head. *Should I keep it?* There are so many reasons why I shouldn't but most of all, this lifestyle isn't safe for a child.

"I'm going to get your arm casted and get you feeling better," she promises, patting my leg, leaving me with my thoughts of neglect.

◆◆◆

Knocking at the door wakes me from my sleep. My body, protesting from its abuse, aches and burns with movement.

"Dani, you have a visitor," a nurse says, turning on the vibrant light, which makes me squint.

I look at the window of the hospital and see the sun is just starting to rise; it could only be six in the morning, if that.

"Sorry to wake you, Dani." My sleep state is wiped clean as my pulse jumps to a gallop.

I turn quickly in the bed, ignoring my hurting body.

"Stevin, what are you doing here?" I ask shocked. Last time I saw him was when my mother hauled me off. I look him over. He's dressed in black slacks and a blue button-down shirt and carrying a cup of coffee, but his face looks like shit. Like he has been over-worked and hasn't had enough sleep.

"You need to leave, now. Security!" I holler, but the door is closed and I doubt anyone can hear me. He needs to get the hell out of my room before a club member sees him.

I look around the bed for the emergency call light but can't find it in the sheets and extra pillow the nurses brought me for comfort.

"I just need a second of your time, please," he begs, walking toward me, I glare at him. I cannot believe he and my mother were together, a common romance at work, only the work was to take down my father, and who cared if I got ran over in the process. I forget the call light and put my hand up for him to stop walking any closer. He stops abruptly and puts his hands up in surrender.

"I'm not telling you shit," I spit, my tone angry and cold.

"Your mom is missing, Dani," he responds loudly.

"She was headed back to New York last time I talked to her," I say, hoping he takes that info and runs out the door with it.

"She was supposed to meet me back in New York, but she never arrived," he exclaims, the lines of stress growing deeper around his mouth when he talks. I sit up a little more, curious. "I talked to her the night before her flight but haven't heard from her since. She and the rental car are both missing from the hotel where she was staying." He's shaking his head as he speaks, seemingly not wanting to believe what he's telling me.

I bite my lip trying to think, but all I can wonder is how he knew I was here. *Is the FBI following me?*

"How did you know I was here?" I ask.

"Your attack was on the news; your coworker was interviewed and everything," he explains, shrugging like I should know this.

"Well, I haven't seen or heard from my mother. Last time I saw her, I threatened to kill her if I saw her again," I say, looking him right in the eye, my tone promising.

He looks at me with a stunned expression. "Should I consider you a suspect in your mother's disappearance, Dani?" he questions, tilting his head to the side.

I laugh. "You can do whatever you want, but I can promise you I didn't kill her." I furrow my eyes at him, "not yet, anyways."

"Right. Well, I will find out what happened to your mother," he threatens, his hand clenching his coffee cup tightly.

"I think you better go," I declare, scrunching my face with anger and pointing toward the door.

He glares at me before turning on his over-polished shoes to leave.

I fall back gently against my pillow. My mother is missing. I wonder if Shadow had anything to do with it, or if the group of people who attacked Babs and me got a hold of my mother.

Shadow

I cannot believe I let this happen, I feel like I'm being kicked when I'm already down. What the fuck? My girl, my ol' lady, is pregnant with my disgraced DNA. I am hardly the man Dani needs let alone one for a child. If I was a man, a fucking man like my father, I would have taken care of Dani when the shit hit the fan. But I didn't; instead, I ran to a bottle of booze and tried to forget her with other women. Dani came home from the hospital today, and I don't know what to fucking say to her. I grab another beer can and pop the top, the delicious bubbles fizzing and popping from the opening. I lie back down on the hood of my Mustang outside the apartment and look at the sky. It's turning that grey color when the sun just starts to set.

I hear heavy footsteps coming toward me but I don't lift my head to look. I just sip on my beer, hoping the answer to how I'm supposed to feel will come along.

"You going to drink yourself to feeling better?" Bull asks.

"That's the plan," I sneer.

"You're going to fuck this up," he declares, sitting on the hood next to me.

"What the fuck are you talking about?" I ask, turning my head to look at him. I don't really care to hear it, but I know he is going to tell me regardless.

"When shit went south with Dani, you drank yourself into oblivion. It didn't make you feel any better, and it sure as shit didn't make you smarter. But it did make Dani run into the arms of another man," he states, looking at me with that 'I know what I'm talking about' smirk.

I look at him, curious how he knows about Dani and Parker. Probably Bobby, that man is as bad as Babs with gossip.

I scoff and look back at the sky.

"I know I did the same thing when shit got hard between me and Dani's mother, and I lost her instead of figuring my shit out," he confides, hitting my leg to get my attention. "Losing Dani's mother was the worst regret I live with."

Knowing Dani's mother, I beg to differ. I think losing her was probably for the best.

"So, what are you saying?" I ask, my voice showing my irritation in his lecturing.

"I know you think you would be a shitty parent, what with how your mother was and all, but regardless of what you think about yourself, you would be a great father. It's not the end of the world; you choose to be in Dani's life, it's just the beginning." Bull starts laughing, making me smirk.

"Do you love her?" he asks.

I sit up and look at him, thinking about his question. I do love Dani, even after everything that has happened. It's fucking crazy. Bull's right. Dani and I know what shitty parents are—we were raised by them. We know what not to do and know how to control urges that arise which may flow in the bloodstream to our child.

"I do," I insist, taking a sip of my beer.

"Then don't let her go. I can tell you, if you don't make amends with this situation, she's going to leave you and never look back." My eyes snap to his. "A mother and child are something no man can make a woman choose between." He scoots off the hood of my car and looks at me sternly. "Don't fuck this up, Shadow." He narrows his eyes at me as if warning me and walks toward the apartment building, to see Dani.

I sigh loudly, crumpling the can in my hand before letting it hit the ground with the others.

Seeing Dani try to move on last time made my heart almost cease beating. I felt the urge to feel again, like I needed to resort to my old ways of feeling—killing. Dani is my life, literally; keeps me alive and makes me feel. Losing her will more than end my existence.

I groan and fall against the hood. I usually talk to Bobby about this shit. He's been my family way before I knew what that word even meant, way before the club. I sit up and slide off the hood of my car. I climb in and start it, the engine purring with rage, wanting to be released. I pop the shifter into first gear and dump the clutch, letting the tires eat asphalt.

I drive toward the club, not ready to talk to Dani. I want to talk to her but I need to talk to Bobby first, and I'm definitely not ready for that. How can I be a good father? I'm a machine, fueled by another's blood. My curse is the need for control, the result, damaging everyone around me.

Mine and Dani's relationship is no love story with some happily ever after. What we have is real. It's dark and it hurts. Dani is angelic on the outside, but she's an angel with black wings. This is the life of hell we've redeemed for ourselves. Dani and I are both destined for nothing better than the road ahead full of twists and turns, and it's no life for a child. Her being off the path her mother tried so hard to keep her on will do nothing but bring the sinner out in Dani, but at least that's something I can relate to. I know a lot about sinning. It's the only thing I can do right. I like to think being together we can navigate each other through the darkness which consumes our rationality. Both raised without the knowing of what love and nurturing is, it's only natural we are going to screw up and lose our footing in the cruel world that consists of love.

I fishtail it in the parking lot of the club, screeching to a halt in front of the doors, not giving a fuck that Bull hates it. I pop it into neutral and pull the keys out.

"Bull is gonna kick your ass, pretty boy," Hawk squawks at me, leaning against the building and coughing on a cigarette.

I huff. "I'd like to see him try," I say.

I push the doors open to the club and hear some of the boys hooting and hollering at the bar. I look over and see Candy lying flat on her back, letting one of the other girls do a body shot off her chest. *How did I ever find her sexy?* She is plain revolting when I see her. I push the doors open to the chapel and sit down in one of the chairs, resting my elbows on the table and letting my head fall into my hands. I'm a mess.

"Wanna play some cards?"

I peer up and see Tom pulling a chair out beside me. He plops down and slaps down a stack of cards.

"Looks like you need to take your mind off things," he says, shuffling the cards.

"Sure," I agree, sitting up.

"Everything okay?"

"Not really," I respond with a clipped tone.

"Yeah, I heard," he tells me, eyeing his hand.

I look at my hand and notice I don't have much of one.

"Yeah and what's that?" I question.

Tom stops and looks at me over his hand of cards. I know what he heard, and he knows I know.

"How about we don't talk about that," I say, eyeing him back.

"You got it," he smiles, picking up a card from the stack.

"Bobby!" Candy cheers from the other room.

"He's in there?" I hear Bobby ask as his footsteps get louder, heading toward the double doors to the chapel.

"Mind if I talk to Shadow alone for a sec?" Bobby asks, walking in.

Tom looks at me for a second before setting his cards down on the table.

"Sure." Tom rises from his seat to leave. Bobby circles the table and sits across from me, his eyes piercing the side of my head.

"Wanna talk about it?" Bobby asks, breaking the silence. His presence makes me angry; I'm not ready to talk about shit.

I pull my pistol from its holster and lay it on the wooden table, the metal clanking against it as it sets.

"Yeah, let's talk," I seethe.

"You're looking at this pregnancy all wrong. You are going to rock as a father, and Dani is going to be hot as hell pregnant," he smirks, my gun facing him but not affecting him. He knows I won't shoot him; not on purpose, anyway. I glare at him, because just the thought of him thinking Dani is hot pisses me off.

We sit silently while I take in what he's said.

"You are going to be a great father, Shadow," Bobby whispers. My eyes snap from my gun to his face. "Going to be a spitfire like his or her momma, and a fighter like you," he says with a smile. I can't help the smile that creeps across my own face at the thought of a little girl who looks just like Dani.

This is going to be okay. Dani and I will be okay. Having a child with Dani is just more of Dani, something I'll never get enough of. I need to go find her and see where her head is at with all this. I sit up and grab my pistol from the table, placing it in my holster. I smirk at Bobby and laugh.

"Dani is mine and that baby is mine, regardless of my corrupted DNA," I say to myself rather than Bobby as I stand.

Bobby's mouth parts with surprise then grins wide.

"So, are we good about before," he asks rising.

"Of course," I respond with a grin. "Having someone else beat the shit out of you for me, was much easier."

I push the doors open and am greeted with a drunk Candy. She slides her hand up my chest and twirls a lock of my hair.

"Hey, so I hear you are single again, baby," she coos, smacking gum in her mouth.

"Not even close," I say, trying to escape her trashy bubblegum smell.

She slides her hand over my crotch and squeezes.

"I heard you and Dani are over," she slurs.

I grab her by the hair hard and pull it back, making her face me. "Dani could burn this club to the ground, and I still wouldn't let you back in my bed," I clarify carefully.

"You gotta be kidding me!"

I look over Candy's shoulder and see a fuming Dani. I unlace my hand from Candy's hair and push her away from me. Fucking great.

Dani stomps toward Candy and me, her face red with anger. She's going to kill Candy if I don't stop her.

"Dani!" I yell, trying to catch her attention, but she doesn't slow down. I knock Candy out of the way and grab Dani by the waist, tightening my grip as I haul her down the hall.

"Candy, get your trashy ass out of my club!" Bull yells.

I push the bedroom door open and shove a hostile Dani in. "You are pregnant; you can't be doing that shit anymore," I say, pointing toward her midsection.

"What do you care?" she mocks, cocking her head to the side. Her eyebrow holds stitches and she has a bruise on her cheek. Even under all the physical pain, she is still glowing. She's pissed I left her at the hospital, and I don't blame her.

"I needed to figure some things out," I justify.

"Right," she mouths.

"Why are you here?" I ask, trying not to sound like a prick but failing miserably.

She whips her head around to face me. "My dad wants me to stay here." She brings her hand up and plays with her bottom lip; she's nervous. "I'm keeping the baby," she whispers.

I walk to her, the sight of her hurting worse than anything I'm experiencing. I grab the nape of her neck roughly, making her suck in a breath of surprise.

I lift her chin so she's forced to look at me. I lean lower and give her bottom lip a tender kiss. "I wouldn't let you choose any other way," I declare, my eyes staring at hers intently. I feel her mouth tremble against mine as tears begin to cascade down her flushed cheeks. The muffled lyrics from "Wild Horses" by The Rolling Stones pounds against the wall from the party.

I rub my rough thumb across her delicate cheek, wiping away her tears; the last thing I want is to see her cry. I grab her wrist and peck gentle kisses on the tender flesh, my eyes never leaving hers. I trail my fingers with my other hand down her broken arm, the pads of my fingertips scratching against the pink cast when it makes contact. I can't help but feel the fire burn deep inside at the thought of her being hurt. I'll kill whoever did this to her.

She grabs both sides of my face and starts kissing my jawline, her caring kisses making my desire for her soar. I kiss her pink lips as I walk her backwards to the bed.

"Dani, you're mine. That hasn't changed and it never will. It just scares the hell out of me that I'm going to have to share your company," I whisper, trailing my finger down her abdomen. "But if you think I was controlling before, you haven't seen shit yet. You are going to start eating and resting more."

"Make love to me, Shadow," she whispers. I want to make love to Dani; I don't do it often enough. I can't help it, though, because when Dani touches me, she releases an animalistic energy from me. I want to claim her ass with my handprint, leave my mark on her shoulder with my teeth, and make her legs tremble after I'm done with her. She kisses my lips and gently sucks the bottom one into her mouth. I growl in response and grab the hem of her shirt, pulling it upward slowly. She raises her arms as I pull it off, revealing her perky breasts. I smirk; she's not wearing a bra. Being around this club has made her wild, I love it.

I lean down and engulf her breast in my mouth, she arches her back in response and entwines her fingers into my hair. Her sweet nipple erects against my tongue, making my dick pulse with excitement. I cup the small of her back and lower her body on the unmade bed as she slides her hands down her torso and undoes her shorts, pulling them off. I suck in a breath at the sight of her bandaged knees; again, I'll murder whoever did this to her. I shrug out of my cut, pull my shirt over my head, and kick off my boots. I pull my loose jeans down with my black briefs, my cock so hard and angry it looks purple. I want nothing more than to take her roughly, but tonight I'm going to make love to Dani. I'm going to show her that depraved rush she brings out of me when she denies me, that corruption of unclarity when she acts like she doesn't need me.

I climb over her small frame, my knees pressing deep into the mattress as my body claims her. I demand her lips, my tongue taking hers hostage with its intrusion. She wraps her arms around my neck and opens her legs, giving herself to me. I grab the base of my cock and guide it into her warm opening. Instantly, my body hums with recognition, knowing Dani's body like a drug addict on a binge. I thrust into her slowly when all I want to do is slam into her and hear that whimper she gives when my cock takes all she has to offer. She arches her back as I slide in deep, her legs tightening around my waist. I suck in a tight breath as her pussy clams down on my cock. I begin to thrust slowly, savoring the feel of her skin against mine. I can feel her breasts rub against my chest as I slide in and out of her sensually. I look between our bodies and notice her perky tits, they look a little fuller. I smirk. Pregnant looks good on Dani.

My dick slides in and out, her arousal guiding my shaft with ease. I run my nose along her neck, giving her skin gentle pecks. She moans lightly as her walls clench around my cock, the tight squeeze amplifying my craving for release. Her breathing becomes ragged as she dives into that realm of ecstasy. My calves cramp as my balls tighten, the feeling almost too much as I lower my face into the crook of Dani's neck while my fists grasp the sheets beside her. My body begins to vibrate with my own undoing as I roar loudly. I pull myself from Dani's neck and look at her beautiful face; she's my Hell and my Heaven. The good and the bad. I can barely handle her, and now I'm going to raise a child with her hellfire spirit. I kiss her lips passionately, silently accepting the challenge.

Dani

I wake up to my broken arm itching like crazy, I try to wedge my finger inside the cast as far as it will go but it's no use. I groan in frustration and look around the room for something to shove down there. I spot an ink pen on the end table and nearly crush Shadow trying to get to it. He moans as I reposition myself in my spot and slam the pen down the side of my cast. I groan with satisfaction when it hits its mark.

Shadow rolls over and grins when he notices why I nearly suffocated him to death to get to whatever was on the nightstand.

"Better?" he asks gravely, his voice heavy with sleep.

"Yes," I sigh, pulling the pen out.

I look over and catch Shadow eyeing my arm in its pink cast. He rolls over, pulls the drawer open on the nightstand, and pulls out a giant, black magic marker.

"What are you doing with that?" I ask nervously.

He grabs my casted arm and positions it just how he needs it, pulls the top off the marker with his teeth and presses it to the hot-pink cast.

As he doodles on my arm, I can't help but interlock my fingers into his thick hair. Just the touch of it has me willing to roll around in the sheets with him. Then again, it could be hormones. *Aren't pregnant women supposed to be horny all the time?*

He pulls back from my arm and applies the lid to the marker. I look down and survey the artwork on my cast as he puts the marker back in its place.

Shadow's Property

Is written in thick black ink with an outline of a skeleton head under it. The pink of the cast fills the skull, making it a pink skeleton head.

I look up at him in shock. I thought he would draw his name or a stick figure, not brand me.

"You never wear your damn cut." He points to my arm, wearing a cheshire grin. "That you can't take off."

He sits up on the bed and rubs the sleep from his eyes like a little kid.

"I'm going to get you and my baby some breakfast," Shadow says.

"Yuck. The thought of food sounds gross," I respond, sticking my tongue out.

"You will eat, Dani," Shadow demands, looking at me with that furrowed eyebrow which leaves that little wrinkle. He looks so cute when he does it that I bite my cheek to keep from smiling at him when he's trying to be serious.

"That reminds me, I got you something," Shadow remarks. He walks over to one of the dresser drawers and pulls it open. I try and look around his body to see what he has, but his muscular frame blocks the view.

He turns around with books and a box on top.

"Got you some books about what to expect when pregnant, a book with baby names, some vitamins, and this is a box with suckers that will help with your morning sickness." He places the books down with the box and tosses the pills beside me.

I pick up the box of suckers and run my finger along the cover of one of the books.

"Why did you get these for me?" I ask in awe.

"Because I knew leaving you at the hospital to figure my shit out was an ass move." He sits down on the bed and grabs my chin, moving my face to look at him. "Because I want you and my baby to be healthy," he whispers. He leans over and kisses my lips tenderly, his sensitivity taking the breath from me.

"I didn't leave you when I left. I just needed to figure out how I was going to be the man you and my child deserved." He brushes a hair from my face and kisses my forehead, his words making my heart swell with affection.

"You going to tell me what happened exactly?" he asks, pointing at the cast on my arm.

I bite my lip anxiously. The pregnancy kind of caught everyone off-guard after the attack, and I should have known it wouldn't last.

"You already know everything," I lie. I can feel my cheeks turning red from guilt.

"Why don't you tell me again?" he insists, his tone menacing.

"I came out of work and was attacked," I tell him, looking at the wall and avoiding eye contact. He grabs me by the chin hard, making me look at him.

"Now, why don't you look me in the eye and try that again," he orders, scowling. I close my eyes, trying to escape those stormy blue ones from penetrating my shell of lies. I shouldn't say anything, but enough shit has rolled after the events of what me and the girls had done.

"Fucking spill it, Dani," he grits.

"I can't," I say, pulling out of his grip.

"You're fucking hiding something from me," he growls, standing. He leans down and grabs my chin. "You belong to me, and you and our baby's safety is mine to look after. I can't do that unless you tell me everything and stop hiding shit from me."

I stand as well, angry and downright pissed off. "Hiding shit? How about the fact my mother's missing! You wouldn't be hiding anything from me about that, would you?" I ask, crossing my arms in front of my chest.

Shadow flexes his hand, and I can sense the anger building within him.

"You got about two seconds to explain, Dani," he warns, ignoring my accusation of him having something to do with my mother's disappearance. I close my eyes, knowing if Shadow *did* have anything to do with it that means she's not alive anymore. I'm not sure if I feel relieved or grief at the thought. I open my eyes to see a very angry Shadow, puffed out and furious, waiting for my answer.

"Fine," I whisper, hoping Babs forgives me. "I walked out to where you have been parking, and a car came hauling ass toward me. The driver door checked me, making me fall." I point toward the road rash eating my kneecaps. "A group of guys got out and said 'this was for Darin' before beating the Hell out of me with a bat." I'm strangely calm as I tell him all that.

"Darin?" Shadow questions in confusion.

I turn my head, not wanting to give him anymore.

"Dani," he threatens.

I won't be a rat; my status around here is already exactly that.

I look him in the angry eyes staring back at me. "You'll have to ask Babs about the rest," I tell him.

The word angry is not even in my vocabulary right now. I'm beyond that. I pull my boots on hobbling down the hall to Bull's room.

I knock loudly, my fist pounding against the old door.

He swings the door open. "What the fuck?" he yells. His hair is a mess and he's wearing nothing but threadbare boxers.

"Get dressed; we need to see Babs now!" I demand before walking away.

I wait out by my car for Bull to crawl his ass out of bed.

"You want to explain what the hell is going on?" Bull asks, walking out of the club and lighting a cigarette.

"Jump in the car. I'll explain on the way there," I tell him, climbing into my car.

"Don't fucking park up here like this again. How many times I gotta tell you, boy?" Bull questions, getting in beside me.

I start the car and pull out of the courtyard, ignoring him.

"You going to tell me why you woke me up, Shadow?" he drills, resting his head back on the headrest.

"Dani and Babs' attacks are related. They have gotten themselves into some shit and Dani won't tell me," I inform. Bull looks at me instantly.

"That one's stubborn like her momma," Bull chuckles. "What did Dani say?"

"That I should ask Babs," I respond, lifting my eyebrows, irritated at the situation.

"Shit," Bull mutters under his breath. "You two figure out your shit?" he asks, referring to Dani's pregnancy.

"Yeah. I stopped at some pregnancy store to pick up books and shit for her," I reply.

Bull laughs. "You're learning."

I remember walking into that damn pregnancy store before heading to the club last night. I knew I fucked up leaving Dani to figure my shit out, but I didn't want to say something I didn't mean, so I left.

"Can I help—" The little lady stops as she notices me standing in a store full of pregnant-women crap, me wearing my cut and rough attitude for everyone to see. I'm sure I looked like I took a wrong turn.

"My girl is pregnant and she's sick all the time," I respond, feeling anxious.

"Oh, congratulations," she chirps. "I've got just the thing."

That lady sat there explaining a box of suckers to me for twenty minutes, and then showed me a shelf full of vitamins for another twenty minutes. I about said 'screw it'.

When I checked out, the lady started talking about baby names and celebrity baby names; she wouldn't shut the hell up. I just wanted my change back.

"There's a spot," Bull says, pointing to a parking spot close to the hospital doors.

I ignore him and park in the 'no parking zone' instead.

We enter Babs' room and see a bunch of nurses and a doctor standing around her bed.

"I'm calling time of death: 4:45," the doctor says, looking at the clock on the wall.

"What the fuck?" Bull questions.

"I'm sorry. Are you family?" a nurse asks, rushing in front of Bull.

"Damn right, I am," Bull yells, pushing the nurse out of the way. He makes his way to Babs and hangs his head low. "What happened?" he asks softly.

"I was in surgery when I got the distress call. She had a stroke; it could have been caused by a brain clot. Her head took quite the impact when she fell, and brain clots are hard to find. We did everything we could," the doctor says, his tone somber, looking at a chart.

"I called the husband ten minutes ago when the patient started having problems," a nurse says, stepping up behind the doctor.

"Did you get a hold of him?" I ask.

"Yes, I did," she responds.

Bull grabs Babs' hand and closes his eyes, his body slumping forward with a sob. I always wondered if Babs and Bull had anything on the side, and now I know they did.

I walk up to Babs and look at her, knowing I will not see the mother of the MC again. Her bright red hair is curled around her face, and her freckles are vibrant against her pale skin. I close my eyes and rub them with my fingers, the emotion of the situation weighing heavy on me. She was like a mother to me and Bobby, the only one I really ever had.

"Someone will pay for this," Bull threatens, his eyes closed and his lips pierced with anger.

He stands up and kisses Bab's lips tenderly. As their lips touch, a slight sob escapes him. I turn and walk out, giving him a minute. Seeing the President of your club—a badass who takes no shit—cry is not something anyone can take lightly.

Seconds later, Bull walks out of the hospital room, his face sad and hung low.

"You get Dani to tell you fucking everything," Bull orders, his tone sharp and demanding.

14

Dani

I RINSE THE SOAP FROM MY FACE AND TURN THE FAUCET OFF, THE smell of Shadow's soap still lingering in the misty air. I grab a towel and hop out of the shower then I peer into the mirror, scared what I might see. I haven't looked in the mirror since my attack. I noticed the little beady, black stitches snaking in and out the corner of my eyebrow and yellowish and bluish splotches on my neck and shoulders where they kicked me. I close my eyes to try to wash the images away but still see them swimming in the darkness behind my closed eyelids. I open them and turn to get dressed, putting on some jersey shorts and a light white tank top—something light and breezy.

The bedroom door opens and Shadow walks in, rubbing the back of his neck.

"Sit down, Dani," Shadow demands.

I do as he says, hesitantly.

Shadow walks up and kneels in front of me.

"Babs has passed away," he whispers.

"What?" I question, shooting off the bed, distraught.

"She passed away today," Shadow affirms, standing with me.

"But how can that be?" I ask, shocked that her health disintegrated so quickly.

"The doctor said she had a stroke, possibly by a brain clot which could have been caused from her fall," Shadow explains, pulling me close. I grab hold of his shirt and pull him close. A strangled cry breaks though my mouth, as Shadow wraps his arms around me while the turmoil of the situation hurls through me.

"Dani, I need you to tell me everything you know," Shadow says, pulling my chin up. "I can't keep you safe if you don't."

"Fine," I whisper as tears slide down my face. That could have easily been me in that bed, and if I don't tell Shadow what happened, it could be another ol' lady.

"Babs had a niece whose boyfriend beat her up for getting into his drugs. So me and the girls went and picked the guy up in the club's van and took him somewhere to teach him a lesson. Now they are coming back for us," I blurt out.

"Where did you pick this guy up?" Shadow questions, his tone serious and jaw clenched.

"I don't know. I was in the back of the van, so I couldn't see anything. We found him behind some building with green lights all around it, and he was wearing a green bandana. That's all I know."

"Fuck," Shadow mumbles.

"What?" I ask meekly.

"I think you girls threw us into a fucking turf war. We are not allowed over on that side of town, and they aren't allowed over here. You girls going over there and messing with that guy was stupid. Why didn't Babs just bring it to the table?"

"Babs said she told Locks but he told her no; that it wasn't club business," I inform.

"Keep your ass in here. I have to go find your father," Shadow commands, pointing to the bed.

I sit back down on the bed, throw my face in my hands and sob. I can't believe Babs is really gone. She has been a friend to me ever since I arrived here, she was family.

Shadow

"I've called you all here because I have some bad news, along with the club being on lock down," Bull states, taking a sip from a full bottle of whiskey.

"What?" Bobby asks, eyeing Bull with concern.

"Babs passed away about an hour ago," Bull reveals slowly, his eyes beginning to glaze over. I can tell he's trying to act tough for the club, but he's failing.

"What?" Bobby exclaims, standing from his chair.

"Stroke," Bull says flatly.

"Where the fuck is Locks?" Old Guy asks.

I look next to Bull where Locks usually sits, but there's only an empty chair.

"I imagine he's probably taking it pretty hard," Bull says. With the way Locks has been treating Babs lately I doubt that.

"Anyways, we are on lock-down because it seems our lovely ladies went on a mission to redeem the honor of Babs' niece without our knowledge," Bull continues, rubbing his hands up and down his face. "We think the guy they attacked is under the protection of Augustus." He looks up from under his hands, waiting for the backfire from the guys which is bound to happen.

"The Kingpin?" Bobby questions.

"Yes. They kidnapped some guy, beat him and left him on the side of the road," Bull informs.

"They picked him up behind a club with green lights. I'm thinking it's The Green Room, which is on the wrong side of town, Augustus's territory," I pipe in.

"Damn women," Hawk gruffs.

"Why didn't they bring it to the table?" Bobby asks.

"Apparently, Locks didn't find it worthy of the table," I seethe. That wasn't for him to decide; he should have brought it to the table for a vote.

"So, now what?" Old Guy asks.

"Going against Augustus and his boys is going to be a hell of a war. I'm not even sure if he is the one attacking. We have to think this through before going on that side of town and making waves," Bull tells us, lighting a cigarette.

"I'll do some digging, see what I can come up with. Until then, the club is on lock-down," Bull finishes.

"Everyone is accounted for but Cherry," Hawk says from the end of the table. I smirk. Cherry is a rebel. She's always against the club, breaking laws left and right. She's the worst pain in the ass this club has had to endure. She's lucky we owe Phillip.

Bull groans a rumble of frustration.

"Of course she's not."

Dani

I sit on the bed and I can hear the club become heavy with idle chitchat as it's filled with family and close friends. Had I known attacking that boy with Babs would have led to this, I wouldn't have never gone through with it. I haven't felt the same since I almost killed that guy. I don't even know if he's alive. Shadow comes in the room and leans against the back of the door; he looks exhausted.

"Rough meeting?" I ask.

"You could say that," he replies sarcastically. "The news that Babs is gone and you ladies threw us in a turf war isn't exactly something to celebrate on."

I bite my bottom lip and look at the ground; he's right.

"What pisses me off more is Locks. He should be trying to avenge his wife's death," Shadow continues, his hands fisted at his side. "He'd be in the ground already if it weren't for the respect I have for your father." He looks at me, his eyes promising me he would do anything to protect me.

The room is filled with tension and silence.

"I'm going to go get something to eat," he ultimately says, changing the subject and leaving, slamming the door behind him.

Minutes later, he comes back into the room with a tub of chocolate ice cream and a spoon. He leans his muscled back against the wooden door and pops the top of the plastic container using his thumb.

I can't help but giggle. He's always eating chocolate ice cream.

"What's so funny?" he asks, stuffing a spoonful in his mouth.

"You," I respond, pointing to his tub of ice cream.

He looks up from under his thick eyelashes with hooded eyes.

"You want some?" he offers, pushing off the door and walking toward me. He dips the silver spoon into the chocolaty goodness and places it inches from my mouth. I look at his mischievous blue eyes and open my mouth slowly, as he moves the spoon forward slightly. I move forward to lap up the chocolate, but he pulls it away before I can make contact.

I toss my head back and laugh at his playfulness.

He glances behind him at the dresser then turns back to me with the look of a man on a mission before grabbing a black bandana off the dresser.

"What do you think you're going to do with that?" I ask

nervously.

Shadow smirks like the devil himself with his eyes hooded. I recognize that look of lust in his eyes, and I second-guess having sex with Shadow after just hearing about Babs' death.

He sits the chocolate tub aside and gestures his hand in a twirling action. "Turn," he says.

I look at him, unsure if I want him to blindfold me. "Trust me," he says softly, his eyes raised with excitement.

"It feels wrong, what with Babs and all," I whisper.

Shadow licks the chocolate from his lips slowly as he fingers the bandana.

"People have different ways to deal with death," he responds. I can't deny Shadow. I crave for his affection in this dark hour—just us together, relieving our grief.

I inhale a deep breath and turn slowly. He wraps the soft fabric around my tear stained face, my vision darkening as it's placed over my eyes. He tugs it as he ties it behind my head tightly. All I see is pitch-black. There is not even a peek of light slithering in. I can feel my breathing go heavy as my heart races against my chest. I trust Shadow, but this is taking trust to a whole new level.

"You think sex was great before, but you have no idea," he whispers into my ear, the smell of chocolate coming from his breath.

His words remind me how much more sex he's had than me. The thought that he has blindfolded others before makes me jealous.

He pulls my shirt above my head, his hands gliding down my body as his fingers interlock with the hem of my jersey shorts. He slowly pulls them off, his nose trails behind them along my legs.

Shadow directs me backward until the backs of my legs hit the dresser. He grabs my hips and lifts me on top of it, its top cold against my rear, making goose bumps crawl across my arms.

He brings his lips to mine, giving me a taste of the chocolate he denied me, his tongue demanding and greedy. He breaks the embrace and starts trailing kisses down my neck, down my collar bone, over the mounds of my breasts. My body hums with desire from the affectionate touch Shadow offers, bringing me from my mourning to elation. He gives my nipple a hard nip, making my body come alive with pleasure. He continues kissing me down the valley of my breasts, across my belly, heading south. My stomach clenches with anticipation, wondering what his next move is.

He grabs the underside of my thighs and scoots me back, jostling my body towards the back mirror, then pulls upward, angling my lower half up. I try to wiggle my head to loosen the bandanna but it's no use. I feel my legs thrown over his shoulders and before I can protest, his mouth crashes against my wet core, the feeling of cold jolting me.

"Oh, my God!" I squeal, as he chuckles against my opening.

He slides his warm fingers into me and begins to pump them in and out painfully slow.

"Never thought chocolate could taste any better," he murmurs, his voice rumbling against my clit.

My hand slams down on his head as he laps at my clit, the intensity of the sensations overwhelming. His ice-cold tongue assaults my pussy and his heated fingers dive back and forth. My body is vibrating with release, as his wet tongue devours my juices, confused with the warmth inside and the blizzard on the outside. I begin to pant in short breaths as I start to round my hips in a circular motion, trying to grab that release Shadows tongue is causing. He stops for a second, making me wither, and my hand loses contact with his head as he dips from his place. Within seconds, he's back, and my hands regain their place. I brace myself for the cold attack that is about to happen but it's no use. As soon as his mouth crashes down on my heated opening, I cry out; it's so cold it's borderline painful. I moan loudly as my waves begin to crash hard. When I think I can't take anymore, Shadow circles his thumb along my clit as his tongue darts in and out, making my orgasm peak. I arch upward and yell with my release, the warmth overpowering the arctic freeze on Shadow's tongue.

I slam back against the dresser, my body heaving, out of breath.

Shadow unties the blackness, which consumes my vision. His hair is in a just-fucked state and his mouth forms a devilish smirk. He slips his fingers into his mouth, sucking my wetness and chocolate from them.

"My turn," he smirks. Shadow grabs me by the hips and flips me over so my ass is in the air and my chest is lying on top of the dresser.

He fists my hair and drives his length deep inside me, making me question when he took his clothes off.

He thrusts hard, his cock insatiable and thirsting for my taking. The pleasure begins to build again. Shadow grunts as he snakes his hand around and grabs a hold of my throat lightly, making me moan loudly. The dresser slams against the wall, making me wonder just how much more it can take. I look into the mirror and watch Shadow—his eyes are looking down at his length slamming in and out of me relentlessly, his mouth parted slightly with eyes hooded. He speeds his hips up as he begins to pulse inside of me. He growls and pulls out then flips me over and sprays his semen all over my stomach and chest. Little jolts of white beads smack against my skin, claiming my stomach. He takes his hand and rubs it around on my skin.

"Mine," he declares as he rubs his hand in circles over me and the baby, laying claim to his property.

A knock comes at the door, making me hightail it to the bathroom. Shadow cups his junk quickly as the door flings open.

"Ahhh, fuck, man!" Bobby hollers, shielding his eyes. I peek my head around the doorframe of the bathroom and see Bobby holding his hand in front of his eyes.

"What the hell do you want?" Shadow asks.

"We got a problem with Cherry," Bobby responds, looking away from Shadow.

"I'll be there in a second," Shadow says. Bobby pulls the door shut, cursing under his breath.

"Do you think she's okay?" I question, walking into the room.

"I don't know. She refused to show up when she was asked to get her ass here," Shadow explains, pulling on his jeans, no briefs. Shadow without underwear is something no woman could get used to.

"I'm coming," I tell him, grabbing my shirt off the floor.

I find my clothes and slip them on quickly, not caring about sticky chocolate between my legs or the fact I have Shadow smeared all over my lower half.

We walk down the hall and see Vera and Molly patting Cherry on the back.

"Cherry?" I whisper, stepping up to the barstool she is sitting on.

She looks up at me and I notice mascara smeared across her face, her greyish-green eyes red from crying.

"Oh, Dani, it was horrible," she sobs.

"What happened?" I ask as she slams her head into my chest.

"I was almost killed. A car chased me," she exclaims hysterically. "I ran into a store and hid there until they left." Her words are so loud I can barely understand her.

I rub the back of her head in support—I can relate. There is no fear like running from a vehicle, looking over your shoulder and knowing it can end your life as you know it any second.

"Church, now," my dad commands, pointing toward the Chapel doors.

Shadow

"This is the third ol' lady who's been attacked," Bull says, lighting a cigarette.

"The attacks are speeding up," Old Guy points out.

"I think we need to get on this and quick," I snap, my fingers itching to kill the man who hurt Dani and killed Babs.

"I agree, but we retaliate smart," Bobby says, eyeing me. He knows I would love to go in there guns blazing, and if it is Augustus, he is protected heavily so we need to be careful.

Bull's phone begins to ring as the boys talk strategy. I can't help but notice the look of shock on his face when he looks at whose calling.

"Quiet, boys," he demands as he clicks a button and lays his phone on the table.

"Augustus," Bull greets.

"Bull," the deep voice replies from the other line, the phone on speaker so we all can hear.

"You have attacked three of my ladies, one of whom is now dead," Bull states, clenching his jaw.

"Ladies who passed their line of territory, and this is news to me that one of them is deceased. I'm sorry to hear that," Augustus says, his tone emotionless.

I grit my teeth at his pathetic apology, he couldn't care less.

"You want a war, you got it," Bull declares, eyeing the phone as he reaches his hand over to turn it off.

"Unless you want me to put that pretty little daughter of yours in the ground along with the rest of those white-trash biker whores, I expect you at my warehouse in two hours." The line clicks, ending the call.

Bull grabs his phone and looks at me, his eyes matching mine, scared that if we don't comply the girl we both care for will pay.

"Let's take care of business, boys," Bull orders, tucking his phone in his pocket swiftly.

"Let's ride," Bobby agrees, throwing his chair back.

I walk into my room and pull a drawer out, grabbing extra ammo and another gun for the waist of my pants before putting my favorite pistol in my holster.

"You're going out?" Dani says, stepping into the room. Her eyes catch my gun in its holster and she stills. "This is too dangerous, Shadow," she tells me, stepping up and fisting my shirt.

"I'm going to prove to you I can protect you and the baby, Dani," I declare, shrugging on my cut.

"What if you get hurt, or worse, die?" she asks, her finger tracing the tattoo on my arm.

I laugh. "The only one who's going to get hurt is the guy who attacked you." I lean down and claim those lips, possessing them and committing them to memory. I'm man enough to say I'm afraid I may not return. Augustus is a hard motherfucker, and we could walk into a trap and not know it but not going ensures the toe tag of Dani and the other women.

"I'm not saying goodbye, because it's not," she states against my lips.

"Fair enough," I say.

"Kill the bastards," she whispers, her face serious. I love her corruption, that girl who knows this has to be done and supports me, yet fears for my safety just the same.

"I fucking love you," I express as sincerely as possible, pecking her lips one more time.

I head out and stand by my bike, waiting for the others when Bobby walks out of the doors.

"I know we have been through some shit together, brother, but I want you to know I have your back tonight," he says, slapping me on my back.

I look back at him—the guy I grew up with, the one who accepted me for who I was, my brother.

"I wouldn't want anyone else," I reply honestly. Bobby smirks as he straddles his bike, just as the others start to pour out of the club.

I start my bike and wait for Bull to start his. I look at the club and see a glowing Dani standing by the other girls, the sight of her in that pink cast fuels my need for redemption.

There will be souls paying their untimely debt tonight.

◆ ◆ ◆

Riding, all I can think about is Dani and the baby. *What if I don't make it back, or what if it had been her who was killed?* My hands squeeze the handlebars in anger. This is all Locks' fault. His ass didn't even have the nerve to answer his phone when Bull called earlier. Bull said fuck it and decided to meet Augustus without him.

Bobby revs his engine as he rides next to me, knocking me from my thoughts.

Night is approaching fast as we ride toward Augustus. When we arrive, we pull into what looks like an abandoned warehouse. We climb off our bikes and stare the joint down while the wind howls, causing a rusty chain-link fence to rattle. Lightening brightens the sky, warning us of a storm. The pavement is cracked with weeds sprouting through the splits.

"Let's get this over with, boys," Bull says, walking toward the building. In passing, we notice a torn blue tarp over what looks like a vehicle. Not giving a damn, Bobby pulls it off to look under it. It's a white Monte Carlo with blood on the windshield and hood. It has to be the car Babs was hit with.

"Jesus," Bull exclaims, his tone cracking with emotion and fists clenching at his sides.

"I guess we know now it was definitely Augustus and his men who hit Babs," Old Guy says, surveying the bloody, cracked windshield.

Bobby lays the tarp back down shaking his head in anger. We walk around, see a doorless entry, and go in. My hand immediately goes to my gun, ready for a shootout.

15

Shadow

"**A**H, THE DEVIL'S DUST IS HERE," AUGUSTUS SAYS, COMING DOWN A railing of stairs and adjusting his tie, which matches his black suit. His long, black hair is slicked back into a ponytail, and his black shoes shine from the florescent light fixture that hangs above. "So nice of you to stop by."

"Someone is going to pay for the life of one of my girls," Bull shouts.

"I see," Augustus says, slicking his hair back with his hand. "George loved playing 'cat and mouse' with your girls, but he didn't follow orders directly. Seems he got carried away with one, and I apologize for that." He gestures in the direction of George. He is short and has a green bandanna on low, so you can't see his eyes. He has tattoos that don't make any sense sketched all along his neck, and knuckles. He will die tonight. He just doesn't know it yet.

"If you'll be so kind as to drop your weapons, boys," Augustus orders, kicking a blue crate toward us.

"Do we look stupid?" Bobby asks.

"Do it," Augustus demands. He snaps his fingers and two guys walk up behind him, pointing a rifle at us.

I pull my gun from my holster and throw it in as the other guys do the same.

"Talk," Bull commands.

"Right," Augustus says, loosening the cuffs on his sleeves. "When your little bitches crippled my nephew, I was going to kill every single one of them."

My nose flares with anger; I'd kill him right now if I could but Augustus is too protected, so if I kill him, I ensure the death of myself and the rest of us.

"I even sent a warning to let you know war had begun." He looks up from his cuffs and sniffles.

"I sure did love that bike too." Locks voice sounds from behind me. I turn and find Locks walking up behind us.

"What the fuck?" I mutter.

"Locks?" Old Guy questions, just as shocked as I am that he's here.

"When I found out one of the girls who beat my nephew was your daughter, a new business opportunity came to light. I thought I would trade you," Augustus continues, straightening his tie.

"Trade me what?" Bull asks, his gaze snapping from Locks to Augustus.

"Your girl's life for a little business," Augustus explains. "You let me run drugs on your side, and you can run guns on my side. You get some cash, and your women get to live." He shrugs like it's no big deal.

Bull turns his head, looking at me, his eyes silently asking me if he thinks we should do it. I nod. I would agree to anything to ensure Dani's safety.

"Then this is over?" Bull asks.

"Over," Augustus says, nodding.

"Fine," Bull says.

"Fantastic," Augustus smiles, but continues casually, "However, I don't condone business with clubs who have rats amongst them."

"What the fuck are you talking about?" Bull questions.

"Why don't you tell them, Locks?" Augustus says, looking at our brother. We all turn and stare at Locks who's standing a few feet behind me.

"What the hell is he talking about?" Bull reiterates.

"You might as well tell them," Augustus smiles.

Locks looks at Augustus then back to Bull.

"You lost your priorities when you let your family into the club. You threw caution to the wind when your daughter came back," Locks spits, pointing at Bull. "Dani was a threat to the club, and she should have had a bullet put in her head." He looks at me, speculating it should have been me to kill her. "When Babs told me about her niece, I told her no, and that should have been the end of it. But because you were fucking her, she thought she could do whatever she wanted to." Bull flinches at his words.

"You never deserved Babs," Bull seethes, his words calm and collected. His face drawn tight, his eyes hooded with hatred.

"Eh, that's up for debate," Locks snarls. "I knew Augustus would be out for blood, so I bought my time. When my bike was blown up, I knew it was Augustus and I knew it was just the beginning of a war.

"How'd you know it was Augustus?" Bobby questions.

"I met the guy Babs' niece was dating once, I knew he was one of Augustus's boys by the green bandana," Locks replies.

If he knew who the boyfriend was, and that Babs wasn't going to let the situation go of the guy hitting her niece, then Locks set Babs up. My fingers twitch with urge to throttle my betraying brother.

"Anyway, I came to Augustus with a deal, and in return I would be protected from his retaliation," he finishes, his tone calm and casual like this should all make sense.

THE SCARS THAT DEFINE US

"What deal?" Bull growls.

"He gave me the location of every one of your girls," Augustus says, stirring the pot of betrayal. "In fact, if Lover Boy hadn't shown up, your daughter might have died in that night club." He looks right at me and then to his left. I follow his line of sight and see the guy who was giving Dani a hard time that night at the club a while back.

"But Lover Boy was a blessing in disguise. If I had killed your daughter, I wouldn't have been able to make this deal, now would I?" Augustus smirks.

"You betrayed me," Bull states through gritted teeth at Locks.

"You did it to yourself. You let club business come second when your daughter showed up, throwing everyone in jeopardy," Locks responds, his lips curled with anger.

"Either way, he has to be dealt with," Augustus prompts, pulling a pistol from his suit jacket.

He aims it at Locks, who stands right behind me. Locks' eyes go wide when he notices the gun is pointing at him and grabs me by the shoulders, using me as a shield. The gun fires, pointing directly at me, and I blink, waiting for the bullet to plow into me. Just as I think I'm about to be shot, I'm knocked to the ground.

The wind is knocked from me when my body hits the gritty warehouse floor, making me gasp. I hear a disgruntled cough beside me and glancing next to me, I notice Bobby lying on his back on the ground. Blood is spilling from his side as his legs kick to try to stand up.

I crawl over to him and pick his head up, laying it on my lap to asses where he's been shot. Right in the gut, shit.

"What the fuck were you thinking, man?" I frantically question him, noticing Bobby's face paling quickly.

"Saving your ass," Bobby replies, coughing. He clenches his eyes and moans in pain.

"I called an ambulance. They'll be here soon, son; hang in there," Bull says, squatting down beside me.

"You called an ambulance?" Augustus cries with disbelief. "Get what you can hidden, boys!" He points at some crates in the building.

"Think I'm pretty fucked-up," Bobby says, his blue eyes looking right at me for the truth.

"Nah, it's just a flesh wound," I lie.

"Liar," Bobby whispers. I notice blood crawling out from underneath him.

"You can't die," I mutter. I feel my eyes prick with tears, and I let them fall. I can't take the idea of losing my brother.

"You take care of Firefly and that baby," Bobby stutters as his eyes start to take a distant look.

"You're going to be fine. You're just going to regret trying to save my ass tomorrow," I tell him, trying to be optimistic, but the look in Bobby's eyes have me second-guessing my confidence.

"No regret in life, no fear in love, brother," he whispers as his eyes begin to close. I can feel the life slipping from him as his body goes limp, the fiery depths of Hell taking my best friend.

"Bobby, hang in there," I say, giving him a shake.

His eyes snap open, and he begins to cough.

"Man, it hurts so much," he whispers, his hands trembling.

"You can do this, brother," Old Guy whispers to Bobby.

Bull leans forward and presses his hand to Bobby's gut, trying to stop the bleeding, but it just gushes between his fingers.

"I stopped it some, but it's not going to help for long," Bull states, applying both his hands to the wound.

I look down at Bobby and notice his eyes are closed.

"No, Bobby!" I yell, my voice angry and forced. Trying to wake him, I give him a shove, but he doesn't open his eyes.

"No. No. No!" I roar.

This can't be happening. My brother, the one person I considered my own family before I was accepted by anyone, has left me to thrive in this callous world solo.

I lay Bobby's head down on the concrete floor and stand, wiping my eyes with the back of my hand and smearing Bobby's blood across my face in the process. I pull the gun I had hidden from my waistband and point it at Augustus. Instantly, weapons from behind Augustus and on the balcony above him are pulled and aimed at me.

"You killed my family," I grit, my finger heavy on the trigger.

"He jumped in front of my bullet meant for a traitor," Augustus replies casually, my gun pointing at his head not affecting him at all. "He killed your brother." Augustus points behind me. I turn my line of sight to follow his gesture and see Locks.

He's right. This is all Locks' fault. He went rogue, went against the club, and got Babs killed and almost killed Dani and my baby, all because he wanted to prove a point. I swing the gun around and point it at Locks, who opens his mouth to speak, but before he can say any last words, I pull the trigger. I watch as the slug slams into his chest, making him fall to his knees. His eyebrows furrow as he looks down at his chest where the blood begins to pool from the bullet wound, seeping down his grey shirt. I promised Dani I would kill him for hurting her, and I'm keeping my word. I aim my gun at Locks, ready to take the last shot, when Bull steps up next to me and pulls a gun from his waistband.

"This is for Babs," Bull whispers as he pulls the trigger, slamming a bullet right into Locks' throat. Locks falls to the ground, landing on his back. Blood splutters from the bullet hole in his throat, followed by gurgling and gasping. He's drowning in his own blood.

"Now that's over, are we done here?" Augustus says, hearing sirens near.

"Not quite," I snarl. I point my gun toward the guy who ran over Babs and beat Dani with a bat, following through on my last promise to take down the person who hurt Dani. The guy reaches for his gun in the front of his jeans as I pull the trigger. The bullet jams right into his skull, spraying brain matter all along the wall behind him as he falls down the staircase like a bag of dirty clothes.

I turn and wait for the return fire from Augustus and his crew. Augustus holds up a hand, holding off his boys from firing at me, looks at the guy I just shot and shrugs. "I was going to get rid of him anyway; he can't follow orders. Call it insurance for our new business transaction," Augustus says with a shrug.

"I'll call you with the details, Bull," he hollers, walking out of the building with his thugs in tow.

"We should have killed him," I say, clenching my teeth as Augustus walks away.

"If we touch him, his men would kill every one of us, and everyone we know," Bull replies, looking down at Locks' dead body.

"Lust like a saint, trust like a sinner," he mutters. I look at Bull and notice his brows pinched together as he looks at Locks with disbelief. Locks betraying the club is going to hit Bull's wall of trust hard. Locks was the ideal club member, and I never saw him turning on the club for a second.

"I'll deal with the police," Bull says, pulling his gaze from Locks.

I look down at Bobby with disbelief. An ambulance comes and collects him in a rush, putting him on the stretcher and running back towards an ambulance. I watch the EMT lift the gurney to place Bobby inside and I step up right behind them.

"Sir, are you family?" a blonde EMT asks.

"Yes."

She looks at me with a cocked head.

"I'm sorry, but immediate family only. You can follow in your own vehicle if you want," she says with a dull tone, like it would be pointless. I step back and run my hands through my hair, trying to get a hold of myself.

When the ambulance leaves without flashing lights or sirens, I watch it bump and hurdle over potholes in the unkempt parking lot and onto the main road. Seconds later, the lights flash and sirens go off as the ambulance bolts towards the highway.

"I should have kept a better eye on him," I mutter to Bull, standing beside me.

"He saved your life; he knew what he was doing," Bull replies, patting me on the back. "He'll never be forgotten," he promises his voice grim as he climbs on his motorcycle.

Bobby won't be forgotten. He is the brother I never had.

"I'm Bobby, what are you in here for?" the blonde, yuppie-looking boy asked me. I stare him down, unsure if I should say anything. Nobody has been friendly to me in here since I got here. I have already been in three fights since I arrived yesterday.

"Some bullshit," I say, shrugging.

"Yeah, I hear ya," he replies, sliding up behind me with his food tray. He smiles at me, revealing a mouth full of braces.

"Hey, you want to be friends?" the boy asks and I look at him, curious what his angle is. And who just comes out and asks to be friends?

"I'm Robert Zane Whitfield," he introduces himself, holding his hand out for a shake, his gesture a little geeky. "But everyone calls me Bobby."

"I'm Adrian Kingsmen," I respond, shaking his hand.

"Awesome, want to help me steal some corn bread?" he asks causally.

I stare at him, trying to read if he's serious or playing a joke, but he just looks back at me, nothing giving away it's a joke.

"How?" I ask, interested. Causing trouble in a place I was sent for causing trouble? I'm game.

"I'll distract the cook, you reach over and grab some extra rolls." He grins with a mouth full of metal.

"Have I mentioned how nice you look today, Mrs. Sangaurd?" Bobby swoons the lunch lady.

I smile. My first real friend I have ever had, and I met him in juvie.

"Let's ride, Shadow," Bull calls, breaking my train of thought.

I look at Bull before climbing on my bike, his face long and held with sorrow such as my own. Living in the malicious world, which is the club, we see brothers fall, and we see families break. But I've never felt the despair I'm feeling right now. Between Dani and Bobby, they brought me out of my life of desolation, they tolerate my indifferences and embrace the beast I am. It started with Bobby, and it grew with Dani. Losing Bobby and Babs' death will not be something the club will move on with so easily. They have brought a spirit to the club, which no one has before.

"Let's ride," I agree solemnly, starting my bike.

I ride back to the club, and the only person I want to see is Dani. I want to deliver the news to her myself. Bobby died rescuing my ass, so it needs to come from me.

I pull into the courtyard to the club and turn the bike engine off.

I swing my leg over my bike and head toward the club to deliver news which will not come lightly. As I enter the club, I hear the bikes of Bull and the other guys pulling in, but I continue on my path toward Dani. Bull can let the rest of the club know what happened. I open the door to mine and Dani's room and see her sitting on the bed, reading a pregnancy book. She peers up at me from behind the book and lights up.

"Thank God, you're alive. I was so worried," she exclaims, tossing the book to the side. She scurries off the bed and clings to my body. I want to hug her back; I want to feel that connection I need so desperately but, I can't. I don't want to give her the false hope that everything is okay—that I'm okay—when in fact everything is far from satisfactory.

She pulls away hesitantly, her arms still wrapped around my waist, and looks up at me. I pull away, the sight of her green eyes making this harder.

"What's wrong?" she asks warily.

"Sit down, Dani," I order, pointing to the bed. I squint my eyes, trying to hold back the emotion, so desperate to escape.

"You're scaring me," she says, sitting on the bed.

"Shit happened, and things didn't go as smoothly as we had hoped," I begin, running my hands through my hair.

"Spit it out, Shadow," she snaps.

I look at her, furious with her tone, but when I see the glow of her skin, the ivy of her eyes, I can't hold it against her.

"Bobby..., he, uh..." I stumble on my words, not sure how to deliver the message without the blow. In the end, there is no easy way to say it. "Bobby was shot. He didn't make it, Dani."

She gasps, the sound making the hair on my arms raise.

"What? What do you mean he didn't make it?" she cries.

"Exactly what I said: he didn't make it. He took a bullet for me and didn't survive the injury," I yell, I don't mean to come off unsympathetic, but I can't help it. I risk a look at Dani, and she has her hands cupped across her mouth and a look of horror on her face.

"I wanted to be the one to tell you," I whisper. "I'm going to head over to the hospital, see about arrangements and all." I lean over and give her head a gentle kiss. I want to be there for her, to be the strong one she needs, but I'm barely hanging on myself.

"I'm coming with," she declares, lifting her chin.

"Dani, I don't think that's such a good idea." The last thing I want is for her final look of Bobby to be one of death. That's not how I want him to be remembered.

"I'm going, Shadow!" she yells. Knowing I'm not going to win this argument, I nod in agreement. When it comes time, I'll make sure she leaves the room.

We exit the room and hear loud cries and sobbing coming from the club—Bull must have delivered the news. I grab Dani's hand and pull her through the club. I don't want her to break any more than she already has, and sitting around all these people will do just that.

We arrive at the hospital and I park in the usual 'No Parking' zone. I grab Dani's helmet and put it beside mine, the sight of her glassy eyes and my cut on her making me second-guess letting her come in.

"Dani, are you sure you want to do this?" I ask, leaning my head against hers and pushing a stray hair behind her ear. "You've already been through a lot today."

"Absolutely," she whispers. She looks at the hospital, breaking our contact. "Besides, someone needs to tell Doc."

I stroll through the sliding glass doors to enter the hospital and hear alarms going off, lights flickering wildly. A rush of nurses in different-colored scrubs along with doctors in white coats come running past us, nearly knocking Dani and me into the doors we just walked through.

"Code blue. We have a code blue," ignites from the intercom.

"Holy shit," Dani whispers.

"Seems the reaper is moving swiftly tonight," I comment to nobody in particular.

We look down the hall to where all the doctors are running and see a blonde in pink scrubs come flying from the room all the nurses and doctors just entered.

"It's Doc," Dani says, taking off toward her.

I run after her, not sure what is going on.

"Oh, my God," Doc cries, holding her face, distraught.

"What is going on?" Dani asks.

"He's lost so much blood. I'm not sure if he's going to make it," she cries. Her words grabbing my attention, I grab her by the shoulders roughly.

"What the fuck do you mean? Is he alive?" I practically interrogate her. She just sobs louder, the sound irritating me. I shove past her and go into the room to see paddles on Bobby's chest and tubes down his throat. A flat tone begins to beep, catching everyone's attention in the room

"We got him back but not for long. We need to get him in the OR, now." a short, brown-haired lady insists, looking at a screen. In seconds, they pull up the bedrails and rush Bobby's bed out of the room.

Bobby's alive—my brother still has a fighting chance. I can't help the rush of hope that flows through me. I once hated that feeling, not caring for its façade, but I'd be a fucking liar if I said I didn't hope to the gods that my brother pulls through this.

Dani

I sit in the chair next to Shadow as Doc hands both of us coffee.

"You two should go home. I'll call you if anything changes," she urges, sitting in a chair across from us in the waiting room.

"I'm not going anywhere," Shadow replies, taking a sip of the hot coffee.

"Is he going to be okay?" I ask.

"He's in a critical condition, the bullet nicked an artery. He died once in the ambulance and once again when he got here. There is no telling if he will make it or not." She looks down at her coffee and sobs.

"Fuck me," Shadow whispers.

Doc sniffs and wipes her nose with the back of her hand. "Take Dani home, get some sleep."

Shadow looks at me, his blue eyes full of hurt, killing me inside. I want to take away the pain he's feeling, add it to mine, but I can't. Shadow is living a Hell I can't imagine. Bobby took a bullet for him, saved his life, and he lost a woman he considered a mother all in one day.

"You will call me if anything changes, right?" Shadow asks, looking at the floor.

"Absolutely," she promises, taking a sip of her coffee.

"I'm fine, Shadow. We can stay," I offer.

"No, you're pregnant and need to rest," Shadow says, standing and turning to Doc. "Call me if anything happens."

"I will," she reiterates, standing with us.

◆ ◆ ◆

I wake to the dark night and slide my leg across the bed, looking for a cool spot. When my leg slides along and I don't feel Shadow, I raise from the bed and pat his pillow. Nothing. He isn't in bed. I slide off the bed and shimmy into some shorts before exiting the room. I pitter-patter my bare feet down the hall and find Shadow sitting on the worn-leather couch which sits diagonally across from the bar. He's adjusting white powder into lines on a mirror on the coffee table using a pocket knife.

"What are you doing?" I ask.

"Can't sleep," he clips, his tone cold.

"So, you thought you would do cocaine?" I question.

Shadow scoffs at me.

"Just come to bed with me," I offer sweetly, but Shadow doesn't budge.

"I understand you're hurting, Shadow—"

"You don't know shit about hurt, Dani," Shadow spits, licking his thumb which the white powder brushes upon. He looks up from the coke and hits me with damaged blue eyes.

"Hurt is watching your mother overdose on drugs and you watch her dying, wondering if reviving her would be a bigger Hell than letting her die. Hurt is having your dad—the only role model you ever had growing up—shot down in cold blood in a third world country. Hurt is watching your brother suffer because he took an undeserving bullet, one meant for you." Shadow's eyes gloss over before he looks back down. His words hit me hard. I bite my bottom lip to keep from putting him in his place, because I know he's hurting. I want to be there for him, but he clearly doesn't want me to be around.

I start walking back to the room, giving Shadow his space.

"Dani, wait," Shadow sighs, but I don't stop. I know nothing good will come of us having a conversation while we are both hurting and he's high.

I walk into the room and slam the door then slide against it, throw my head into my hands, and sigh heavily.

I crawl across the floor and up onto the bed and curl myself into the sheets. The door opens, painting the wall with light from the hall before slowly closing. I feel the bed dip down and a hand is placed on my back.

"You okay, Doll?" my dad asks. I flinch, surprised it's my father and not Shadow.

"Yes," I lie.

"This is just the process of healing, Darlin'," he exasperates.

"With drugs?" I question.

"Unfortunately, the ways of healing are different for everyone. The boys of the club are not men of many words when they're hurting, and drugs seem to help with the overthinking of things." My dad pats my back, and he talks as if he's speaking from experience. "Just be glad he's not drowning in girls, or—" he pauses. I know what he was going to say: girls and killing. He's right, though; Shadow could be doing a lot worse things right now trying to forget Bobby took his life to save his.

The bed dips as he brushes his lips against my temple. "Just for the record, I didn't want any of this for you. But I know you're strong enough to survive this world, Dani, You grow stronger with pain. You just have to survive it." My dad gives my back one more pat before leaving me in the dark with my thoughts.

◆ ◆ ◆

I feel warmth cocoon my body, waking me from my sleep.

"I'm sorry," Shadow whispers in my ear.

"It's okay," I whisper back.

"Bobby took a bullet for me, saving someone who doesn't deserve the act of saving." His words are edged with sorrow but make me angry. I turn around in his hold where are noses are nearly touching.

"You are worth saving, Shadow. You mean something to me and your baby," I clip.

Shadow pulls me in and kisses my forehead, tucking my head under his chin.

"Do you think it's a boy or a girl?" he asks.

"I don't know," I respond against his neck.

"If it's a boy, I want to name him after Bobby," Shadow suggests. I lift my head up and look at him, his eyes hooded with emotion.

"What is Babs' real name?" I ask.

"Delilah," Shadow mutters.

"If it's a girl, we should name her that, after Babs," I whisper. Delilah is a beautiful name.

"I think that is a great idea," he agrees.

"Kiss me, Firefly."

Without a second thought, I smash my lips to his, my mouth trying to overtake his pain and drown it with love.

16.

Shadow

"SHADOW, YOUR PHONE IS GOING OFF."
I open my eyes to a half-naked Dani holding my phone inches from my face. I grab it and answer, hoping it's good news from Doc.

"Hello," I say, half-asleep.

"He's awake," Doc chirps.

"I'm on my way," I exclaim, jumping out of the bed.

"What is it?" Dani asks.

"He's awake," I tell her, grabbing clothes from the dresser.

"Really?" she asks with excitement.

"Hurry up. Let's get over there." I'm pulling my jeans up as fast as I can. I couldn't sleep at all last night, but to be fair I didn't want to sleep. I thought I would fall asleep and not hear my phone go off if Doc called me. I kept thinking of things I wanted to tell Bobby before he left this world, words I was afraid would have to wait and be spoken at his eulogy instead. I wanted to tell him I was sorry for acting like such a pussy when shit went crazy with Dani. That he's the only family I ever considered to be my own aside from her. The idea that someone I considered a brother turned on the club is a shock on its own. And a woman I looked at as mother is now gone because of that asshole. I prayed, something I've been doing a lot of lately.

I grab my cut and throw it on. I look over at Dani to see if she's ready, and she looks absolutely stunning this morning. Her skin is glowing and she just has this energy about her. I fucking love her pregnant.

We ride over to the hospital quickly. When we pull up, we rush inside, afraid Bobby's moment of alertness will pass and I'll miss my chance to talk to him.

I grab Dani's hand and run in the direction of his room. As soon as I enter, Bobby slides his head from looking at Doc and turns to me. He looks pale as Hell.

I walk up to the side of the bed and grip his hand firmly.

"Brother?" I question, wondering if he can hear or answer me.

"All his vitals are rising slowly. I think he's going to make a full recovery," Doc informs us with a smile.

Bobby smirks. "You fucking owe me, man," he says with a low rasp, his energy weak. All I can do is laugh and nod. The asshole has my emotions running like a teenage girl who's been dumped at prom.

I feel Dani tuck her arm around my waist as she slides up next to me.

"Firefly," Bobby whispers.

Dani smiles that drop-dead-gorgeous smile.

Dani

The next couple of days Bobby is nothing but a tornado of angry. He refuses treatment and tries to check himself out of the hospital early. He doesn't want to see anybody, unless they are there to take him home. Doc says she has tried to reason with him, but he just won't listen. So I'm going to try and work my magic today to see if I can persuade him to stop being an idiot. Shadow stays at the club, his only solution to the problem is to shoot Bobby in the leg to keep his ass in the hospital bed.

I step into the hospital room and see Bobby lying in bed watching TV. His face is pale and he has machines hooked up to him everywhere. He looks like shit and that's putting it lightly.

"I hear you're being stupid and trying to check out early."

Bobby looks at me and raises a brow. "I'm fine. I don't need to be here," he says, his tone bitter. He takes his gaze from me back to the TV, dismissing me altogether.

"He needs to be here," Doc says, walking in the room.

I reach over and grab his hand, giving it a friendly squeeze. "Bobby, you died. You killed us along with your death. We can't have you back only to lose you again because of your stubbornness." Bobby's gaze remains on the TV, pissing me off by ignoring me.

I reach over and punch him in the arm.

"What the fuck, Firefly."

"You think that hurts? Think about what's it's going to feel like when the wound on your side is infected," Doc yells. I take a deep breath, he's trying my patience.

Bobby smiles, his eyes crinkling at the side. "You love me and you know it." Doc rolls her eyes and starts fiddling with the sheets on the bed.

I grin. "You're not leaving until you're released," I state, making no room for argument. "You're going to be an uncle. You need to start thinking about that role."

"She's right," Doc remarks.

Bobby shakes his head, his smile turning into a full-on grin.

"Fine, I'll stay, but only because I don't want Dani to kick my ass," he jokes, making me laugh. He winces from his own laughter, gaining Doc's attention.

"Any regrets?" I question, staring at Bobby holding his bandaged side.

Bobby grins. "Nope."

epilogue

Dani

a couple of years later

I LAY BACK ON THE BEACH TOWEL AND LET MY BODY SOAK UP THE SUN'S rays—it feels good.

Zane tugs on my arm and points at the water. He turns two in a few months; he's getting big too fast. I giggle and start to stand when a hand is placed on my shoulder.

"I got it, Big Momma, you sit back and relax. I don't want my little girl coming any sooner than she needs to," Shadow insists, leaning down kissing my growing belly. Shadow wanted to knock me up as soon as I had Zane, but I made him wait. Having Zane was rough: my blood pressure got really high so they had to induce me early, ending up in a C-section birth. Zane had everyone scared when he arrived, but he made his entrance into the world one to remember.

Shadow and I have decided to name our soon-to-be little girl after Babs, calling her Delilah. Babs was a motherly figure we never had, and she is truly missed at the club. Her funeral was beautiful, and I go to visit her grave often.

My dad took the biggest fall after Babs' death. I never knew the two of them were secret lovers—Shadow was the one who told me. Shadow took over the club when my dad bottomed out, but I think my dad is finally starting to get his footing back and is taking charge of the club again. Shadow gave the position back, no questions asked. He has a lot of respect for my father.

"Come on, son," Shadow says, taking Zane's hand and running off toward the water. Shadow has been Zane's hero since day one. He's a great father, just like I knew he would be. I watch Zane giggle and laugh, his dark hair which matches Shadow's, shift in the wind as the breeze blows. He is Shadow made over: dark hair, blue eyes, and an attitude to match.

"Hey, wait for us!"

Sand is kicked up and sprayed across my legs as Bobby takes off toward the shore, his tanned and tattooed back and yellow swim trunks nothing but a blur. I notice Doc go running off into the water right behind him.

I laugh and brush the sand from my legs, watching my family play in the water. It seems so surreal. I never thought I would be this happy, or that Shadow and I would find this place. We still have our dark tendencies, but together we help each other get through them. Mostly with the remedy of angry sex.

Bobby and Doc stomp back up from the shore laughing, Bobby's scar silver and standing out against his tanned body, catching my attention.

"Your scar is looking very angry today," I point out. Bobby looks down at it. "Yeah, I love it when it stands out, and the girls love it, too," he says, grinning, gaining an eye roll from me and a scoff from Doc.

Shadow comes up behind Bobby, brushing sand from his legs.

"That kid has way too much energy," he says breathlessly. "What are we talking about?" he asks, pulling a water from the cooler.

"How you thought I was dead but didn't get that lucky," Bobby replies, raising his eyebrow at Shadow.

Doc starts laughing as she sits down next to me. The swimsuit cover she's wearing slips off her shoulder, showing fierce-looking, silver scars slashing down her back. My eyes widen, and my mouth parts in horror. I open my mouth to ask what happened, but Bobby catches my attention standing above her. I look up and see him shaking his head with a stern look on his face. I snap my mouth shut and look at the scars again, but Doc pulls her cover over her shoulder, hiding them.

"We've been through this," Shadow says. "I'm not a fucking doctor; how was I supposed to know you were still alive?"

"Zane, don't get too close to the water, Bug," Bobby yells. I glance around the boys and look to see how close he is. He's not close at all; he's making a sand castle feet away. With a dad and an uncle more protective than a mother, and both in a motorcycle club, I'll be amazed if Zane doesn't hate them both by the time he's ten.

Shadow, Bobby, and Doc take off toward the water, and I lie back down and stare at the clouds passing in the sky. Things have been peaceful around here: nobody has been shot or hit with a car, and I haven't seen or heard from my mom, making me one hundred percent positive Shadow had indeed taken care of her. Now that I have children, though, I'm glad she's gone. Who knows what kind of messed-up scam she would try and involve them in to get what she wanted. She was cold-hearted and only cared about her scorned heart.

"You look deep in thought," Shadow says. I look over to see him lying back on a towel, staring up at the sky.

"I think it's time I claim you outside of the club," Shadow declares, smiling. I scrunch my nose, unsure what he means, but then it hits me.

"Are you serious?" I ask.

Shadow smirks. "I want everyone inside the club and out of it to know you're mine. I want you to be my property and my wife," he replies, brushing a hair from my face.

"Are you asking me to marry you?" I question, sitting up on my elbows.

Shadow laughs. "When have you known me to ask? I'm telling you, you're going to be my wife," he insists with a stern voice.

I throw my head back and laugh.

"I can't wait to be yours, both inside the club and out," I tell him with a smile.

THE END

...for now

THE FEAR THAT DIVIDES US

(The Devil's Dust #3)

M. N. Forgy

PROLOGUE

six years earlier

BOBBY

As I take a sip of what's left of my beer, my eyes catch Babs coming through the kitchen over the top of the bottle. Her red hair is sticking to her face from the summer's heat, and she's mumbling about something. I set the empty bottle on the counter and watch her put up glasses and fill the ice bin. It's quiet here, too quiet. Nights in the clubhouse are usually filled with easy women and drugs. Well, somewhat easy. Seeing as I'm still a prospect I don't get anywhere near the amount of ass the patched in brothers get, but I do alright. I peel the label from my beer and start folding it in on itself.

Old Guy crashes through the club's front doors, catching everyone's attention.

"Where's Bull?" Old Guy asks, his voice frantic.

I shrug, not sure.

"I think he's in his room. You want me to grab him?" Shadow asks, sitting next to me. I look over my shoulder at Shadow and grin, ever since we became prospects he's been kissing ass. I can't help but make fun of him, and I can get away with it because I knew him way before the club.

"Yeah. Hurry up," Old Guy demands. He runs his hands along the sides of his head, smoothing back the long hair that's escaped from its ponytail.

I slide off my bar stool and toss my bottle in the trash. I'm curious as to what has Old Guy in such a state. Bull comes out of his room, buckling his belt.

"This better be good, goddamn it," Bull mutters as he makes his way toward the front door.

Before we make it to the door, Old Guy comes in carrying a woman. She's curled up against his chest making it hard to see whether I know her or not. She has blonde hair, stained with blood in some spots, and clothes that look like they haven't been washed in days.

"What the fuck?" Shadow whispers, with disbelief. My eyes widen, shocked at the state the woman is in.

"Who is she?" I ask.

"Not sure. She pulled up in a nice car and kept asking to talk to whoever was in charge about wanting to make a deal before collapsing to the ground," Old Guy informs.

"A deal?" Bull asks. He walks up to the woman and brushes the hair from her face. "Someone did a number on her."

"There's more," Old Guy says. He shifts his feet, and looks downward. Movement catches my eyes, I look down at his legs to find a child clinging to Old Guy's legs.

"Fuck me," escapes from my mouth in shock. A little kid with long, blonde hair and red cheeks hugs onto Old Guy's legs. I notice her pink dress, and kneel down to the little girl's height. She has blonde hair like the woman who I'm assuming is her mother.

"Hi there, sweetie, is this your momma?" I ask, in a soft voice. I notice her left cheek is a little redder than her left, making me wonder if she fell down, or ran into something. Her face is stained from tears, and she has snot running down to her lips. She blinks her eyes a couple of times, as her bottom lip pouts. She looks at her mother and begins to wail.

"I don't think she can talk yet," Old Guy says, shifting the unconscious woman in his arms. I shrug, I know nothing about kids.

"What do you want me to do, Prez?" Old Guy asks.

Bull nervously runs his hands through his black hair. "Shit, just take her to one of the rooms." Old Guy heads down the hall with the little girl clinging to his legs, crying.

"What are you thinking, Prez, taking in a stray?" Shadow asks, shaking his head.

"That woman obviously has nobody else. I'm not about to throw a child, with a passed out mother, out on the street," Bull says, his voice sharp and angry.

Shadow nods, knowing he overstepped his boundaries.

"What the fuck, man?" I ask Shadow. I know he has issues, but I'm surprised he has no compassion for the woman and child.

Shadow glares at me with those evil-as-shit blue eyes.

"I'll clean her up and take care of the child," Babs says, skipping off down the hall.

I follow her down the hall into one of the empty rooms. Babs starts applying a wet cloth to the woman's face. I get a better look at her as she's lying on the unmade bed. She has a round face, with pouty lips, long, blonde hair, and a thicker figure than most girls around here. Her rack is nice, too. Her white top has blood and dirt smeared over it, and her jeans are just as bad. The woman's eyes flutter open, catching my attention. They're blue and bloodshot.

Instantly, the little girl clings to her mother, the contact making them both cry.

"What's your name, beautiful?" I ask the woman, as I sit on the bed.

Her eyes shoot to mine, her long lashes sticking together from crying.

"My name's Jessica, are you in charge?" she asks, her voice cracking. Her eyebrows crease and she waits for my answer.

"No. No, I'm not," I say, with a kind smile.

"This is Bobby. I'm Bull, I'd be the one in charge," Bull says, stepping up from behind me. "Who did that number on your face Darlin'?" Bull gestures toward her split eye.

"I need protection." Jessica looks over at her daughter. "*We* need protection."

"From who?" I ask.

She looks up from her daughter who is straddling her lap and her eyebrows furrow. Her lips part as tears begin to cascade from her blue eyes, like what she's about to say is the hardest thing she's ever done.

"From my husband," she says softly.

ABOUT THE AUTHOR

M.N. Forgy was raised in Missouri where she still lives with her family. She's a soccer mom by day and a saucy writer by night. M.N. Forgy started writing at a young age but never took it seriously until years later, as a stay-at-home mom, she opened her laptop and started writing again. As a role model for her children, she felt she couldn't live with the "what if" anymore and finally took a chance on her character's story. So, with her glass of wine in hand and a stray Barbie sharing her seat, she continues to create and please her fans.

stalk me

Website:
http://www.mnforgy.com

Goodreads:
https://www.goodreads.com/author/show/8110729.M_N_Forgy

Facebook:
https://www.facebook.com/pages/M-N-Forgy/625362330873655

Twitter:
@M_N_FORGY

ACKNOWLEDGEMENTS

Acknowledgements are a bittersweet moment for me. I love to give thanks to those who have helped me, but I'm always afraid I'm going to leave someone out that has helped me along this journey. So if I left you out, I apologize.

First I want to thank my husband, he has helped me in more ways than I count. He has also had to put up with my crazed state trying to get this book to perfection.

Next I want to thank the unlimited supply of Oreos I have stocked in my cabinets. They have been the perfect bribe for five extra minutes, when it comes to my children.

I also want to thank my parents, they have listened and helped so much.

I want to thank all my Little Devil's in my street team, you guys rock and I love every one of you! A big thanks to the admins of my street team, Awhina, Keisha, Nisha, and Kat.

A big thanks to Love Between The Sheets for the cover reveal, the blitz, and more. You have been great putting up with my unorganized self.

There have been so many blogs that have helped me and become some of my good friends. I wouldn't be where I am without you and you're amazing. Forever Me Romance, Kitty Kats Crazy About Books, Rock Stars Of Romance, Give Me Books, TheSubClubBooks, Submit and Devour, Kelly's Kindle Confession, Twisted Sister Rockin' Book Reviews, Bare Naked Words, A is for Alpha B Is For Book, Red Cheek Reads, Bad Girl Books, Reading past my bedtime, and more.

A very big thank you to Hot Tree Edits. You have been so helpful in editing my manuscript and teaching me how to be a better writer. Also, Arijana at Cover it! Designs for the amazing book cover.

Thank you so much to my beta readers. Tracey, Nisha, Kat, Awhina, Bel, Fran, Anitra, Emily, and Jennifer.

And most of all, my readers. This book wouldn't have happened without out you ❤